C000126744

WANT TO KNOW MORE?

Head over to the link below and get your copy of the exclusive short story prequel THE BOY AND THE MIRROR.

This is a subscriber exclusive and is not available anywhere online other than via my website.

Discover where the story began for Timothy's family and see how an unsuspecting chimneysweep set a whole family on the most enchanting adventure imaginable.

GET YOUR COPY NOW

subscribepage.com/theboyandthemirror

REAPER'S JOURNEY BOOK I

Dedicated to those that take the time to see beyond the masks and madness that the world gets to see.

Chris sat at the small table in the apartment kitchen, staring into space. Steam billowed from the boiling pan of water, but he hadn't noticed. An open bottle of half-drunk vodka sat on the scratched table in front of him. He looked lost in thought.

The surrounding kitchen, increasingly filling with steam, was inconsequential. The hob could have been engulfed in flames, and he would not have noticed. Chris was, as always, trapped in a memory, refusing to let him go.

Sat alone in the apartment, he often remembered the funeral.

Even on the day, he had resented the weather. As he stepped alongside the immaculately polished hearse, the sun shimmered on the glass. Chris remembered thinking it should have been raining. Funerals were synonymous with rain, and he had always pictured them that way.

Instead, as he hoisted Ash's coffin onto his shoulder, the sun was beating down on him.

Carrying the coffin had been the hardest thing he had done. Chris had never expected to have to carry Ash in this way. No husband could ever prepare for it.

Crossing the threshold, he remembered fighting back his emotion just to make the walk along the aisle of the small church.

Chris had never been religious. He had found no solace in religion, but Ash had. He respected Ash's beliefs enough to pass amongst the angel statues and ornate stained-glass windows without a second thought.

Reliving the painful moment as they lay the coffin for all to see, Chris was ripped back to the dreary apartment kitchen.

The billowing steam had activated the smoke alarm on the ceiling, and the shrill noise blared around him. Shaking off the haunting memory, Chris looked around in confusion until he realised what was happening. Pushing his chair out from beneath him, he stalked across the kitchen and ripped the pan from the hob.

Immediately he regretted his action. Bare skin on the metal handle had not been the best idea as he felt searing pain as heat transferred into his palm. Instinctively Chris released his grasp on the pan; the boiling contents tumbled over the lip of the pan and down his arm.
'Son of a-' he scorned as the pan fell to the floor.

Coiled pasta and boiling water spread in every direction across the floor as he turned towards the sink. Slamming his hand on the tap, Chris thrust his burning arm beneath the cascading water.
'Just what I needed,' Chris spat as he rested against the worktop and glanced across at the vodka bottle.

Pulling his arm free from the water, Chris moved quickly to retrieve the bottle. With the bottle in hand, he slid his arm back beneath the water.

Watching the skin as he drank from the bottle, Chris

saw his arm begin to blister and swell.

With no lid on the bottle, Chris took a long draw from the bottle. The fiery liquid rolled down his throat, but he accepted it and almost welcomed it. The numbness drinking brought him was all he wanted nowadays. Although it had been six months since the funeral, he still had not moved on and every night was the same.

Without Ash, Chris had lifted himself from their home and moved across State. Still working in the same job, he had kept himself busy. That being the case, even in a small cramped apartment, he felt more alone.

It had been Chris' desperate attempt to free himself from the painful memories of his loss, but it had done the exact opposite.

Selling their home, he had hoped to cut ties and move on. Instead, the loneliness felt all the more in the unfamiliar and generic apartment he now rented.

Losing patience with the cold water, Chris draped a cloth over his arm and walked through to the living room. Equally as dreary as the rest of the apartment, Chris slid himself down into a chair with a sigh. Chris looked across to a framed photograph on the coffee table in front of him, feeling a lump form in his throat as he did.

Tears welled in Chris' eyes as he leant forward and picked up the photograph.

Chris and Ash dominated the picture clad in padded jackets, sunglasses and winter hats. Behind them, the impressive profile of Mount Everest dominated the skyline and landscape.

It had been the most perfect of honeymoons for them. It had been Ash's idea, but turned out to be a perfect adventure. Four weeks away from the bustle of everyday life. They had found themselves surrounded by mountains and landscapes of unparalleled beauty.

The trip had taken them through impressive peaks but also allowed them to stand amongst the tents and flags of Everest Base Camp.

They had both looked up in wonder at the mountain but knew their place in the world. The mountain was something far beyond their abilities. When they had spoken eagerly with those waiting to summit the formidable peak, they knew it best to leave it to the professionals.

The picture now staring back at him showed the pair of them at a happier time. The love between them was easy to see, the smiles on their faces warm and loving.

'You weren't supposed to leave me yet,' Chris whispered as tears rolled down his cheeks.

Still holding the picture, Chris took another swig of vodka. The bottle caught his attention as he lowered it to his side. Held beside the photograph, he was suddenly awash with guilt.

'What am I supposed to do?' He asked the two faces smiling up at him. 'It's difficult. You should be here with me.'

The guilt pooled inside him, and instinctively Chris tossed the near-empty bottle at the far wall. The glass shattered as it hit, and the remnants of the vodka dribbled down to the floor slowly.

'It's not fair,' Chris sobbed as he hugged the photograph to his chest.

He hated being lonely. There was something about the night that made it all the worse. Every evening as the world slept, all he could think was how quiet the darkness was. What friends he had left behind had told Chris the grief was consuming him. It had been one reason for going.

Rather than face the truth, he had chosen to run from it. Severing all ties to his past in the hope he could emerge out the other side.

From the outside, it was easy to see Chris was drowning in his loss and in the throes of depression. But, from the inside, Chris found it impossible to know and accept. He knew something was amiss, but considered it all part of grieving.

Hugging the picture close, he leant his head back and let the tears flow. Chris had spent the first few weeks trying everything to hold the tears in, as if he could bottle up what he felt. That had soon ended. He had quickly come to accept crying was necessary. Sometimes it helped and others, much like tonight, it made no difference.

Lifting the frame, he looked at the smiling faces beaming back at him and longed for those feelings again.

Ash's death had brought with it a level of guilt for Chris. The night of the accident Ash had been covering a shift for Chris so he could meet up with some college friends and have a night to himself. They rarely had time aside for friends and Ash had been insistent Chris take the opportunity.

It should have been the other way around. It was Ash's night off, but Ash had been insistent that Chris enjoyed his time catching up with old friends. The regret plagued Chris. He should have insisted, somehow made Ash keep his night and worked the shift as it should have been. If it had been that way around perhaps, Chris would have replaced Ash in the pine coffin.

Or perhaps it would have all been different and they would both still be happy together.

It was impossible guilt filled with improbable possibilities, yet it haunted Chris every day.
'Enough,' he finally stammered. 'It can't stay this way.'

At that moment Chris decided he would return to Ash's hometown and see if that would ease his mourning. Ash's family had been nothing but kind to him but deep down his guilt tainted that with feelings of worry that they blamed him.

Not wanting to move, the vodka having dulled his coordination just enough, Chris remained in the chair until a drunken sleep washed over him.

In the morning he would make his excuses at work and travel to Mount Shasta in the hope in some way he could find the strength to move on.

It was a painful visit, but something Chris needed to do.

Arriving at Ash's family home, they welcomed him with open arms and love. That was what hurt the most. The hours driving across California had given him enough time to dread what was going to welcome him, and the fact Ash's mother had embraced him like a son had shattered all his expectations.

Crossing the state and travelling the I-97 was long and tedious but gave him time to think.

There was an end in sight as he pulled into the small town. Navigating the narrow side streets, he had finally pulled into the driveway and sat for a few moments. 'Christian?' the elderly female voice bellowed from the porch. 'You should have said you were coming.'

Chris had been sitting in the car trying to talk himself

into walking up to the house. It filled him with dread and fear at something so simple, but knew he had come too far now. With the engine idling, Chris had sat staring at the house before Martha had finally appeared on the wooden steps and looked across towards his car.

'Too late now,' Chris sighed and killed the engine.

Reluctantly, he stepped out of the car and looked across at his mother-in-law.

'Martha,' Chris greeted as he stepped up to the house. 'I'm sorry, I wasn't sure I was going to come.'

Standing at the bottom of the steps, he could see the same sadness in her eyes as his own. While Martha greeted him with warmth, he could see the same futile look of loss, the same look he tried daily to hide.

'Little bit far from home to just be out for a drive though, isn't it?'

Martha beckoned for him to join her, and he reluctantly stepped up onto the porch. Coming only to his shoulder height, the old woman grabbed him in a warm embrace and hugged him tightly.

'I'm glad you've come, Frank will be happy when he gets home.' She whispered to him as she held him. 'It's been too long, you know.'

'I know,' a lump caught in his throat. 'I just didn't know if it was right to come.'

'Don't be stupid, there's always a place for you here.'

Suddenly awash with emotion, Chris once again sobbed. Held in the warm embrace, he could not hold back the tears. He had vowed not to do this, to be strong, but seeing the familiar features in Martha reminded him of Ash. It was simply too much.

'Now come inside you silly man and make yourself at home.'

Releasing him, Martha wiped her own tears away and

brushed down her floral dress. Opening the door, she welcomed Chris into the house as a bedraggled and sluggish Labrador trundled towards him.
'Toby still going strong, I see.'

Dropping to his knee, Chris welcomed the elderly dog. Misty eyes looked up at him, Chris suddenly felt a little more human. He had always enjoyed visiting Ash's family. They had always welcomed him warmly, like one of their own, and recently he had forgotten how that felt.
'I take it you'll stop for dinner?' Martha asked as she walked through to the kitchen.
'I hadn't made plans to,' Chris confessed, and Martha suddenly turned to face him.

Drenched in the artificial light, Martha looked older than she was. The lines in her face seemed more profound, and her eyes narrowed as she looked at Chris.
'What brings you here, Chris?' There was a softness in her voice. 'We haven't heard from you since...'
'The funeral,' he confessed. 'I know, I haven't known what to do and to be honest, I just drove and ended up here.'
'Divine intervention?'
'Muscle memory.' Chris quickly corrected. 'I was thinking about the time we spent in the mountains. Just walking and being with each other. I missed it.'
'You're going to walk the mountain?'

Chris and Ash had spent many hours meandering the various routes up and down Mount Shasta that dominated the horizon. The snow-capped mountain climbed skyward. Clouds ambled slowly across the lower peak, hiding the summit from view. It was a sight Chris had become familiar with over the years and when he had driven along the I-97, the mountain in sight, he knew why he had come.
'Why?' Martha pressed.

'Since Ash died, I've done nothing. Work has been great, but something is missing, I don't feel anymore.' Chris moved to sit on a stool by the worktop in the kitchen as Martha followed and began preparing food as they talked. 'And you thought coming here would make you feel closer to Ash again?'

Martha had always had a way of reading Chris. It often worried him how quickly she could understand what he was thinking, but right then he was grateful for it. Casting his gaze to the panoramic window, he saw the sun beginning to set, painting the mountain in a glorious hue of orange light.

They talked while Martha prepared dinner, and the time seemed to pass quickly. As she put the final touches on dinner and pushed it into the oven, a sound interrupted their conversation.

'Martha,' a gruff man's voice bellowed from across the house. 'Whose is the car on the driveway, they're blocking my space.'

A familiar face joined the voice as Ash's father walked into the kitchen.

'Chris!' The old man beamed and thrust a hand out towards Chris.

As Chris took the hand, he felt pulled into a tight embrace as Frank, his father-in-law, hugged him.

'It's been way too long Christian, how have you been?'

Chris pulled himself free and feigned a smile at Frank.

The man was in his mid-sixties, his skin was weathered and tanned. Frank had always been active and still maintained a smallholding of land on the far side of the town.

'Pretty terrible, if I'm honest,' Chris answered truthfully. 'I was saying to Martha I came here to get away from things and try to find some peace.'

'Peace, here? Wrong place for that son.'

Martha threw Frank a glare and shook her head, warning her husband. The interaction went unnoticed as Chris sat back down on the stool.

'How long you staying for?' Frank mumbled as he washed his hands in the sink and pulled two beers from the fridge.

'Martha's offered for me to stay the night, but I'm planning on hiking Shasta in the morning.'

Chris took the beer as Frank snapped off the lid on the edge of the worktop. Frank had a look of concern on his face as he looked from Martha to Chris.

'Son, it's not climbing season, and it's been a while since you've been up there.'

'I know,' Chris tried to play down the old man's concern as he took a long drink. 'I just wanted to clear my head, get myself back to nature and what better place?'

'The summit and glaciers aren't the greatest at the moment.' Frank continued to protest.

'I know, I may not even summit, but I just want to be out there. I'm sure you can appreciate why?'

Chris worried he had been a little too defensive as Frank's face twisted with a painful memory.

Dinner was a sombre affair. The mood between the three of them was quiet, they shared only a handful of words as they ate in almost silence. By the time Martha and Frank finished cleaning the pots, Chris had finished three bottles of Frank's beer and was feeling a little lightheaded.

As Frank handed him another bottle, the old man invited Chris to join him on the porch.

Leaving Martha in the house, the two men wandered out onto the wooden porch. The air was icy, filled with a fall chill, and Chris folded his arms across his chest. The night sky was cloudless, a blanket of stars twinkled enchantingly. In the darkness, Chris could see no sign of the impressive mountain in the distance.

'Why did you come, Christian?' Frank asked him flatly, snatching Chris' attention back from his musing.

'I don't know, it just felt right.' Chris rested his bottle on the bannister. 'I didn't want to come, I didn't want to upset you or Martha.'

'Have you spoken to your parents lately?'

The question caught Chris off-guard, and it filled him with a wave of guilt. The knowing look on Frank's face told Chris he already knew the answer.

'No, I don't know what to say to them.' Chris held back his tears again. 'I didn't know what to say to you. If I had been thinking clearly, I wouldn't have even turned up.'

Frank stepped up to him and placed a firm hand on his shoulder.

'There's always a place for you here, it's what Ash would have wanted.' He said comfortingly. 'You should never feel afraid to come here, this is your home as much as it was, Ash's.'

'Thank you.'

'And, your parents are worried,' Frank continued, his voice becoming a little sterner now. 'We all have been. They told me you've sold the house and moved across state?'

'I needed to be free, I couldn't live in the house we built together and not hear or feel-' The words caught in his throat.

'Grief is natural, son. You don't think me or Martha don't stare at empty chairs and wish our baby was with us, do you?'

'I know,'

'Ash wouldn't want any of us wallowing in sadness and self-pity.'

'I am trying.'

Frank was quiet for a moment and merely looked at Chris. Tears streamed down Chris' cheeks as he moved out of Frank's grip and retrieved his drink from the bannister. Unable to look at his father-in-law, Chris leant on the wood and drank the remainder of the bottle.

'Maybe the mountain is what you need,' Frank added. 'I hope you can leave whatever darkness is haunting you up there and come down the young man my Ash fell in love with.'

Frank offered his own bottle towards Chris, and the pair chinked the bottles together.

'It looks like you need some time alone,' Frank walked towards the door. 'Don't stay out here too long, the temperature really drops. Martha and I will make the sofa bed for you.'

'Frank?'

The old man paused as stepped through the door and turned to face Chris.

'What is it?'

'I'm sorry.' Chris stammered.

'For what?'

'If I had gone to work this would never have happened, maybe it would be Ash stood here now and not me.'

'Don't live regretting a past you can't change Christian.' Frank answered. 'And you have nothing to be sorry for.'

Stepping through the door, Frank allowed the fly screen to close first and then offered Chris one final thought.

'I hope you find whatever peace you're looking for up Shasta, I really do.'

Closing the inner door, they left Chris alone on the veranda as he stared up at the stars.

There were no sounds other than the gentle rustle of

foliage and the distant noise as cars rumbled along the I-97 far off in the distance.

Raising his bottle towards the stars, Chris offered a silent toast to his lost love.

Chris left the house long before Martha, and Frank
woke. He had wanted to avoid the expected attempts by
his in-laws to convince him to hold off on his climb. Their
best intentions would be there, and Chris knew that, but it
was something he needed to do.

Leaving them a brief note on the worktop, he made his
bed and disappeared out onto the veranda.

The morning air was bitingly cold as he edged the
outer door closed as quietly as he could. A slight breeze
fluttered the flag hanging from the front of the house.
Zipping his quilted jacket tight, Chris walked over to his
car and slid into the driver's seat silently.

Removing the handbrake, Chris rolled the car down
the driveway and only once he was clear of the house did
he start the engine. Pulling out onto the road, Chris didn't

see the lights come on the home or Martha step hurriedly out onto the veranda as he drove off.

Leaving the past behind, Chris made it to the narrow approach road to Mount Shasta within the hour. Being the middle of winter, the way was peppered with tracks of snow, but nothing offering Chris any issues. Another fifteen minutes ascending the narrow road and Chris was satisfied he had gone far enough in the car. Pulling into a small layby, Chris settled the car and killed the engine.

With the headlights extinguished, it plunged Chris into darkness and almost immediately felt the cold seep into the car with the heaters now switched off.

Cracking the door, Chris stepped out and took in a long breath. He had always enjoyed the sense of freedom in the mountains. The sun had still not peeked above the horizon yet, but the sky was lightening. Looking around Chris felt surrounded by peace. He could taste the cleanliness of the air and listened to the sounds of nature.

All Chris could hear was the sound of branches rustling in the breeze. Tall trees flanked the road, and as he peered closer, Chris could just about make out the profile of the mountain above.

'Time to get started,' Chris said to himself as he moved towards the rear of the car.

Opening the boot, he had already prepared his climbing bag. Dropping himself onto the lip, he quickly swapped his shoes and tied the laces of his well-worn boots. Attaching the gaiters, he smoothed down the fabric and pulled the rucksack up onto his back.

The rucksack hadn't been his, it had been Ash's, and it took some time to adjust the straps to be comfortable with his frame and size. Locking the car, Chris set off into the early morning and began his hike up towards the slopes of Mount Shasta.

The climb was uneventful. The snow had thickened on the ground early on, and the barely trodden paths slowed his pace. It was an uneven climb filled with rises and falls along the way, but Chris pressed on unperturbed.

Soft music played in his ears as he adjusted the volume on the MP3 player in his pocket.

The music matched his pace perfectly, the steady rhythm to the classic ensemble was his favourite tracks to listen to as he walked. Usually, he would take the silence of the mountain as his company, but today he needed the distraction from the music.

Chris could not help but admire the beauty as the sun crested the horizon in the first half hour of his walk. Casting the mountainside in a vibrant red glow the individual crystals of ice on the path in front of him. The light danced as the sun rose higher until, casting his gaze towards the summit, he finally saw the snow-covered peak high above him.

There were no other hikers on the path, no signs of anyone having even breached the snow as he walked. The first sign of life was a small camper van parked in the ample open space above the ski resort. Passing by the front of the van, Chris could see the trailer was occupied by the heavily condensated windscreen and side windows. There was a smouldering fire in the snow outside the door, but otherwise there were no signs of life within the camper.

Passing by unnoticed, Chris continued on his way, recalling his path from memory, all the while absorbed by the gentle music playing in his ears.

Chris pressed on relentlessly through the day. His calves screamed by the time the sun peaked in the lunchtime sky. The thick snow was taking its toll. In places the depth reached to his knees but Chris continued on.

He made no time for breaks. The rucksack on his back contained only essentials, but not the essentials of a regular hiker. Tugging on the straps subconsciously, Chris looked around for a place to rest.

'Morning,' a voice suddenly announced from behind him as Chris removed the headphones from his ears.

Turning Chris was surprised to find a man almost twice his age waltzing smoothly along the path he had taken. Muttering a greeting, he hoped the old man would walk on, but unsurprisingly the older man stopped at the same time as Chris.

The older man was dressed in a thick coat with a scarf across his face and a hat pulled tightly down his forehead. All Chris could make out of the man's face was the grey eyebrows and wrinkled eyes that peered between the fabric of his face coverings. He was dressed for the weather and felt utterly familiar with their surroundings. 'Cold day for it, I'm guessing you're not going to try to summit today? Weather should be closing in before sunset.'

The old man rested himself against tree trunk and sipped from a metal water canister. While Chris was not in the mood for small talk, he knew he had to engage the older man, or at least humour him a little.

'I'm not sure,' Chris muttered. 'Hadn't really planned how far to go. The snow's a bit deeper than I thought it would be.'

'Walked her before?' The old man pressed as he replaced the bottle in his bag.

'A few times, not in the snow though.'

'Whole different animal in the snow, you'd probably be better finding somewhere to camp at the base of the Avalanche Gulch, any higher when the weather closes in, and you'll be exposed.'

'How far off am I?' Chris already knew the answer but fed his newfound friend's curiosity.

'Another hour at most, there're some caves you can take shelter in,' the older man said as he replaced the bag on his back. 'Either that or, if you start now, you can make it down before nightfall.'

'I'll head for the caves,' Chris answered confidently. 'I've not come this far to turn back now.'

The older man appeared to weigh Chris up for a moment, looking at him with curiosity.

'In that case,' the old man paused and placed a pair of Oakley glasses over his eyes. 'I may see you at the top, or when you come to rest.'

Without another word, the older man raised a hand as he turned and set off up towards the steep slopes ahead of them.

Giving the older man enough time to put some distance between them, Chris finally set off along the same route. Curiously, it did not take long for Chris to lose sight of the man's tracks in the snow ahead of him.

'What the hell?' Chris mumbled to himself as he looked at the path in front of him.

There was no sign of tracks in the snow. The powdery white landscape was completely undisturbed, yet far off in the distance Chris could see the dark speck of the older man meandering off ahead of him.

'Which route did you take then old boy?'

Looking around Chris tried to find the route but saw nothing in the snow, no marks or scuffs where the older man had walked, just an expanse of undisturbed snow in front of him.

Casting aside his thoughts towards the old man, Chris restarted the music and set off across the snow.

The other walker had been right. As the sun began to

drop, Chris cast a glance behind him and saw the massive clouds rolling in from behind him. Dark grey clouds lumbered slowly towards him, and it cast the land beneath in shadow. Even from this distance he could see the haze of rain and knew, by the time it reached the mountainside, the raindrops would fall as snow.

Returning his attention to the mountain, he saw the Avalanche Gulch rising high in front of him. Off to the eastern side, he could see the openings amongst the snow marking the crevasses and caves the other man had been talking about.

Honestly, Chris had already been aware of the caves, it had been his destination all along. With the weather closing in behind him, he increased his pace and made a beeline across the open plain towards the caves.

As the first flakes of snow tumbled from the sky, Chris reached the cover of exposed rocks capped with snow. The cold was biting, his lungs burned with each ragged breath. His hike across the open had taken its toll, and his body was telling him he had walked enough. Looking around the snow, mostly, disguised the jagged rocks and spattering of cave entrances.

Clambering over the increasingly uneven surface, Chris finally found an entrance into the mountain. The cloud base had swallowed the mountain, Chris no longer had any view out towards where he had come from. A torrential deluge of snow had replaced the flutter of flakes, but everything felt peaceful.

Standing at the entrance of the cave, Chris removed his headphones and looked out at his surroundings.

He could hear the flakes of crisp snow landing all around. What trees were scattered about rustled in the gentle breeze and everything was quiet. Nothing disturbed nature other than the falling snow and rustling branches.

'Perfect,' he sighed to himself and stepped between the rocks and into the dark cave.

The narrow fissure between the rocks was a tight squeeze at first. Removing the bag from his back, Chris pressed himself close against the rough stone and passed between them with little trouble. After a short length, the rocks opened up until suddenly he found himself stood in the mouth of a giant cavern.

Fumbling in the top part of the rucksack, Chris found a head torch and pulled it onto his head. Cycling the light through the various lighting types, he settled on one and panned around the vast cavern in front of him.

Icicles dangled precariously from the jagged ceiling. The torchlight struggled to reach the far extremes of the cave, and Chris suspected the hole stretched deep into the mountain. Knowing Shasta was still considered an active volcano, Chris' imagination wondered exactly how deep and how far into the mountain's core the tunnel systems led.

Lifting the bag from the slippery floor, Chris moved deeper into the cavern until he reached a broad fissure stretching the entire way across the floor. Leaning precariously close to the edge, Chris peered down into the darkness. There seemed no end to the blackness below, and he quickly stepped away from the side.
'Nice and quiet, I suppose,' Chris murmured to himself and sat down against the wall of the cave.

Although the floor was cold, it didn't matter to Chris. Opening the bag again, he pulled out a large battery powered camping lamp. Bringing the bulb to life, it bathed a significant portion of the cave in the eerie white light. Glad for the illumination, Chris removed the head torch and dropped it on the floor beside him.

Setting the lamp down on the ground, he pulled an unopened bottle of vodka from the bag and unscrewed the lid.
'To you, Ash,' he raised the bottle towards the icicles above and quickly downed a good portion of the container in one deep swig.

The warmth of the liquor was a welcome feeling against the cold. It warmed him from the inside, and he took comfort from the strength of the drink. This particular bottle was sentimental to him; it had been a gift from Ash for their first anniversary. Imported especially for the occasion, Chris had promised to save it for a particular time.

Admiring the ornate label and crest emblazoned on the shaft of the bottle, he took another long drink.

It didn't take long for the strong liquor to have its effect. The light danced around slowly, and Chris felt his eyes start to roll around drunkenly.

'Excellent stuff,' he chuckled as he tried to take another swig but missed. Instead, he poured a mouthful down the front of his jacket.

Wiping the liquid from his top, Chris placed the bottle on the ground with a loud *clink*.

Looking around slowly, Chris suddenly noticed the surrounding noises. The vodka, somehow, seemed to have enhanced his hearing. Far off he could hear the rhythmic drip of melting ice forming droplets which tumbled from the ceiling above. Deep within the fissure, he could listen to the sounds of cracking and even beyond, he could hear the whistle of the wind.

The cave was alive with sound when Chris really listened. Water, movement, echoes and distant noises seemed to reverberate all around.

Then he picked out a curious sound, something that did not fit with the rest.

It was a familiar sound, but in his current setting, he could not place it.

Finally, as a dark shadow passed in front of the lamp, Chris realised what the sound was. *Footsteps.*

Snatching his gaze up, he was surprised to see a figure stood before him. As his drunken vision settled on the person towering over him, a strange sense of dread washed over him.

'You'll not likely freeze to death drinking this,' the voice sounded familiar, but Chris could not place it. 'Stuff like alcohol will keep you warm for days out here.'

'Won't take too long I'm sure.' Chris replied, his words slightly slurred and laboured.

The figure stood before him did not fit, it seemed wrong. Dressed in a long flowing black hooded robe, there was no sense to their attire. No quilted jacket or cold weather clothes. The hood itself drooped over the head and completely concealed the face beneath in dark shadow. The robe stretched all the way to the floor and hid whatever boots or shoes the new arrival was wearing.

Whatever material it was made of was dense. The folds and ruffles in the fabric barely moved as they edged closer to Chris as he sat, still slumped, against the wall.

'Did you come here to die?' The familiar voice pressed. 'Is it the reason you didn't dare let them talk you out of it?'

The sudden realisation the new arrival knew him snatched him back a little from his drunken state. Using the wall to steady himself, Chris stood up and turned to face the robed figure.

'Just who the hell are you?' Chris snapped.

'Who I am is not really important, I'm more interested in who you are.'

'You seem to know enough about me,' Chris said accusingly. 'How about you take the hood down and let me see who you are.'

Eerily, a pair of eyes pierced the darkness of the cowl and suddenly came into view. They were cold and stared emotionlessly at Chris from the shadow. The blue iris seemed to match the cold of the cave, and Chris felt an involuntary shudder trickle down his spine.

'Who are you?' Chris asked again.

The mysterious robed figure stepped forward to stand right in front of Chris. Whoever sat beneath the material was slightly taller than Chris, he had to look up to see the shrouded face.

Curiously, no clouds of breath emerged from the hood. Chris pressed himself back against the wall as the figure towered over him imposingly.

'Mind stepping back?' Chris said, more to end the uncomfortable silence than anything else.

'You seem nervous.' The voice grumbled.

'Wouldn't you when some clown in a gown comes to talk to you in a cave?'

It dawned on Chris he was still holding the vodka bottle in his hand. Dropping his attention from the figure to the bottle, he realised what the issue was. Dropping the bottle to the floor, he moved himself to the side and stepped away from the looming new arrival.

'It's clearly the drink,' he chuckled and stepped slowly across the width of the cave.

'You could be right,' the shrouded figure agreed. 'Or else it could be more than that.'

Chris turned and stumbled backwards as the figure was once again stood uncomfortably close, looming over him.

'Jeez,' he stammered. 'Give a man some space.'

The demeanour of the figure suddenly changed, and the air felt colder. The pair of vibrant blue eyes disappeared as the figure pressed Chris backwards with its presence. Quickly Chris' back was pressed against another wall of ice, allowing the hooded head to lean in closer.

Peering into the impossibly black space beneath the hood, Chris could see nothing of a face.

'You came here to die, Christian Thomas, but you lack the honesty to admit it.' No air moved across his face as he peered into the hood. 'If you lack the honesty, I expect you also lack the resolve.'

'I didn't come here just to die.'

'But you came here for it, perhaps amongst other things. But Christian, you came here with no intention of descending the slopes, didn't you?'

Although the eyes had disappeared, Chris dropped his gaze. From the dark he felt, whoever was beneath the hood was staring at him. It made him feel uncomfortable.

'You know nothing about me.' Chris snapped.

As soon as he had said it, he knew he was wrong. Whoever sat behind the cowl certainly knew him. They knew his name, his reasons, his intentions and who knew what else.

'We both know,' the voice answered ominously. 'I know more about you than you would like and the bottle over there is one of your last comforts.'

'What I choose to do with myself is of no concern to you,'

'It concerns me,' there was a menace in the words. 'I am here at your end to show you things you would not wish to see.'

'You're a figment of my drunk imagination trying desperately to talk me out of ending this pitiful life I've come to inhabit.'

In one fluid movement, a pair of gloved hands reached upwards and pulled the massive hood. Ripping the material back Chris stood mouth agape at what looked down at him.

There was no face, only the sickly pale bone of a human skull peering down at him. The same chilling blue eyes stared from the sockets. As Chris stared in horror, the skull changed. Pasty skin covered the pale bones until a human face appeared. It grew from behind the cavities of bone spreading slowly in every direction.

Feeling his heart racing and staring in utter disbelief, Chris watched as the boned head became a recognisable face. After a handful of sickeningly long seconds, a face now accompanied the voice that spoke to him.

It was male, weathered and aged in his early sixties. A straggly goatee sat around his narrow mouth, and a head of neat greying hair hung from his head. The face had a handsome look to it, a rugged aged appearance taking Chris by surprise.

'That's better,' the man said as he traced a gloved finger across his newly formed forehead and down his cheeks.

Chris was gob smacked and shocked into silence. His mouth opened and closed comically as he tried to comprehend what had just happened. It was impossible, utterly unthinkable: a face had grown on a skull before his very eyes.

'Mind wiping that ridiculous look off your face?'

Chris was finding it impossible to form words.

'I suppose introductions are in order,' a forced smile appeared on the rugged man's face. 'I go by many names, some less likeable. The one I've come to like most is Azrael.'

The robed Azrael held out a gloved hand in greeting. When Chris finally took the hand, it surprised him how thin the fingers felt in his grasp, but before he could think anything Azrael pulled him closer until their faces were almost touching.

'Do you know what it means?'

Chris shook his head, transfixed on the materialised face now so close to his.

'It is another name for who I really am,' Azrael drawled. 'It means death. I am death.'

Pulling his hand free from Chris' grasp, Azrael allowed the glove to slip free of his hand. Raising it upwards Azrael waved a hand of bone, no skin, muscle or blood, just white ivory bones that somehow held together and moved.

'I am death, and I am here to take you.'

The words echoed as darkness washed over Chris. He felt himself fall, tumbling backwards through the air. The last sensation was when his head slammed roughly down on the floor. After that there was nothing.

Chris awoke with a start. Eyes wide, he looked around the cavern for a moment. There was a wave of relief when Chris realised he was alone in the cave. Resting his head back on the floor, he looked up at the ceiling above him.

Somewhere high above, a crack of light could just be seen on the ice. It suddenly dawned on him he had been inside the cave for a long time if he could see sunlight. 'Feeling better?' The voice asked, and Chris sat up in shock.

Looking around, Chris desperately tried to find the source of the voice but saw nothing. The words still echoed around, but there was no sign of the robed man. 'Christian, you'd better pull yourself together a little if you want to understand what's happening to you,' the voice was mocking him. 'Come over here, and I'll show you something.'

Reluctantly, Chris stood up and walked across the cavern. The voice sounded like it was coming from the vast fissure in the ground he had seen earlier. Inching closer to the jagged edge, Chris peered over and was surprised to see the robed man, Azrael, sat on a ledge of ice ten feet below.

'Care to join me?' Azrael asked as he tapped his bony fingers on the ledge beside him.

'I'd rather not,' Chris answered flatly. 'I wouldn't want to fall down there.'

'Won't make much of a difference,' Azrael said as he stood himself up on the ledge. 'It's not as if it'll do you much harm.'

Clambering up, Azrael soon pulled himself up over the ledge and stood up a little off to Chris' side.

'What do you mean by that?'

Azrael didn't offer an answer. He looked across at Chris for a few seconds before a wry smile appeared on his face. Those cold blue eyes stared at Chris intensely, and once again he felt as if Azrael was peering inside him in some way.

'Look,' Azrael finally replied and pointed back to where Chris had walked from.

Turning with purpose, Chris panned around his surroundings until it drew his attention to a lifeless figure on the floor. Wrapped in the same quilted jacket Chris was wearing, he stared across at the impossible.

'This can't be,' Chris struggled to finish his sentence as he stepped tentatively across at the lifeless body.

The trousers on the body matched his own, the scuffed gators and boots were the same. Chris knew what he was looking at, but the impossibility of all of this told him it was not true. Moving around the corpse, the face finally came into view, and Chris could only stare down, mouth agape and head spinning in confusion.

'This isn't possible.' Chris gasped.

Dead and motionless on the cold icy floor was his body. The skin was pale and cold, lips tinged blue with the lack of oxygen and the cold. Lifeless eyes stared up at the roof of the cave, and his lips were slightly parted.

One hand gripped the bottle of vodka while the other held onto a folded photograph. Leaning closer, Chris immediately recognised the picture and recoiled back.

'It seems you got your wish, Christian,' Azrael said as he moved to Chris' side. 'Death indeed has come for you.'

'How am I looking at myself, why am I looking at myself?'

'Because you need to see your own end, you also need to hear what I have to say.'

Chris spun to face Azrael, whose blank expression was impossible to read.

'What is that supposed to mean?'

'What did you expect to happen now, Christian? In death, did you expect the heavens to open and you somehow climb towards the clouds for an eternity of peace?'

'I don't know,' he confessed and turned back to look at his own body in death.

His skin looked pale and waxy. Chris did not dare reach out and touch his own corpse, but something inside him wanted to know how it felt.

'Tell me,' Azrael began as he watched Chris peering at the body. 'Why did you do it?'

Chris knew the answer; anyone who knew him could tell Azrael the answer.

Having climbed up the slopes of Shasta, Chris had not made his decisions to end his life. He would have been lying if he had said it was not on his mind, but he had not decided his course of action. Even now as he looked at himself, he wasn't sure it had ever really been his end game.

'Ash,' he finally replied. 'But I'm guessing you knew already.'

Chris reached out to touch his dead face, but his fingers passed through. There was no contact, just the ghostly materialisation of his fingers passing impossibly through the physical skin. He could feel nothing, no resistance or sign the body beneath him was real.

But he knew it was.

'Ash is not waiting for you where you are going.'

Chris turned to look up at Azrael.

'Meaning what?'

It dawned on Chris he did not know what to expect from death. When he had been alive, the only thing he had wanted was to see Ash again. Now stood beside the robed figure of Azrael, the guardian of death. He had no idea what was really going to happen.

'What did you expect, Christian?'

'I don't know,' he confessed. 'Nobody does I expect, we have preconceived notions, but what is there beyond that?'

'People face me with ideas of angels and demons, heaven and hell, but I can tell you this is not true.'

'Why are you here?' Chris pressed beyond the riddling thoughts the afterlife. 'What is your purpose in all of this?'

'Finally,' Azrael beamed and offered out a re-gloved hand towards Chris. 'A real question.'

Azrael pulled Chris up and replaced the hood up over his head. With his face shrouded in the shadow of the hood, Chris could no longer see the face or piercing blue eyes.

'Forget this,' Azrael pointed to the corpse on the floor. 'You've made your decision now, and there is no turning back from it. From this moment the decisions you make will decide where your future lies in this plane of life.'

Azrael stepped away from the body and walked towards the cave entrance. Torn between the body he was leaving behind and curiosity of what lay beyond, Chris eventually committed and fell into place beside Azrael.

Reaching the narrow opening in the cave wall, Chris allowed Azrael to go first and followed close behind, squeezing between the jagged walls of rock.
'What sits beyond the cave is not the world you left behind,' Azrael announced as he stepped towards the bright opening of the cave. 'What lies here is the place which exists between life and death, a place we call Altum.'

Announcing their arrival, Azrael moved aside, allowing Chris to see the world before them.

It was not as he had expected. Having entered the cave, he had admired the thin trees clambering skyward, bathed in the blizzard and snow. Instead of the mountainside, the view before him was breathtaking in beauty.

The light was bright and as his eyes adjusted Chris could make out the detail of the impressive structures which stood before him. Buildings built in the style of Ancient Greece surrounded a massive domed structure dominating the centre of the city. There was little sign of life, and the buildings looked to be glowing pearlescent in the bright light beaming down on Altum.
'What is this place?' Chris asked, his voice filled with awe at the sight in front of him.
'Altum is a city of judgement, over there is the Hall Of Souls And Scales.'

A strange feeling of concern welled inside him as Chris looked across at the impressive domed structure.

A structure similar to the Pantheon sat next to the

dome and looked to be the entrance to the Hall. Whatever material the buildings were made of appeared to shine in the light, the faces of all the buildings appeared glassy smooth and pearlescent to the eye, casting a faint shimmer of a rainbow to the naked eye.

'Is that where you're taking me?' Chris' throat was dry, and it filled his voice with nervousness as death turned to look at him.

'Not yet, Christian,' Azrael began slowly. 'I brought you here to offer you a choice.'

'What choice?'

'In time,' Azrael said coolly. 'First, I need you to see the world through my eyes and only then can you make your choice.'

Azrael turned to face Chris and raised his hand towards Chris' chest. Reaching out, Azrael pressed the tip of his gloved finger where Chris' heart once beat.

'Go back to your life and see your world as I see it. Only then will you understand the gravity of what I will offer you.'

A burst of pain erupted inside his chest as Chris was propelled backwards by some unseen force. As the world span dizzily around him, Chris struggled to catch his breath and felt a burning fire inside his chest. He had felt nothing so intense in his life and as the air caught in his chest and his throat contracted painfully, he panicked.

When the pain finally subsided, Chris blinked away the disorientation and let himself come around slowly.

He was no longer stood at the mouth of the cave, nor within it as he had been. As he blinked away his blurred vision, his surroundings came into focus.

Chris was once again inside his bleak and dreary apartment. The shattered glass from the vodka bottle he had thrown at the wall remained piled on the carpet. It was exactly as he had left it three days before. In the apartment's silence, Chris suddenly felt very lost and very much alone.

Rubbing his hand against his chest, Chris could still feel the dull ache of pain where Azrael had touched him. Beneath his fingers, the skin felt tender and bruised. 'I need to lie down,' he whispered to himself and moved through the apartment to his bedroom.

As he lay down on the mattress, he closed his eyes and drifted into what felt like sleep.

The quilt had wrapped itself around Chris, and he awoke with a feeling of being trapped. Wriggling and writhing, he desperately tried to pull his arms free of the bedding. Slipping his hand free of the sheet, he pulled himself out and shrugged himself free of his cocoon. 'What a night,' Chris sighed as he opened his eyes.

The sun peeked through the curtains and, if he listened carefully, Chris could make out the sounds of the city outside the window. Rubbing his eyes, he brushed away the sleep and sat himself up on the edge of the bed. Stretching out his arms, Chris looked around the bedroom slowly and took in his surroundings.

The room was untidy and messy. Piles of clothes littered the floor, and the draws hung open with barely anything left inside them. Walking across to the drawers,

Chris stripped down and grabbed a handful of clothes before stepping into the bathroom.

Pushing open the bathroom door, Chris turned on the shower and tested the water with his hand. Making adjustments to the temperature, Chris pulled open the shower curtain and stepped into the stream of water.

It surprised him how sore his muscles felt. The aching in his calves told him the climb in the mountains had been all too real. The events in the cave he was less convinced about but, as he washed his aching body, he somehow felt different.

As he lathered the soap across his chest, his fingers touched the patch where Azrael had touched him. Immediately he recoiled his fingers as the skin beneath felt frozen to the touch. Pulling aside the shower curtain, Chris reached across to the steamed mirror and wiped his wet hand across the glass.

For the first time, Chris saw his haggard appearance. A face of rough stubble looked back at him; his eyes were black and bloodshot. Taking his gaze slowly down towards his chest, he felt a wave of revulsion wash over him.

Stretched across his chest between his pecs, a curious patch of black skin stood out. Brushing his fingers against the dark piece of skin, it felt bitterly cold to the touch. The spot was the size of his palm and a spider-web of blackened veins traced out in all directions. Tracing along one of the veins, Chris reached all the way to his throat before the black faded from sight.

'What the hell is this?' He mumbled to himself as he felt the skin again.

While it was cold, the skin felt rough and tight to his touch. The presence of the black scarring filled him with a strange feeling, and he quickly turned his back to the mirror and returned to his shower.

Enjoying the solace of the shower, Chris cleared the stubble from his face and washed away any remnants of the mountain climb. Stepping free from the shower, Chris dried and quickly dressed in the clothes he had brought with him from the bedroom.

With the strange black scarring covered, Chris quickly forgot about it. As he stepped out into the narrow hallway of the apartment block, he turned and locked the door.

The hallway was dark and dreary. Chris hated everything about the apartment block, including his room. Having lived there for less than three months he was still yet to meet any of his neighbours. The only way Chris knew he had neighbours came from the cacophony of noises they made, generally in the middle of the night. Other than that, the block itself could easily have been empty.

Descending the well-worn staircase, Chris emerged in the lobby and pushed the heavy doors open. Almost immediately he was welcomed by the sounds of flowing traffic and footfalls of people walking along the pavement.

Chris enjoyed the anonymity of New York. The constant flow of people allowed him to move around, completely ignored by everyone around him. The city was alive with people, all of them focussed on their own journeys and paying little attention to anyone else unless they had to.

For the first time in days, it filled the sky with dark clouds, but the sidewalk remained dry and what water the clouds held seemed secure in place. Pulling the collar of his coat higher, Chris watched for space and seamlessly slipped into the flow of people as they meandered past the door to his block.

Chris had no destination in mind. All he wanted, more

than anything, was to be free of the claustrophobic apartment and hopefully find some way to clear his mind. It always amused him how much he enjoyed the isolation of the mountains and countryside, yet the first place he thought of when he had lost Ash was New York.

Neither of them had any connection to the bustling city. Ash had come from rural Shasta and Chris from even further afield, yet New York had called to him. Chris realised he wanted to be alone and surrounded by people at the same time, New York indeed offered him that.

Cars rumbled slowly along the roads as Chris weaved around the streets aimlessly. As his legs carried him along the sidewalks, he soon found himself in the nicer areas of the city. The high-rise buildings looked cleaner; the ornate facades showed less tarnish from the pollution of the streets, and soon Chris emerged into Times Square.

Flickering lights from the enormous screens drew his attention from the floor. He had not realised how far he had walked. Pushing himself through the main flow of bodies, Chris stepped between a pair of bollards and onto the pedestrian section of the square.

The flow of people was less now; instead of meandering locals, the square was dotted with tourists who seemed mesmerised by the cascade of images on the giant screens. Couples stood together as they handed around phones and cameras to snatch their moment among the advertisements and trailers.

'Five dollars off pizza?' A youthful voice interrupted.

Chris turned and looked at a young man standing next to him. In his gloved hand he held out a poorly printed pamphlet, but it was something different which had caught his attention.

Looking down at the young man in his early twenties, Chris could see something odd about his face. The man's eyes did not appear normal, somehow they seemed to be smoking. Tendrils of black smoke floated from the corners, and the whites of his eyes looked bright red and bloodshot.

'What's wrong with your eyes man?' Chris stammered as he stepped back away from the man.

'You been smoking something, dude?'

'Your eyes,' Chris repeated and stared in horror at what stood before him.

The red eyes glowed brighter, and the smoke seemed to billow thicker from the corners. As the young man stared at Chris, he could hear something in the surrounding air. The rumble of engines and patter of footsteps on the sidewalk became muted and instead the air was filled with a rhythmic beating sound.

Distant at first, the sound grew louder and louder until it was unmistakably the beating of a heart. Focussing on the heartbeat, Chris realised it was coming from the young man standing in front of him. Staring intently at the young man, Chris realised the world around him had frozen in place.

Cars sat stationary on the road and pedestrians stood, mid-movement frozen in place by some unseen force.

'What the hell?' Chris muttered as he turned around slowly in place.

Even the advertisement boards and televisions were motionless now. Turning full circle, he returned his attention to the young man holding the leaflets and realised his eyes were no longer smoking or glowing.

Unnerved by the strange world around him, Chris stepped back away from the young man, putting as much distance between them as he could. The sound of the beating heart still echoed all around him until he reached the far side of the square.

Bumping into a young woman, Chris comically apologised to the stationary woman. No sooner had the words passed his lips than the world broke out once again into a flurry of motion.

The woman he had bumped into snatched her stern face around to look at Chris scornfully and cast aside his apology blankly.

Peeking between the moving people, Chris caught sight of the young man who looked around in a state of confusion. Where Chris had been stood was now an empty space. Retracting his hand back fearfully, the young man scanned from left to right and quickly disappeared again into the crowds of people.

Whatever had happened to Chris in those few seconds had left him feeling strangely cold. An icy feeling across his chest reminded him of the obscure black markings above his heart, and suddenly he needed to be away from the crowds.

Merging into the flow of pedestrians, Chris made his way through the main roads until he crossed the street and entered Central Park. The outer track was peppered with runners, but as he ventured deeper into the park, he was glad to find fewer people gathered around the banks of the lakes and boathouses.

With the weather so overcast and cold, the park held little appeal other than to hardcore runners and a light spattering of tourists. Even they moved through the open park with haste, searching out the coffee shops and stores for warmth and protection from the cold weather.

Venturing along the western edge of the park, Chris found his way to Hernshead and the outcrop of smooth rocks edging out into the water of the lake. Two old women sat inside the small gazebo, but they paid him no attention as he walked by them and across the narrow path towards the rocks.

Chris had been here a dozen times before. Clambering over the rocks, he positioned himself on the far side and looked out across the water. In summer the stones were littered with people, but now, in the colder weather, he found himself alone.

'What's happening to me?'

The view across the lake was peaceful. The water rippled in the gentle breeze and far off in the distance Chris could make out the movement of the city beyond the walls of the park. Strange as it was, surrounded on all sides by skyscrapers, buildings and city life, the park was a tranquil haven in the centre of it all.

'Confused yet?' Azrael asked, his voice disturbing the peace Chris had sought.

'I'm guessing this all has something to do with you?' Chris touched his fingers to the clothes above the strange black marking on his chest.

'Indeed,' Azrael answered slowly. 'The mark and what you saw with the man in the square.'

'What was that?'

Chris was reluctant to turn his attention away from the rippling water. The motion had caught his attention, and he hoped, by not looking at Azrael, perhaps it was not happening.

'Soul Sight,' Azrael paused for a moment. 'I think it is time for you to see exactly what it is I do and then, perhaps, you can make your choice.'

'My choice?'

Chris finally turned to face Azrael, and it surprised him to find him dressed in regular clothes.

Azrael, his grey hair and goatee now neatly trimmed, was dressed in a tight-fitting suit with a long jet-black coat stretching down below his knees. There was nothing on

first sight that would tell anyone that Azrael did not
belong, that he was, in fact, an agent of death.
'Care to join me?'

There was something sinister in Azrael's voice. Chris
sensed that by accepting the imposing man's offer, he
would agree to something he did not quite understand.
'And if I decline your offer?'

Azrael raised his hand into the air and straight away a
pain erupted in Chris's chest. The black mark on his skin
no longer felt cold. Instead it burned furiously and
painfully as if it any moment his skin would burst into
flame. Clutching desperately at his searing chest, Chris
fought to catch his breath as Azrael stepped closer.
'You need to understand Christian,' he intoned, his words
calm and measured. 'You are already dead, the only thing
keeping you alive is me.'

Azrael bent down to whisper in Chris' ear as he tried to
fight back against the pain.
'What do you want from me?' Chris gasped.
'You'll see soon enough.' Azrael barked, and suddenly the
pain in Chris' chest stopped.

The burning pain subsided, and Chris slowly opened his eyes. It took a few seconds for him to gather himself and to realise he was no longer stood on the rocks at Hernshead. He was now crouched on golden sand. His knees had sunk down slightly, and he felt unbalanced. 'Where am I?' He asked as he rose to his feet, rubbing gently at where the searing pain had been.

'Altum,' Azrael answered as he stepped away to look across towards the shimmering dome.

Still massaging his chest, Chris followed Azrael's gaze and looked at the grand dome. As Chris moved to stand beside Azrael, he watched as the other man's appearance changed. The smart clothes and knee-length coat changed shape until he appeared in his more traditional garb.

The hood of the imposing black cloak remained folded

down his back, but the long sleeves now covered his hands. The hem of the cloak dragged on the floor as Azrael set off toward the great hall.

'We are early,' he began. 'But they expect us.'

As they walked across the soft sand, Chris felt his shoes sink into the sand with each step. Mesmerised by the iridescent beauty of Altum, he struggled to listen to anything Azrael was saying to him.

The dome of the Hall Of Souls And Scales grew ever more extensive, as they walked nearer. As the smooth roof dominated the skyline, Chris could, at last, see the more delicate details that made up the impressive structure.

Where the surface had appeared to shimmer from a distance, it was now apparent as to why. The entire surface of the curved roof was moving as water rolled across the polished surface. The sunlight high above reflected from the water, giving the dome its shimmer and shine.

They finally reached the side of the building and Chris could not hold back his wonder. The edge of the roof stopped a metre from the floor, and Chris watched as the water cascaded into a small gulley like a flowing waterfall. Bending down, he placed his hand beneath the flowing water and was surprised how warm it felt.

Rolling his hand over slowly, he pulled it back and stared at his fingers in surprise. The water had left an oily trail across his skin. Raising his hand to the light, he saw the same pearlescent rainbow on his skin as he did on the surface of the great hall.

'What is this?' He asked in wonder.

'Nobody really knows, it flows from the very tip of the Hall and always has done since the inception of The Enlightened Council.'

Azrael was cautious not to bombard Chris with too

much information too soon. Teasing Chris with just enough, he believed, would cement Chris' curiosity enough that The Council would consider Azraels' intentions.

'Come,' Azrael interrupted abruptly. 'There is something else I would wish you to see.'

Shaking the oily water from his hand, Chris wiped it clean against his clothes and quickly followed behind Azrael. The other man walked with more pace, and Chris struggled to keep up. Billowing fabric from Azrael's robes threatened to trip him, so Chris moved out to the side to steer clear of the material.

'The Council are in session, and I would have you see a judgement with your own eyes.' Azrael explained.

As they followed, the wide rim of the dome around the small, Pantheon building came into view.

Two guards stood either side of a wide opening. Both were dressed in green robes with hoods laying over their heads. They concealed the hands of the guards beneath the sleeves of their robes, but from each sleeve a strange blade that pointed out the back of their hands and curved sharply towards the floor.

'Who approaches the Great Hall Of Souls And Scales when The Enlightened Council are in session?'

Neither of the green-robed guards looked up, and Chris could see nothing of the features of their faces.

'Azrael Deliverer of this soul in need of judgement.'

Immediately the nearest guard snapped his head upwards and turned to face Chris. To his surprise, the space beneath the hood was empty. Although in the hang of the fabric Chris could clearly see the outline of a head, inside the hood itself, was devoid of anything. That being said, Chris could feel unseen eyes staring at him from beneath the gown.

'Is this your latest offering?' The form inside the hood asked.

'Not today, his judgement is postponed, but I would seek an audience with The Council.'

'Are you expected?' The second guard interrupted.

'I am.' Azrael quickly replied. 'The Council are aware of my arrival, and I wish to present Christian before the Council if our path beyond is granted?'

It all seemed farcical and almost like an elaborate act to Chris as he watched the interaction between Azrael and the guards. It was hard to decide what was theatrics and what, if anything about this place could be labelled as such, was a regular practice.

'The Council will accept your presence.'

Both guards turned to face one another, allowing both of them to pass into the spacious interior of the Pantheon beyond. Azrael led the way, and as Chris brushed past the further of the two guards, he felt something grab at his wrist.

'Your judgement may be held but remember, everything and every sin can be seen by The Council. You would do well to stand quiet or else face truths your heart would wish concealed.'

Chris pulled his hand free of the guard's grip and gasped as he looked down. Although a hand had clearly grabbed him, he had felt the fingers wrapped around his skin, nothing was protruding from the sleeve.

'What are you?' Chris asked as he peered curiously at the guard.

'We are the protectors of the great hall.' The first began.

'Unjudged souls offered a hope of redemption and ascension,' the second interrupted. 'Our time amongst Altum will bring us closer to eternal peace.'

'How long have you been here?'

Neither guard offered an answer. Instead, they turned to face back out towards the rest of Altum, leaving Azrael and Chris to walk beneath the high roof of the Pantheon building.

'What were they?' Chris pressed. 'I mean, I know what they were doing, but what *were* they?'

'You mean their appearance?' Azrael continued as they walked across the polished marble floor.

'Or lack of it!' Chris smirked.

'They are empty vessels, the remnants of souls that have perhaps faced judgement before. Beneath the robes, I expect you would find something of a decaying corpse to tell you they were once human.'

'They've been there that long?'

Azrael seemed uncomfortable at the question, and as they neared a pair of enormous wooden doors, he directed Chris' attention away from his line of questioning.

'Beyond these doors sits The Enlightened Council. Three members preside over all judgements, and it is their decision that will see a soul ascend, return or descend into darkness.' Azrael reached and gripped a large metal ring on the door. 'As the guard said, your place is standing in silence among the shadows. The Council will call you forward if they wish to speak.'

'And if they don't?'

'Then you escape their gaze.'

Pushing through the heavy door, Azrael allowed the momentum to open the door fully. What lay beyond was a vast open space that represented the inside of the massive dome Chris had been mesmerised by.

'Enter Reaper,' a commanding voice bellowed from the centre of the domed hall. 'Bring your prey and wait amongst the pillars.'

The voice was male and extremely well-spoken with a

strong accent. The acoustics of the hall echoed the voice around until the repeated words faded into nothing. To Chris' amazement, the interior of the dome appeared exactly the same as the exterior. Water inexplicably cascaded along the face of polished stone and disappeared into a narrow crack where the walls met the floor.

Following the contours of the roof high into its peak, Chris finally brought his gaze down towards a trio of strange seats that seemed to have grown from the floor.

Made of polished cream marble, three stems protruded from the floor. The centre of the three sat slightly higher than the two on either side. At the top of the stem sat an intricately carved flower of some description. The peeling petals flexed down towards the floor, and as if born from the carved flower, a single person sat in the centre of the three stems.

A fourth pillar sat shattered and broken beside the taller of the three. The remnants of the carved flower lay smashed and dusty on the floor below. Before Chris could say anything else, the central figure rose to their feet.

Clad in a gown of vibrant yellow and blue, the standing figure was distinctly female. A head of long red hair seemed to compliment the bright colours of her robes perfectly. Her face looked to be in her late fifties, yet there was a beauty and youth to her, something regal and almost enchanting.

'You stand before us,' she began, and for the first time, Chris noticed a diminutive figure stood beneath the three podiums.

At first, the other man within the hall was unfamiliar. It was not until the young man looked around nervously that Chris placed the face and recognised him to be the leaflet vendor from Times Square.

'Why is he here?' Chris whispered, but Azrael silenced

him with a stern look.

'Your time has been called, and you have been delivered to us for judgement.' The regal woman continued. 'Do you know why you are here?'

'No ma'am,' the young man's voice quivered.

'We present the sum of your life before us and we, The Enlightened Council, must decide your fate.' She motioned towards the other two members who remained silent and seated. 'This life is not your first, your soul has been encased in other forms and each time you have been given a chance to redeem yourself by returning in another form.'

'You mean I've lived before?'

The confusion on Chris' face was mirrored on the young man's face.

'Your soul has failed judgement three times, this will be your fourth.' The woman said, her words full of disappointment. 'It will be the decision of this council if your soul has anything left to save or else be banished to Descent and Eternal Darkness.'

'Please,' he suddenly pleaded. 'What can I do, what have I've done to deserve that?'

Chris watched curiously as the woman raised her hand and an image flickered into existence as if projected between the two furthest pillars.

'This shows your life, your wrongs, and your achievements. Decide for yourself if your lives have been of worth or waste.'

All eyes within the great hall were now focussed on the playback of the young man's life. It depicted a flurry of images, things the young man had done during his life. For a moment it showed him, in his younger years, breaking into a dark apartment.

Chris could sense where this was going and as the

young man sobbed he suspected he did too.

'We have seen enough,' the male council member to the left declared, and the images disappeared.

As the male council member rose, the red-haired woman sat down, their movements perfectly timed to one another. He was round-faced, his grey hair cropped short against his head, yet his face seemed warm. Dressed in the same yellow and blue robes, the man pointed a short finger towards the young man beneath him.

'This life and the ones before showing your true nature. A thief, a man who sought the easiest route for everything and yet worst of all, across all your existences you have taken the life of another.'

The man spoke as a teacher would when scorning a pupil. The air in the room was electric and tense.

'Our judgement is final,' the male councillor declared, and the red-head woman stood again and continued his sentence.

'Our judgement is just,' the red-head woman said as the third councillor, another woman with short cropped white hair, stood next.

'Our judgement is-'

A fourth voice finished the sentence of The Enlightened Council.

It was a younger voice, a woman's voice, and her arrival appeared to catch Azrael and The Council by surprise.

'Descent!' She declared as she materialised from the space beneath the three tall pillars.

The mood in the hall transformed with the woman's appearance.

'Amber, your presence here contravenes the rules of the Hall Of Soul And Scales, what reason do you have for standing within our halls?'

It was the white-haired Council member that spoke now. Her face was weathered and lined, showing her age, but she spoke firmly, her voice commanding and authoritative. Her gaze was fixed on the new arrival, her face filled with scorn and anger.

'I have a right to claim my souls,' Amber, the new arrival declared confidently. 'Too long have you denied us the souls you judge, and today I thought I would ensure your own rules are honoured.'

Amber was youthful in her appearance. Her light brown skin seemed radiant in the hall's light, and a head of jet-black hair appeared neatly unkempt as if styled to look messy. Standing tall, she was a lean figure, confident in her stature and dressed in a form-fitting catsuit that hugged her athletic frame. She looked in her mid-thirties, piercing eyes scanning all around until her gaze settled on Azrael.

'I might have known this Reaper would be lurking in the shadows,' Amber smirked as she half-skipped across the hall towards him.

Her demeanour was playful, her tone one of confidence, but there was something about the way she moved and spoke that unnerved Chris.

'You shouldn't be here,' Azrael growled as she came to settle in front of him.

She circled around Azrael slowly. Although he stood slightly taller, she held herself well in his presence. Raising her hand to his face, her light brown skin contrasted against Azrael's paler complexion. Walking around him, she seductively stroked her fingers across his cheeks and around the back of his head.

Chris could see her touch was uncomfortable for Azrael. The older man tensed as her fingers inched across his face, and Chris could sense his discomfort.

'I have every right,' she murmured as she circled him slowly, never removing her touch from his head. 'Your corrupt masters have manipulated the rules for too long, denying Eternal Darkness the souls it should have.'

'The judgements are fair,' Azrael snapped.

'Fair?' Amber countered quickly. 'You consider it fair to send the souls that should be judged for Descent to return below for a chance of redemption?'

Amber returned to her place in front of Azrael and took a step back. The two of them glared at one another intently for a few moments before Amber finally pulled her gaze across to Chris.

'Another soul for biased judgement?' She asked, her focus now on Chris.

'A soul you will not touch,' Azrael snarled and stepped between her and Chris.

Peering around Azrael, a look of curiosity appeared on her face. The playful look reappeared on her face, noting Azrael's protectiveness over him had piqued her face, her interest.

'Something more then, Azrael?'

The air became tense between them, and after a few seconds Amber turned her attention away from the two of them and back towards the judged man.

'Keep your victims as you see fit Azrael,' she sang as she skipped back towards the centre of the hall. 'I'm content to claim this young man and welcome him into the fold.'

Reaching the young street vendor, Chris saw him recoil at Amber's touch.

'What will you do to me?' He stammered.

'Oh my dear,' she whispered in his ear. 'I will let you be what you want to be. Forget their judgmental snares, we embrace you for what you are and let you be free as you should be.'

Turning to offer one last glare towards Azrael, she quickly turned to address The Council.

'May I claim the soul you have rightly judged into my care?'

'Take him Dark Angel and remove yourself from our halls.' The white-haired Councillor spat angrily. 'Grace our halls again without reason or invitation, and you shall feel the wrath of this Council.'

'I'm sure to some that threat may carry weight,' Amber grinned. 'For me, I just want to be able to claim what is rightfully mine.'

Before the white-haired Council member could

respond, Amber and the young man disappeared in a cloud of black smoke. As the smoke dissipated, leaving behind it an empty space where they had stood, the Councillor appeared on the verge of wanting to scream. 'Reaper!' The male Councillor shouted, breaking the tension in the hall.

'Yes My Lord.' Azrael quickly answered and stepped out of the shadows.

Azrael had regained his composure from his interaction with Amber and carried himself purposefully across the hall. Taking his position beneath the three pillars, he looked up towards the Council members high above.

'We see you that you have brought a new face into our halls, would we be right in assuming this is your nomination?'

'That is correct,' Azrael answered. 'I bring a soul that has yet to grace these halls, clean and untouched by the process of your judgement.'

'Present him,' the white-haired Councillor interrupted.

Azrael turned and beckoned for Chris to join him. A sudden wave of nervousness washed over him as he stepped out from the shadows. Bathed in the bright light of the hall, he felt all eyes on him. Doing his best to look calm, Chris made his way across the room to join Azrael beneath the flowered pillars.

Standing beneath them Chris realised how tall they were and how intricately they had been designed. Veins of ivy were carved into the shaft of the pillar, stretching upwards and around until it reached the open bud of the flowered seating. Chris could just make out the head and shoulders of the two standing Council members. Having remained seated, he could see nothing of the red-haired woman who seemed to pay him no attention.

'What makes you think he is worthy to follow in your footsteps, Azrael?'

As the male Councillor spoke the pillar on which he was stood lowered into the ground, slowly bringing him down to their level.

'I believe him to be torn; we would not make a clear judgement. He has lived but one life and has a strong desire to be reunited with one who has ascended.'

Chris watched as the pillar ground to a halt, and he could see the male Councillor stood in front of him. Standing a little shorter than Chris, the man was in his seventies, round-faced but warm in his look Chris watched as he stepped between the folded petals of his pillar and crossed towards Chris.

'Do you know who we are?' He asked, his voice level and calm.

'No,' Chris answered quickly.

'We are The Enlightened Council, three members whose job it is to judge those presented before us.' Chris watched as the Councillor came to stand in front of him. 'The souls we see are in a place where a decision is hard to foresee, their actions in life are not clear and we need time to decide where they should ultimately be.'

Chris hung on his every word. The man commanded his presence, and although smaller he carried a strange sense of presence. His bright robes seemed to glow, and every inch of Chris' attention was locked on him.

'We have no names but represent all four elements to allow fair judgement.'

'Four?' Chris pressed and quickly felt Azrael glare at him.

'Astute,' the Councillor smirked. 'Indeed, the Council once sat at four members, but now we sit at three. Three to judge the souls presented before us.'

Stepping closer, Chris felt self-conscious. The old man

stared at him, Chris felt as if he was peering deep inside him, deep into his soul and seeing things Chris would not want to be seen.

'Do you know why you have been brought here and put before us?'

'Not really.'

'Azrael here believes you possess the balance and character to follow in his footsteps and become a Reaper as he is.'

'Reaper?'

'An agent of judgement. One who locates those souls that require our intervention and places them before us. Azrael has been our most trusted servant in that respect for more than his term would have demanded.'

'Why me?' Chris interrupted, directing his question at both the Councillor and Azrael.

'Azrael?'

'Because you have a strong connection to your fallen love. It gives you passion and drive that will be needed to do what we do. The promise of being reunited will bring you focus and purpose.'

'Will it bring me, Ash, back?'

The question hung in the air unanswered for a moment, and Chris feared where it was going.

'In time you will be reunited, yes,' the Councillor answered slowly. 'It will not be quick, your time in service will be long, but it will guarantee you one thing.'

'And what is that?'

'Ascension,' while Chris assumed what this meant, the look of confusion on his face did not go unnoticed by the Councillor.

'Your own soul remains in a state of question, there can be no decision without judgement by the Council. If you are clean, then you're soul can Ascend to eternity, if it is dark and deceitful you shall rest in the embrace of Eternal Darkness.'

'And if you're not sure about me?'

'Then you can be given the chance of redemption. Another life upon the earth to better show your true nature and intention.'

'Than I will do that.' Chris answered quickly.

'Don't be so hasty Christian, redemption comes at a price.' Azrael paused. 'You will have no memory of your previous life. Any new action must be done with a clear conscience and not tainted by the actions of your life before.'

'Would I remember Ash?' Chris knew the answer already.

'There would be no memory, nothing left to remind you of the life you lived and the love you had.'

Chris felt like his world was crumbling around him. The expanse of the surrounding hall seemed to close in, and he could not accept what they were saying. A thousand questions ran through his head as looked from the Councillor to Azrael and back.

'Can I not return as I am and finish my life?' Again he knew the answer before it was given.

'Your choice upon the mountain made that impossible. You ended what you had, and now you face your own choice.'

'But remember, you are only here through your own choices and the consequences of those actions.'

The implication of what they were saying hung heavy in the air.

Suddenly Chris felt very vulnerable and very much alone.

Chris stepped away from Azrael and the Councillor.

They watched him as he moved, but he was oblivious to them. The world swam around him, and there was a sudden realisation that Chris was facing the consequences of his own actions.

The voice inside his head muttered questions at him.

Did you really want it to end?

What did you think was going to happen?

What did you expect to come?

Did you think it would bring you closer to Ash?

Did you want to die?

The questions raced at a sickening speed, words becoming mixed until it was nothing more than a cacophony of noise. Chris span on the spot and squeezed his palms to his ears to try to drown out the voices but to no avail.

Turning around in place, it all became too much. He needed to escape, be free, be anywhere but in the open space of the great hall.

'Chris?'

It wasn't the same voice.

'Chris?'

It was familiar, yet distant. The echoes of his own questions threatened to drown it out, but he knew the voice.

'Stand still,' the voice breathed as a hand touched his shoulder.

Chris stopped spinning and allowed his view to settle.

The gentle touch on his shoulder brought with it warmth and comfort. He knew the softness of the hand well, and it had been far too long since he had felt it. Stood before him, entirely beyond the realm of possibility and comprehension, stood Ash.

'How can you...' Chris started, but the emotion stopped him from speaking.

'You need to see why,' Ash answered lovingly.

'I'm sorry.' Chris wept. 'I didn't mean for it to be like this.'

Chris could not decide how he felt. Seeing Ash stood before him was the one thing he had wanted, more than anything, yet now he was filled with guilt. As Ash raised a hand to Chris' face, he could not pull himself to look.

'You shouldn't be here, you know.' Ash's words were calm but laced with disappointment. 'I had so much hope for your life beyond me.'

'There was no life beyond you, there never could be.'

'You're wrong.' Ash replied flatly. 'You chose there to be no life beyond me, you chose only to mourn when you could have moved on.'

'A life without you was not worth living.'

'And so here you stand.' Ash released the grip on Chris' face and took a step back away from him. 'By your own choices, you stand here, offered an eternity to save the memory of me.'

What would have had me do?'

'Move on, Chris. Accept the past and move on.'

'But I loved you, you were my love and my life how could there be anything without you?'

'There is always more beyond,' Ash whispered. 'You were not supposed to be here now.'

'And now I am, what now?'

Chris longed to reach out for Ash but dared not. The essence of Ash was just that, and he knew it. Holding onto the memory was enough. To reach out and feel nothing would be impossible to accept.

It tore him apart as he looked at Ash.

'You have a choice, Chris, a choice you should never have had to make. You should have bypassed this place, in my eyes, your soul was never in question, a judgement would never have been needed.'

'I did what I did to be with you, to hold you again and know you were real.'

Chris's face was stained with tears, his lips quivered, and his body shook uncontrollably.

'What you did was betray my legacy to honour my memory.'

Ash's words stung, there was no malice in the voice, but words carried with them a painful bit of realisation and truth.

'I just wanted you back,' Chris' voice faded.

'And now where are we? I'm here, but I cannot stay, you're here but not to join me.'

'What would you have me do?' Chris bit, wiping the tears from his eyes. 'I'm here now, what would you have me do?'

Ash took a step back away from Chris and looked at him for a moment. Before his eyes, Chris could see Ash's presence fade. The gentle features of Ash's face disappeared, but the piercing eyes remained.

'Do what you feel is right. To see me again, you must face an eternity of slavery to The Enlightened Council or else face forgetting me and the pain I've caused, forever.'

'It wasn't your fault,' Chris protested as he stepped towards Ash's fading image. 'You were taken; it wasn't your choice to leave me.'

'But it was yours to come here.' Ash's words were full of sadness and regret. 'Do what you think you must. You have the chance to escape the pain of losing me.'

As Ash's voice faded so did the appearance before Chris, leaving nothing behind to tell him Ash had ever been there.

Chris felt alone stood on the far side of the hall. As he slowly wiped the tears from his cheeks, Chris remembered he was not alone in the room. Doing the best he could to hide his emotion, he turned to see Azrael and the Councillor watching him intently.

'What would you have me do?' Chris finally asked as he walked back towards them. 'What price do I pay to return to the one I love?'

'Azrael,' the Councillor began. 'I leave this to you.'

Chris watched as Azrael respectfully bowed his head, and the Councillor returned to his seat.

As the pillar rose back up, Azrael returned his attention to Chris and looked down at him curiously.

'I believe it is time for you to understand what my role is in all of this. Come.'

As the pillar ground to a halt and all the Councillors disappeared as they sat back down, Chris followed close behind Azrael. He did not lead them back towards the main door but, instead, he led Chris to another smaller door. Reaching the door, Chris cast one last glance back towards the three pillars of The Enlightened Council and followed Azrael through.

Stepping through, Chris found himself in a much less impressive room. Unlike the Hall Of Souls And Scales, this was more an annexe of the primary structure. They emerged into a long and narrow corridor which stretched out in front of them. Moving along its length, Chris admired the ornate carvings on the wall on either side of them.

Peering at the images, Chris realised it told a story of some sort. Stopping partway along the hallway, he leaned in close to look at the carvings.

'What are these?' Chris asked as Azrael stopped to look at him.

'They show the journey from chaos into order.' Azrael explained as he joined Chris. 'This is where we have recorded our efforts over the centuries.'

Tracing his fingers across the intricately carved images, Azrael seemed to be lost for a moment in his own memories. Chris watched as his guide tracked around a figure on the mural that had the same appearance as Azrael. Robed and hooded, the depiction stood atop a mountain of crumpled bodies. One arm was stretched out and holding a frail figure.

'You must understand Christian; your world has always been protected by the balance of my kind. Reapers are there to ensure balance before death, we provide the Council with souls that need judgement.'

'Doesn't everyone need that?' Chris interrupted. 'If what you're saying is true, I would expect there to be queues of people waiting for judgement.'

'Not every soul is imbalanced. There are many whose fates are decided by the actions as clearly as night and day.' Azrael retorted. 'Souls that are unclear are the ones that we must present before the Council.'

'Am I such a soul?'

'No,' Azrael turned to face Chris. 'You're soul is in a state of fracture. Your actions, most likely your decision to embrace a death of your own creation, has left your fate undecided.'

'And if I hadn't done it, what would have happened then?'

'It is impossible to determine, considering.' Azrael trailed off.

'Considering what?'

'Your life was incomplete, you were not supposed to be at this place for some time.'

The gravity of Azrael's words sank in quickly. Chris turned to look at Azrael who, for the first time, did not seem to want to meet his gaze.

'How long should I have had?'

'Longer than this.' Azrael replied noncommittally.

'How much longer?'

'It doesn't matter, we are here now, and you must make your choice.'

Azrael turned and continued along the length of the passageway away from the great hall. Still wanting more answers, but knowing he would get none, Chris quickly followed behind Azrael. Completing the length of the passageway, Azrael pushed open another set of double doors, and they emerged back out into the bright light of Altum.

They walked silently for some time. Casting the occasional look behind them, Chris was surprised to see how far they had travelled from the dome of the Hall Of Soul And Scales. As they had walked, they passed through what Chris would call a village. With wide open spaces of pale sand, they only caught sight of a few houses and other structures along the way.

Finally, after a long and uncomfortable silence, they reached a darker structure. The building felt at odds with the bright airiness of Altum. Jutting from the sand at odd angles, the building appeared to be made of crystal and stone.

'What is this place?' Chris finally asked, breaking the silence.

'This is my home in Altum, it is the one place all Reapers begin.'

'There are more of you?'

'There was. A long time ago there were many of us, now there are far fewer.'

'What happened?'

Azrael paused, his hand wrapped around the handle of the door leading into the dark building.

'All in good time, Christian,' Azrael began slowly. 'If you step in here beyond, then you agree to join me.'

'I thought I was here to learn more before I decided?'

'You made your choice when you followed me from the halls,' Azrael smirked. 'But I think deep down you knew that, didn't you?'

There was a look on Azrael's face that told Chris he knew the answer. Leaving the hall, Chris had understood he had already shown his intention. Having seen Ash before him had told him all he needed to hear. Although Ash had told him to make his own choice, Chris had no choice.

He had come this far, been thrust into an underworld of life between death, by his own hand. He had done it all in the name of love and loss.

There was no way now, faced with a chance of being

reunited with Ash, that he could turn back now.

Sub-Terra differed greatly from Altum. As Amber brushed off a fine layer of smouldering dust from her shoulders, she looked around slowly, feeling instantly at home. Unlike Altum, the light spreading all around came from the slowly snaking molten rock that flowed in channels all around.

Buried beneath the earth, Sub-Terra was a place many would associate with hell. In truth, however, hell's myth was a perversion of the truth. Sub-Terra was the shadowy depths where souls of questionable motivation and action came to reside.

'Where am I?' The young man's voice was barely above a whisper as he picked himself up from the dusty ground.

Looking around, he was in awe of his surroundings. Far off, a stream of molten rock cascaded like a waterfall off the edge of a jagged cliff. All around the landscape was burned and charred, giving the world around him a darker appearance.

'Sub-Terra young David,' Amber answered with a wry smile. 'You're home now, for eternity.'

'Am I in hell?'

Amber spun around to face him quickly, the smile on her face gone. She pushed her face close to David's and glared at him angrily.

'Hell does not exist, save for in the twisted minds of the weak and fearful.' She growled angrily. 'Sub-Terra is a consequence of your actions, but it is nothing more than a place to end.'

'So it is hell then?' David pressed and suddenly felt the sting on his face as Amber struck him hard.

'You would do well to forget the preconceptions of your life before.'

Staring at him for a moment, she finally turned around and stalked off across the uneven floor towards an enormous structure on the far side of the open space. 'Follow me,' she barked as she set off at a swift pace.

Reluctantly David followed Amber but kept his distance away from her. He could barely keep his attention on Amber as the vast city of Sub-Terra came into view over the crest of a small rise in the ground.

The structure that had been the focus of Amber's direction seemed to grow as they reached the crest of the hill. From his vantage point, he saw a pair of entwined pillars rising high towards the unseen sky high above. Surrounded by the rock he knew somewhere above there was a roof of jagged stone, but regardless of his effort, he could see nothing but darkness above them.

The twisted structure looked to be their destination was imposing and eerie. At its base, the channels of molten rock seemed to meander into a bubbling pool surrounding the twin twisted towers.

David could not conceive the size of Sub-Terra as it stretched out before him. Between them and the towers, he could see hundreds of smaller buildings, all looking to have been carved from the jagged rocks. Fires burned and shadowy figures meandered all around, paying him no attention.

'Eternal Darkness awaits you,' Amber interrupted. 'It is not wise to keep him waiting.'

'Him?'

'You'll see.'

Walking down the steep slope into the central part of the city, they were met with no resistance. The shadowy figures he had seen from above disappeared as they approached. Although they passed nobody along the way, David could feel the curious eyes of whatever people resided there peering from the shadows.

Passing between the twisted rock structures, they finally made one last turn and found themselves in the shadow of the curious towers. This close, David was forced to crane his neck to see the pair of spike pinnacles pointed up towards the dark sky. Jagged veins of glowing red rock stretched from the very tips down into the boiling pool of molten rock.

David could feel the heat; at least he thought he could. Since materialising within the depths of Sub-Terra, he had felt nothing. Although the world around him was filled with fire and lava, he had not felt the burning heat upon his skin. He had merely felt nothing.

'I bring before you the latest judgement from the corrupt Enlightened Council.' Amber declared, projecting her voice across the bubbling pool of lava separating them from the twisted towers.

For a few seconds, nothing happened. Across the lake of lava David could make out a space at the base of the twin towers. Amber seemed to be directing her announcement towards the very area between the two bases. As he waited for something to happen David chanced a look behind him and gasped in surprise.

Lined up behind him were the charred and scarred faces of at least a hundred people.

Each of them looked to be in a different stage of burning decay. David could make out their human features, faces half-scarred or consumed by the fierce heat of Sub-Terra. Some appeared less damaged than the others, but all of them had at least been touched by the searing heat in one way or another.

One face which caught his attention seemed to glare at him, lips upturned in a twisted snarl as a single eye glared at him. The rest of the man's face was burned and charred beyond recognition, the entire right side of his face was twisted and black. With his only in-tact eye, David could feel a genuine hatred burning out towards him.

Instinctively David took a few steps backwards and suddenly felt Amber thrust her arm hard into his lower back.

'Mind your step, you fool,' she snapped as she spun David on the spot. 'Another step and you would have been swimming in there sooner than you should.'

Facing back towards the towers, David realised he had almost tumbled into the boiling lake of lava. Forgetting the glaring demon behind him, David stared down in terror at the closeness of the fiery lake.

'What is that place?' David asked as he stepped back from the crumbling edge beside the lake.

'Furca Tower, the resting place of Eternal Darkness and the place you shall only visit once.'

As Amber spoke, the ground shook and shuddered. Taking another cautious step back, David watched as the bubbling lake boiled more violently. Starting at the far side, the lava bubbled and spit, sending sparks of fire in every direction.

Slowly emerging from the lava, a bridge of smooth black stone appeared. Unlike the jagged primal bedrock that made up the landscape of Sub-Terra, the bridge seemed to be polished and smooth, flawlessly carved as it rose slowly from the molten rock.

'Come.' Amber barked and stepped onto the still rising bridge.

Tentatively, David followed and stepped up onto the bridge. Avoiding the puddles of lava, David walked cautiously across the bridge and towards Furca Tower. Moving close now David could see the veins of red were in fact lava which defied the concept of gravity and flowed upwards along narrow channels carved into the face of the structure.

'How is that possible?' David asked as he peered at the veins.

'You will soon come to accept Sub-Terra is a place defying the logic of your past world.'

They passed beneath the arch created by the two bases of the towers crossing one another and continued along, dwarfed by the thickness of the towers. The hallway was tight and claustrophobic, sending a chill down David's spine until they finally emerged into the centre of the tower.

Looking up, David could see the corkscrew effect created by the intertwined buildings as they stretched high above them.

'Welcome, David,' a voice boomed from the far side of the open space.

Snatching his attention down, David could not see any source of the voice. The only thing different on was a black void on the far side of the room.

Stepping towards it the void looked to be made of black smoke seeming to hover just above the floor and dominate a significant portion of the chamber ahead of him.

'Who's there?' David asked tentatively as he stepped towards the hovering black smoke.

'I am Eternal Darkness, and I welcome you to my kingdom.'

The voice came from the hovering smoke, and David stopped dead in his tracks. Staring wide-eyed at the smoke, he could not quite fathom how it was possible the sound was coming from inside it.

'I am certain you have many questions to better understand what you have become.'

David stood in stunned silence, and the smoke merely laughed at his silence.

The laugh was thunderous and menacing.

'For the first time in your life, you find yourself unable to speak?' The smoke chuckled. 'A life of venomous words and actions, yet you stand before me silent?'

Tendrils of snaking smoke emerged from the centre and stretch out towards David. Unable to move, he felt rooted to the spot as the smoke made its way towards him slowly.

'Let me see the darkness that tainted your life and understand why the Enlightened Council sent you to dwell in my kingdom of Sub-Terra.'

Now David could feel.

Fear coursed through his veins and as the smoke wrapped itself around his body, he could feel the heat burning against his skin. As it slowly wrapped itself around him, David was pulled towards the dead black centre of the smoke.

Try as he might, David could not move. Fear gave way to panic as he struggled against the smoke as it tied itself around him. Although the light smoke would typically have no physical presence, David could feel it like a coiled rope tight against his body.

Drawn closer and closer, he was consumed by the lifeless black centre of the smoky apparition and was swallowed into a world of nothingness.

'Your life's choices brought you here,' the Eternal Darkness whispered. 'The actions of your life culminate here, this place is the consequence of your decisions. You are here for the life you took.'

In an instant, David was cast back to a time in his life he had desperately tried to suppress.

David had spent his life regretting his choice that night. He could hear the rain, feel the panic as his racing heart beat in his chest.

'Stop, Police!' The voice echoed around him, but he dared not look back.

David did not want to live through this again.

'Please no.' He screamed into the darkness. 'It wasn't meant to be that way. I didn't mean to do it. Let me go.'

David's pleading screams echoed through the chamber as Amber watched.

Amber remembered her own arrival at Sub-Terra, long before they had elevated her to the role of Dark Angel. She knew the pain and fear David was feeling. She did not envy it, but understood the reasons it had to be done. By facing the very thing that had seen a soul cast into Sub-Terra, it allowed a realisation that this was the end brought about by a person's own actions and nothing else.

Before Amber could reminisce about her own exposure

to her dark deeds in a long forgotten life, David was thrown back out from the smoky apparition.

Landing heavily on the floor, Amber watched as David crawled across the floor.

'You are ready,' Amber declared as she watched David take in his own appearance.

Amber could see both David's hands were now burnt and charred black. His left arm had taken on the same appearance of charred flesh that smouldered and smoke as she watched him looking at it.

'The scars remind you of your past, your punishment for past deeds.'

She watched as David stared at his hands and screamed.

David's body was twisted and scarred, both hands, one arm and the lower third of the left side of his face were all twisted and charred black. In the confines of the open room, David wept at his new twisted appearance and Amber, from across the room, smiled.

'Another member of the rank and file of Sub-Terra,' she said, and looked towards the hovering smoke.

'Did the Council offer you any resistance at claiming the soul as our own?' The bodiless voice boomed.

'Not as much as you would expect,' Amber began. 'But Azrael was protective of a soul within the hall. A soul yet to face judgement.'

'Twisting the rules to keep us weak, I expect.' The Eternal Darkness groaned.

'There was something different about this one, Azrael was too protective of him.'

'A successor to the great Reaper himself?'

'Perhaps,' Amber murmured as she walked past David. 'I sense a change is coming.'

Ignoring David as he struggled to accept his

appearance, Amber stared into the blackness of the hovering smoke.

'I feel the tides are turning,' the voice declared. 'In time we may redress the corruptness of the Enlightened Council and return once again to a time of power within Sub-Terra.'

The stone and crystal building was spookily silent as they stepped through the jagged door. Chris followed close behind Azrael as he passed through a short corridor which opened out into a large training room.

The high ceiling was almost transparent as the crystal allowed the outside light to pour in. The natural hue of the stone tainted the natural light, giving it a tone of emerald green.
'This will be your home until I consider you are ready.'
'How long will that be?' Chris pressed as he walked around the edge of the large room.
'As long as it takes.' Azrael replied, his words flat and without emotion.

The main floor was made of polished wood, complimenting the dark stone and crystal walls. Eight columns stood around the edge of the room, supporting the fantastic clear ceiling above. Against the far wall, three stone plinths stood proudly. Each was bathed in a beam of white light, channelled through a series of holes bored into the wall.

'What are they?' Chris asked as he walked towards the plinths.

Only two of them had anything mounted on the top. The middle of the three sat empty. A thin layer of dust lay on the smooth surface. Stood to the right as Chris looked was a pair of weapons mounted on the flat face. Each carried a large curved blade at ninety degrees from a handle of carved wood. They seemed to be a pair of scaled-down scythes, the edges smooth with the handles treated and stained rich mahogany.

To the left a pair of curious daggers stood, their blades crossed just below the tips, balancing precariously. Unlike the scythes, someone had scored the blades of the knives with an intricate pattern around the edge of the blades. The handles were made of the same rich-stained wood and seemed to blend perfectly with the shimmering metal of the blade.

'They are the weapons of a Reaper.'

'Why would you need weapons?' Chris asked curiously. 'I always thought the scythe was just for show, to add some fear to the visage of death.'

'Human ignorance, that is something we will certainly need to help you forget.' Azrael sighed and walked away from the stone plinths. 'We charge a Reaper with directing lost souls to the Hall Of Souls And Scales. Along that way, some forces would seek to claim the souls for themselves, to other ends.'

'Like the woman back there?'

Chris' attention was drawn to the pair of scaled

scythes. There was something hypnotic about them, the way the light caught on the metal. Peering closer, Chris could see his own reflection staring back at him from the polished blade.

'Amber is a Dark Angel, she seeks souls set for Descent, but she observes the rules. Mostly.' Azrael eyed Chris as he spoke. 'She comes from Sub-Terra, a place beneath the earth where souls who cannot find Redemption are sent.'

'So this is heaven, and that is hell?' Chris muttered, his attention continuing to be drawn towards his own reflection in the blade.

'More human notions that mean nothing in our world.' Azrael grimaced. 'Heaven and hell are concepts, there is simple Ascension, Descent and a chance at Redemption. I have not been above or below, and this is the price I pay. Instead, I service the Council who would best see judgement for those whose fates are undecided.'

Chris could hear Azrael speaking, but the words made no sense to him. It drew his complete attention to the weapons. Stepping closer, he had no control over his own actions as he raised both hands out towards the weapons.

As his fingertips brushed the warm wooden handles, his eyes rolled into his head and he felt thrust backwards.

Screams filled his head. A thousand voices from every direction spoke and shouted above the screams.

Then silence.

Nothing moved as the world around him came into focus.

Chris found himself in an unfamiliar place. He stood facing out towards a vast lake in the depths of a cold winter's morning. Flakes of snow fluttered lazily from a heavy sky, and a light mist rolled along the shores of the lake on the far side.

Looking down, Chris found himself stood on a long

jetty of mossy wood. The pier was narrow with a barrier at waist height to either side and in front of him. Looking back, he could make out the shore away behind him, partially obscured by the same rolling mist.

In the silence, he could hear the crackle of the falling snow. Occasionally he could hear the gentle tap as the flakes landed on the glassy surface of the lake.

It was comforting to be alone. Everything that had happened to him over the last few days seemed a lifetime away, and Chris inhaled deeply as if drinking in the moment's peacefulness.
'Who are you?' A voice whispered from beneath him.

Casting his gaze down towards the wooden planks, Chris did not know how to answer.
'Why do you come here?' The whispering voice pressed. 'Can't you find the answer within yourself?'

There was a mockery in the words as the whispering voice pressed on.
'Look at yourself, and perhaps you will see the answer.'

Awash with curiosity, Chris took the handful of paces to the end of the jetty and peered down towards the water. The barely felt breeze kept the surface of the lake in constant motion. Steady ripples danced across its surface, but as Chris looked down the water became still and motionless.

As his own reflection came into focus, Chris was confused by what he saw.

His own face did not stare back at him. Looking back at him was a dark hooded figure, their face obscured by the dense shadows created by the loose material.
'What is this?' Chris finally asked, raising a hand to his head and finding no hood obscuring his face.
'Your future,' the voice whispered again. 'Your past and your present. This is you as you will become if you follow

the path laid out before you.'

'Who are you?'

'Who are *you*?' The voice retorted. 'We are the same.'

Chris watched as the reflection in the water pulled back the hood revealing Chris' reflection. Leaning closer, Chris felt, at last, comfortable with what was looking back at him. He knew his own face, and the reflection matched all his movements.

'You will become,' the voice pause for a moment as Chris leant closer to peer at his reflection. 'Death.'

In an instant, the face looking back at him changed. Bone emerged from the skin, and a sickening skull stared back at him. The screams returned as the head breached the surface of the water and flew up towards him.

Instinctively, Chris jumped backwards. As soon as he did, he was drawn back to the crystal-roof room and to the sound of the two scythes clattering to the floor.

Disorientated Chris' vision saw as he now found himself stood in the centre of the room with his back to the trio of stone plinths. Both the scythes now lay discarded on the floor by his feet, and his hands shook as he looked down at them.

'What did you see?' Azrael asked as he stood looking at him.

'I saw my reflection in the water,' Chris panted. 'Except it wasn't me, and then...'

His voice trailed off as he played back the gruesome vision erupting from the water.

'And then what?'

'A skull jumped out from the water, and I came back here.'

Raising his gaze, he finally looked across at Azrael. The older man stood watching him curiously. Chris could see something in his expression that unnerved him.

'It was you,' Azrael declared. 'You must understand, the

life you had is no more. Everything you do from this point is in service to the Council and to the traditions of Altum. Having agreed to continue the line of Reapers, you agree to serve the Council until your time for judgement arrives.'

'My memories?'

'They will be yours to keep as long as you need them.'

'How long will it take?' Chris pressed. 'How long until I can see Ash again?'

'A question best forgotten. There is no answer other than as long as it takes. Every person's journey is determined by their actions in life and their service in death.'

'What have I really agreed to do, Azrael?' It was the first time Chris had used his name.

'In time you will understand,' Azrael began. 'But for now, I think it best we start simple and then, along the way, I can tell you about the world you now inhabit.'

Chris was tired of the mystery. All the breadcrumbs and snippets of information told Chris there was a whole new world he needed to understand. Azrael's talk of Dark Angels and things trying to steal souls only added to the intrigue.

Azrael could see the confusion in Chris' expression as he tried to cope with everything he had seen so far.

'Pick them up.' Azrael instructed, disturbing the awkward silence in the crystal room. 'We might as well begin somewhere.'

Looking from the discarded scythes and back to Azrael, it shocked Chris to see the older man remove his outer robe and hang it from one of the columns. Reaching behind him, Azrael removed a dagger, much the same as the ones remaining on the stand behind Chris.

'How much experience do you have with weapons, Christian?'

'Not much.' He confessed.

'Then I have picked the right place to start.'

Chris watched as Azrael tossed the dagger from his left hand to his right and then sprinted across the room towards Chris. Acting purely on instinct, Chris snatched up the nearest of the two scaled scythes and raised it into the air just in time.

Azrael's dagger sliced through the air, and Chris only just managed to deflect the mighty blow by thrusting the wooden handle of the scythe into Azraels' wrist.

'Good!' Azrael snapped and quickly adjusted his attack.

There was no time to think as Azrael launched a flurry of attacks at him. The blade of the dagger came from his left, then right and then directed towards his face, and again Chris did his best to deflect each attack.

In no time at all, Chris had felt the sting of the smooth blade across his skin more than once. As Azrael tossed the weapon into the air and grasped it in his other hand, Chris knew what was coming.

Before he could do anything to deflect the attack, the dagger sliced through the air and Azrael plunged it towards his face. Chris had nowhere to go, Azrael had forced him so far back across the room he could feel the polished stone of the wall behind him.

Azrael stopped his attack with timed precision. Snatching the blade still in the air, Chris stared at the knife hovering mere millimetres from his nose. The tip of the blade shook slightly in Azrael's hand, but the older man held the tip perilously close to Chris, who pushed himself hard against the wall.

'You show a little promise at least,' Azrael smiled. 'With training perhaps I will make a Reaper of you yet.'

Azrael flipped the dagger over in the air and caught it by the blade. In one swift movement, he replaced the dagger in the conceal sheath mounted at the small of his back.

'The dagger is a Reaper's last line of protection. The scythes are our primary weapon, but you can never underestimate the power of such a small weapon. Keep it with you at all times and always be prepared to use it.'

The speed and grace of Azrael's movements had been impressive. Chris could not help but admire the man stood in front him. To look at him, he appeared too old to move with such agility, but Chris was fast learning appearances as they had been in life meant nothing here. 'Rest,' Azrael finally added. 'Tomorrow we begin your training, and you will begin to learn the answers to all those questions racing through your head.'

Leaving Chris alone in the room, Azrael retrieved his cloak and threw it over his shoulders. Pulling the hood up over his head, he moved towards the door and stepped out into the bright light of Altum. As the door closed, Chris looked down at the scythe in his hand.

'What have I got myself into?'

Yet again his question went unanswered.

Time had no place in Altum. Although the sun rose and set, it did so with irregularity and unpredictability. Since arriving in the crystal building, Chris had witnessed only three sunsets, yet he knew all too well that his time had been longer than three days within the grand city.
'How long have I been here?' Chris asked as he laid the pair of scythes to rest on an outcrop of rock beside him.

Azrael had told Chris the name of the crystal building that had become his home, it was known as The Altar, and it had become very familiar to him. As he stood looking back towards The Altar, he watched as the sun danced across the glassy roof and appeared to twinkle in the sunlight.
'What does it matter? Time takes no meaning here.' Azrael answered as he too laid his weapon upon the stone.

On this occasion Azrael trained with a massive broadsword, the heavy blade had been expertly wielded in his hands. Between them, they had spent countless hours practising with weapons, yet Chris still struggled to master the pair of scythes he had adopted.

Deep down it had frustrated him. On most occasions, during their training sessions, Chris would find himself planted on the floor staring down the blade of whatever weapon Azrael had wielded.

'Because I seem to learn nothing!' Chris snapped, his frustration bubbling over uncontrollably. 'We practice for hours, yet I can barely hold you back for a few seconds.'

Chris kicked out at the outcrop of rock, sending chunks of stone flying in every direction.

'You hold on too much to your past, something distracts you.'

Azrael could see the emotion in Chris and knew all too well it was a distraction.

'I'm here because of that distraction, it's not in my nature to just forget it. It's what brought me here.'

'Harness it,' Azrael comforted as he perched himself on a large stone.

Azrael had discarded the traditional garb. He was now dressed in a fitted piece that only dispelled Chris' misconception about his age and ability. Although looking old, the outfit showed him to be in good health and fitness. A mixture of interlaced red and black weaves gave the clothes a strange look.

'You say forget it and yet harness it.' Chris had been suppressing his frustration, and now it flowed freely.

'What am I supposed to do? All we have done is fight and train, and I know nothing more of what you expect me to do.'

Chris watched as Azrael shook his head from side-to-side slowly, a look of disappointment painted on his face. 'You need to be ready, these are the early steps of your journey.'

'And just how long will this journey be?' Chris barked, his voice louder than he had intended.

'As long as is necessary.'

Azrael's frustration now matched Chris' as he launched up from his seat. Stalking across the golden sand, he came to stand in front of Chris and gripped his shoulders.

'Just what is it you think you need to know to succeed, Christian?' Azrael braced him in his powerful grasp. 'If I begin to explain to you the nuances and details of this world of death, how will that help you in this arena?'

Chris did not know the answer. By knowing more, it would do nothing to aid his training but perhaps do enough to settle his mind to learn.

In the time he spent alone inside The Altar, he resented his lack of understanding. Chris had never been in a position at such a disadvantage, and it was this that unbalanced him the most.

'I don't know,' Chris finally sighed and Azrael pushed him backwards, releasing his grip on his shoulders.

Azrael stalked back to his resting broadsword and snatched it from the floor. Settling it in his hands, he turned to look at Chris and dropped his bodyweight into a ready stance, the weapon tipped towards Chris.

'Best me, at least once before the sun sets, and perhaps I will consider a day of rest so you can learn a little more about where you lie in all of this.'

Not waiting for Chris to reply, Azrael charged across the gap between them.

Thrusting the sword outwards and upwards, Azrael made his attack. Chris had no time to reacquire his own weapons and instead dropped himself to the floor and rolled out of the way just in time to avoid the attack. As the weapon buried in the sand, Chris heard the vibration of the blade as Azrael struck.

Flicking the sand from the floor, Chris shielded his eyes as he rolled away.

Gaining his footing, Chris righted himself and lunged across the floor. He landed roughly on the floor within reach of the twin scythes. Snatching them up, Chris rolled onto his back as Azrael slashed the blade down once again towards his head.

Crossing the curved blades, Chris pinched the broadsword between the scythes and held it just above his face.

'Better,' Azrael growled as he pressed his weight further onto the sword.

Chris struggled to keep the sword from his head. Every ounce of effort was needed to keep Azrael from plunging the weapon into him. Scanning around desperately, he made a decision and acted.

Scooping his leg underneath Chris kicked out hard and took Azrael's legs from underneath him. Off balance, by his attack, Azrael tumbled to the floor, and Chris scuttled free from the next attack.

'Keep going,' Azrael commanded.

Chris spun the two scythes around in his hands and feigned a lung forward. Still righting himself, Azrael jerked backwards to protect himself and stumbled back. Launching no attack, Chris followed through with an alternative attack.

Having feigned an attack from the right, he quickly changed direction and used the momentum of his movement. Slicing the scythe through the air, he aimed it low and scooped the wooden handle across the back of

Azrael's knees. Buckling beneath him, Azrael once again tumbled to the floor, and it was now Chris' turn to strike.

Pivoting around, Chris drove the weapons upwards, over and around to the point where Azrael had fallen.

Both blades buried in the sand.

Azrael was gone, no longer sprawled on the floor. Confused by his opponent's disappearance, the first thing Chris knew about where Azrael was, came from a sharp blow to the back of his head.

Caught completely by surprise Chris jolted forward and landed heavily on the ground, his chin sinking into the sand sending it spewing into his mouth. Coughing and spluttering, Chris rolled himself to see another vigorous attack from Azrael.

Closing his eyes, he waited for the strike to land.

It never did. All he could do to protect himself from Azrael was cross both his arms across his face in defence from the attack.

Opening his eyes cautiously, Chris was stunned by what he saw. The long blade of the broadsword was buried a third of its length into the sand to the left side of his head. His own weapons were in line with his forearms, with each of the curved blades pointing from his elbows. Pinned between the centre of the two tips, Azrael's face hung motionless, and the metal hung a hair's breadth from his skin.

The pair remained in their position for a handful of long breaths.

'May I move?' Azrael finally asked, a smile appearing on his weathered face.

'Yes.'

Chris had not realised how focused he had been, how dangerous the look on his face must have been. Deep down, he felt a wave of relief as Azrael removed himself from the quivering blades Chris was still holding.

Overcome with pride and surprise at his own performance, Chris lowered his arms and accepted Azrael's hand.

'See what you can achieve?' Azrael grinned. 'When given the proper motivation.'

Chris could not suppress the pride at what he had done. It had been a single victory against a torrent of defeats, but it felt, to him, as a step in the right direction. Until that moment Chris had felt ill-equipped and out-manned in every respect when facing Azrael.

But not now.

Now, there was hope that in time he could grow and train until his single victory could be joined by many more. He could prove himself worthy to Azrael.

'Rest.' Azrael said as he slapped his hand on Chris' shoulders. 'Tomorrow I shall show you things that will explain our place in all of this.'

Guiding Chris to a raised section of earth, Azrael left him alone to consider what was to come. Looking out across Altum, Chris could not deny its beauty and majesty. The shimmering dome of the Hall Of Souls And Scales dominated its surrounding. It drew his attention in as people meandered through the wide streets leading up towards the hall.

There was so much he did not appreciate and understand.

'Tomorrow,' Chris whispered to himself. 'Maybe this will start to make a little more sense.'

As Azrael disappeared, Chris gathered his things and returned to The Altar to rest and recover himself. Quite unexpectedly, the exertion of training still took its toll on him. Chris still felt his body ache and his senses dulled by the effort of his practice.

It was funny, in death he had expected to remove himself from such feelings. He had very quickly learned that his body in Altum was as prone to injury and fatigue as it had been when he had been alive.

There really was so much that made no sense.

And tomorrow, he hoped, would start to give him answers.

Beneath a blanket of stars, Chris felt oddly at peace.

Although his body ached and groaned at the exertion, he had suffered with Azrael before he had finished their last encounter on somewhat of a high. Laid out on top of the emerald coloured crystal roof of The Altar, Chris stared into space.

Wherever Altum was, it existed on a plain where the stars appeared in their purest form. Streaks of twinkling light infrequently moved across the blanket of space. The haze of distant galaxies was a mix of vibrant colours against the black canvas of space.

'Beautiful, isn't it?'

Chris sat up quickly and turned to find the old-man Councillor striding confidently across the uneven rooftop towards him.

'I'm sorry?' Chris floundered, somewhat taken aback by his interruption.

'I said,' the old man repeated. 'The view is beautiful, isn't it?'

'Without a doubt.'

'May I?' The old man asked, pointing towards the edge of the roof where Chris now dangled his legs.

'Not at all.'

Curious, Chris was silent as the old man dropped down to the ledge and admire the view of Altum stretching out in front of them. Firelight danced in the gentle breeze, and the streets were silent and undisturbed. 'It is easy to forget how beautiful this place can be.' The old man mused. 'I've spent too many hours locked in the Great Hall, I often forget to appreciate what we have here.'

'It is quite something.' Chris agreed.

'I do apologise,' the old man's voice became softer. 'I am yet to properly introduce myself. We have all gone by many names over the centuries, but I have become quite fond of Osiris.'

'As in the Egyptian God?' Chris asked, perplexed.

'Indeed, you are quite right. The other Councillors have grown fond of other names for us, but for me, that seems to roll off the tongue nicely.'

'I can't say, honestly, that any of this is making sense to me yet.'

'I suspected as much. I spoke with Azrael a little while ago.' Chris was suddenly nervous, it revealed in his expression. 'Dear boy, don't worry, he spoke highly of you in fact. Believe me, from Azrael that in itself is a compliment.'

'Thanks, I think.'

'Perhaps we should walk and talk?' Osiris motioned to the floor below them. 'Appreciate the city and indulge the flights on an old man that spends too much time sat in high places.'

Chris nodded and watched in surprise as Osiris dropped himself from the edge of the roof and landed on the floor beneath them. The drop was easily twenty feet, yet the old man landed with the grace of an agile feline. 'Well, come on then,' Osiris mocked. 'You can jump or else waste time climbing down the same way you got up!'

Unsure of the consequences, Chris edged himself over the ledge and reluctantly dropped himself down. At the last minute, he gripped the edge of the roof and awkwardly dangled, much to his embarrassment.
'Too late now, just let yourself drop.'

Knowing the Councillor was right, Chris closed his eyes and allowed himself to slide down the rough wall of The Altar.

To his surprise, Chris landed firmly on the floor and felt little of the impact.
'See,' Osiris chuckled. 'Not everything is as it seems. Shall we?'

Dressed in the bright robes, Osiris walked at a steady pace as Chris positioned himself at his side. For the first few minutes of their journey, neither of them said a word. Instead, both of them admired the shimmering dome of the Hall of Souls And Scales now bathed in firelight from the torches mounted around its base.

As they reached the edge of the houses at the side of Altum, Osiris finally broke their silence.
'Do you know what we do here, Christian?'
'Chris, I prefer Chris.'
'Ok, Chris. Well?'
'I can make guesses on the little bits I've seen and heard, but I don't really know, no.'
'The Enlightened Council has been with humanity since

the dawn of time. It is our job to bring an end that reflects a soul's actions in their life or lives.' They continued deeper into Altum, their pace slow and gentle. 'A soul can occupy many lives until its true nature can be seen and judged.'

Osiris continued to speak as they meandered through the streets. Chris hung on his every word, drinking in the rich tapestry and history Osiris explained.

Osiris detailed the process of judgement. The Reapers would seek each soul which remained undecided. Pulled from their lives at a point when their soul was in its purest form, they would each be presented individually before The Council. Then, and only then, between the three Councillors, they would test the worth of a soul's actions or inactions.

The process had been what Chris had witnessed in the hall with the young man. They were only ever three outcomes of judgement and as they walked along the primary avenue towards the Hall Of Souls And Scales Osiris detailed them.

'Ascension comes where a soul is judged as pure. Your misconceptions may label it as heaven, Elysium or some other fanciful construction of peace and tranquillity. It may well be that, but for each soul, it is a place of eternal rest taking the guise of whatever they wish. I am sure for many of them its representation would be similar, enforced by religious expectations, but that is not for me to judge.'

'Have you never seen it?'

'Not myself no, I gave up my chance at the dawn of my own death to sit on the council. Perhaps, one day, I shall see my own Ascension, but for now, it remains an unseen mystery.'

There was something in Osiris' words that piqued

Chris' curiosity. Not wanting to interrupt the torrent of information, Chris bottled his curiosity and listened intently to his companion.

'Descent comes at a price of dark choices and actions.'

Chris sensed Osiris' pause was aimed towards him, giving him time to consider what fate he would face if he were to be judged.

'You would label it was hell or purgatory, but it is a place of consequence. Much as Ascension brings you peace, Descent to join Eternal Darkness leaves your soul to pay for the deeds of life. Where rest comes to those who Ascend, Descent brings with it labour. An eternity working to keep the fires of the earth burning.'

'It sounds a lot like hell to me.'

'Misconceptions, my dear boy, feeble attempts to explain the unknown. Believe me, we have fed these ideas and fables through the centuries to encourage a sense of consequence to people's actions. The niggling fear of what is to come at the end of life is often enough to make some people think twice.'

'Is everyone that is judged destined for one or the other and nothing else?' Chris pressed.

'There is Redemption, a chance to live another life. It comes at a cost, you cannot recall your past life and transgressions, only the one you inhabit at that time. Sometimes memories leak between lives, but mostly, it is a chance to reset and let a person's natural balance show.'

'But why let someone try again?'

'Because a single event in life is not enough to judge a soul's true nature.' Osiris scorned. 'You of all people should understand that.'

'Meaning what exactly?'

Chris stopped and waited for Osiris to turn and face him.

'Where do you think your soul would lie, having taken your own life?'

Chris suddenly felt very conscious of Osiris' gaze. The Councillor stared at him intently, and Chris felt as if the old man was peering into his very soul. Chris could not deny his actions on the mountainside had haunted him. 'A single action is not enough to offer proper judgement.' Osiris continued. 'Yet you have not been judged.'

'Feels like I have,' Chris snapped, his words more ferocious than he intended.

'You should consider your position carefully,' Osiris said calmly. 'Azrael sees something in you that saves you from judgement. I would vote to send you back in the hope of Redemption, I'm sure the others would agree, but that is not your path. Redemption for you comes in the guise of service to Altum and The Enlightened Council's quest for balance.'

'I get to keep my memories.' Chris sighed.

'Your past will become your motivation. Memories of your beloved Ash will drive you to survive all of this, will drive you to become a Reaper.'

Looking across at Osiris, the old man did not seem so frail and delicate anymore. The Councillor was calculating, and Chris resented that. He had been drawn in by the man's kindness, but it had all been a veiled offer to manipulate Chris just enough to entice him in. To show him that in reality, he had no choice.

'You do not know the torment and pain that races around my head.' Chris growled and closed down Osiris. 'You've not seen what I have seen or felt the pain and consequence of my decisions. Stand in my shoes, live my life and perhaps one day I may respect your opinion of me.'

Chris towered over Osiris, his words filled with passion and anger.

The old Councillor held his position defiantly. Slowly he tilted his head, just enough to peer up at Chris whose face was contorted with anger and frustration. Leaving him to stew a moment, Osiris stood silently before choosing his words carefully.

'I am not your enemy in all of this; Azrael will educate you about those in good time. You need to cast aside all this anger and hatred and embrace what you will become.'

Chris could not fathom the manner in which these words were offered. On the one hand, he saw Osiris' concern and care at his position. On the other, he saw the skilful manipulation of a wise old man.

'Return to The Altar, rest and recover. Embrace the teachings Azrael offers and perhaps you will find your place in all of this.'

Osiris took a step back away from Chris and turned, leaving him alone on the broad avenue in front of the domed hall. Still seething with anger and frustration, Chris watched as Osiris walked back through the Pantheon building and disappeared between the columns.

Once again alone, Chris moved to the nearest wall and slumped against it. Sliding down the wall, Chris rested his head on his knees, trying to make sense of everything he had learned.

One thing that Chris had always done to clear his mind was sketch. Finding the tools had been easy enough and having returned from his encounter with Osiris, he set about decluttering his thoughts. By the time Azrael arrived and the night gave way to another day, The Altar's floor was littered with half-drawn pictures spread across dozens of sheets of paper.

Chris laid on the floor in the foetal position in a deep sleep as Azrael flowed into the room. Silently he navigated the images, admiring each one in turn.

The sketches showed everything that Chris had seen since arriving in Altum. A rendering of the Hall Of Souls And Scales dominated one sheet. The dome and Pantheon neatly sketched with a rendering of the Councillor's seats set to one side of the sheet.

One particular image caught his attention. Leaning down, Azrael brushed aside some sheets to expose something that had been peering up at him. Buried beneath a handful of leaves, all Azrael had seen was a sketched eye staring up at him.

The eye, although a hand-drawn image, was familiar. Moving aside the sheets that covered it, Azrael immediately recognised the sketched face on the page. 'Amber.' Azrael gasped as he lifted the sheet from the floor.

Mesmerized by the picture, Azrael sat on his haunches, oblivious that Chris had stirred and was now watching him curiously.

'Who is she?' Chris finally asked as he stretched out his aching muscles.

The sketch transfixed Azrael and he rubbed his fingers along the contours of her face on the sheet.

'Come,' Azrael announced suddenly. 'We have much to discuss after your introduction last night.'

Allowing the page to flutter to the floor, Azrael made for the door back out into the open air.

As the door closed, Chris gathered himself and quickly made his way out behind Azrael.

Azrael waited in the rising sunlight just beyond the door to The Altar. As Chris stepped out, it relieved him to see that Azrael was unarmed. Even though his mentor had promised a day of knowledge over training, he had expected Azrael to withdraw his offer considering his encounter with Osiris.

'How did you know about last night?' Chris asked as he stepped out into the sunrise.

'I asked Osiris to speak with you; I knew you needed someone other than me to begin your journey.'

As Chris stepped up to Azrael, he watched the older

man lift a bound bundle from the floor beside him.
'It's time you dressed more appropriately,' Azrael
declared as he tossed the bundle at Chris' feet.

Unravelling the binding, Chris lifted up a jet-black
gown of heavy fabric. He could see what it was
immediately. The material was a tailored hooded cloak,
the same as the one Azrael had worn when he had
presented himself to Chris as death.

A shiver danced along Chris' spine as he looked at the
dark material. Jerking the cloak, Chris allowed the full
hood to flip over and hung in front of him.
'I don't think it's my style,' Chris mocked as he turned the
cloak over and around.

Looking down, he saw there was more from the
bundle. A pair of black trousers and wrap-around top sat
on the floor by his feet.
'Dress yourself and join me when you're ready.' Azrael
said and scooped up his own hood to obscure his face.
'You'd do well to move with some haste, we have a lot to
discuss.'

Returning to The Altar, Chris quickly removed the
remnants of his past life and slipped on the clothes Azrael
had given him. The material was soft to his skin and felt
oddly warm to the touch. The top half of the outfit folded
across his torso like a samurai kimono, and it took a few
attempts to secure the material in place.

Stepping back into his boots, Chris secured the laces
and looked down at the hooded cloak.
'Not today.' Chris said as he considered donning the gown
and stepped back towards the open door.
'Missing something?' Azrael asked as Chris stepped out of
The Altar.
'Small steps,' Chris defended. 'There's only so much
change I can take at one time.'

Azrael peered from the shadow of his own hood for a moment before he agreed with a curt nod. Taking Chris' cue, he pulled down the covering and once again revealed his face to the sunlight.

'Shall we make a start?'

They did not walk far before Azrael led them towards a small building of red marble. It was only a simple box, barely large enough to hold the wooden door in place. Chris was most positively underwhelmed by the simplistic nature of the building.

'What is this place?' He asked as Azrael placed his hand against the door.

It was only then that Chris noticed there was no handle to the door. Aside from a small carving depicting sunshine raining its rays down upon a mountain, there was nothing of note about the door. The building, however, seemed to be attached to a large section of vertical rock, showing it led into the land beneath the jagged stone.

'This is a handy place, somewhere that I think you will appreciate.'

With his gentle touch, the door unlocked and drifted open of its own accord.

'After you,' Azrael motioned, his hand outstretched towards the utterly black interior of the small building.

Taking his cue, Chris stepped past Azrael and crossed the threshold. Instantly he was transported somewhere he did not recognise. As soon as he had stepped over the line of the door, Chris found his feet landing, not on the dark floor, but onto a well-trodden pavement.

'What the hell?' he gasped and turned back to look towards the door he had stepped through.

People meandered past him, paying no attention to either Chris or the curious, open door where Azrael still stood. In a panic, Chris launched himself back through the open door and returned himself to Altum.

'That's not a pleasant feeling,' Chris declared as he fought to steady the dizziness that filled his head.

'Come on,' Azrael jibed. 'Let's get moving, shall we?'

Not waiting for an answer, Azrael stepped through the door, and Chris quickly followed behind.

The same wave of dizziness washed over him, yet Chris found himself no longer standing on the pavement, nor in Altum for that matter. Now, instead, he was positioned by Azrael's side looking out across a vast landscape of the desert.

'Where are we?'

Chris was once again mesmerised by the beauty of his surroundings.

'A place I have come to love over my years.' Azrael explained thoughtfully as he walked towards the edge of the cliff top where they now stood.

Chris drank in the iridescent beauty of the world before him. An arid landscape of desert and jagged rocks stretched out as far as he could see. Irregular patterns of weathered stone littered the landscape, yet he noticed very little sign of life and greenery. Although majestic and inspiring, it felt somehow devoid of habitation.

'This is the Atacama Desert, more importantly, this is Death Valley.'

Azrael allowed the name to hang in the air for a moment, letting the words sink in as Chris stared out across towards the distant horizon.

'Fitting place then,' Chris finally replied.

'Indeed. My mentor brought me here to show how beautiful death can be.' Azrael gripped Chris and jerked him suddenly towards the crumbling edge of the cliff. 'And also how dangerous.'

Chris was held at forty-five degrees, staring down

towards the uneven floor far below. Held in place only by Azrael's grip, he could not shake the feeling of mortality as he stared at the incalculable height he was above the desert floor. Ridiculous, he thought to himself, considering the fact he was already dead.

After a few seconds, Azrael pulled him back and released the grip on Chris' top.
'Lucky you tied it up properly.'
'Sure is.' Chris straightened his clothes and stepped back from the ledge. 'So when do we begin?'
'Now is as good a time as any, I suppose.'

Azrael watched as Chris pulled his attention away from the view to focus solely on him. Before he began, Azrael span his right hand slowly in the air until a spiral of fire appeared in his palm. Seeming the entice the flame into life, Chris watched on in shock as the tiny spark grew until it danced from his palm, contained by Azrael's outstretched fingertips.

Looking around, Azrael moved across to a small patch of ground surrounded by a crop of jagged rocks. Somewhere, roughly in the middle, Azrael flicked his wrist down, and the flame flew onto the ground.

The fire landed as if someone had tossed a rock into a lake. Droplets of shimmering fire splashed around to create a substantial patch of fire on the sandy ground.
'Come, sit with me.' Azrael invited and sat himself down, leaning against one of the rocks.

Chris walked across to join Azrael, finding his own natural seat on the opposite side of the dancing flames. Getting himself comfortable, Chris looked at his mentor expectantly. Chris could not deny his curiosity had been piqued. Everything from Osiris' conversation, the curious teleportation stepping through the door of the red building to the dancing flame that Azrael had magically manifested in his hand.

'Where do you want me to begin?' Azrael offered, a wry smile appearing on his house.

'The beginning?'

Azrael could not help but laugh. Sitting forward, he waved both hands above the hypnotic flames. Peering closer, Chris noticed that the fire moved differently. Leaning in towards the fire as the flames separated and the shape changed.

As Chris watched the flames, they moved away from the main pool where the fire had been born. Staring in disbelief, Chris saw the flames take the unmistakable shape and appearance of miniature people. No details on the face but the head, arms and legs were all in place. 'Here we have The Enlightened Council, four members when times were simpler.' Azrael smiled at Chris' wonder at the fiery representations standing proudly on the dusty floor. 'I will begin with the formation of the council and let the flames do the rest.'

Chris could only stare at the flames as Azrael narrated history of The Council, Altum and Eternal Darkness. His words brought the flames into action and very quickly Chris was absorbed, not noticing anything else around him on the cliff top.

The four apparitions of fire became more detailed, and finally, Chris could recognise three of the four figures. They represented The Enlightened Council and the three faces which had observed him in the Hall Of Souls And Scales.

'The Council was formed to offer judgement when humankind became more ambiguous in its decisions. As temptations increased and morality shifted, so too did the ease at which Ascent or Descent could be determined. To maintain balance The Enlightened Council formed.'

The fiery manifestations of the Council re-enacted Azrael's narration as he spoke.

'Their judgements became a stable process that at first was of minimal interaction, most living lives clear in their judgements. Over the centuries though, it changed.'

The fire became the recognisable shape of Altum. As the city took form, Azrael continued his retelling of their history.

'The souls presented before the council, at first, were few. Ascent and Descent was a lengthy process requiring careful consideration. Over the centuries, however, things changed, and the number of souls requiring judgment increased, placing an incredible strain on The Enlightened Council and filling Altum with unjudged souls.'

The flaming streets became filled with wandering figures, all meandering aimlessly through the streets yet all focussed on the Hall Of Souls And Shadows. Everything seemed centred on the high dome however for every one stepping into the hall two more would appear on the streets.

'As the streets filled, Altum became a holding place, for souls. Soon the city was incapable of holding the sheer numbers, and the earth below suffered as a result.'

The fire mutated again, the dome of the Hall Of Souls And Scales peeling open and pouring back out, washing aside the crowds of gathered figures. Once again exposed, the four members of The Enlightened Council now huddled around in the throes of heated debate.

'The earth was filled with years of darkness, the Dark Ages being just one example when the streets of Altum swelled beyond the Council's capability to hold them. After long deliberation, it was decided the answer was Redemption.'

Azrael lifted Chris' attention from the flames, and he was surprised to find the sun had almost set on the distant horizon.

'And so you see, The Enlightened Council are a stop gap for souls who have not achieved a clear fate. Those whose lives reflect a straightforward decision never pass through the Great Hall. Instead, they make their journey with no requirement for judgment or intervention from The Council. But not all The Council agreed with redemption.'

For the first time a voice, utterly unfamiliar to Chris, projected from the fire. As he returned his attention to the flames, he saw the faceless fourth Councillor speaking to the others.

'Our role is clear, we offer judgement on a life of choice, nothing more. Who are we to create another step and deny whatever fate should be given?'

'As humanity continues to develop the ambiguity of their choices becomes more so,' the white-haired fiery representation argued.

'But we have no right to intervene and add another step. What if those destined for one fate were suddenly changed, would that be fair?'

'We cannot continue as we are.' Osiris declared angrily. 'Altum was not designed to hold so many, we are but four members charged with the judgement of millions.'

The outspoken fourth Councillor did not seem to agree. As the three Councillors talked amongst themselves, it was apparent the fourth had detached himself from them.

'The Council sat, but they sat divided. More often than not the four could not agree, and the judgements rarely passed with simple decisions towards Ascent or Descent without at least having been given a chance of Redemption.'

As the fire changed again, it now showed the solitary faceless Councillor pacing the length of a long hallway, evidently deep in thought.

'The fourth Councillor took note, those who could return often came back for judgement and ascended. Balance had always been in the Council's nature, yet he resented, what he believed to be a new biased system.'

'This cannot be right,' the fiery voice was filled with

frustration. 'They cannot accept their ill-informed actions are creating an unnatural imbalance. I cannot sit idly by wait for them to distort this.'

'The Council has always proffered an impartial standpoint. No more and no less than the seat of judgement, offering no interference with the actions of those returned to earth for Redemption. He, however,' Azrael pointed to the fourth Councillor. 'Decided the actions of The Council had invalidated that mandate and he walked the earth amongst those souls returned for a second chance.'

Once again the fire changed and showed the fourth Councillor walking amongst the streets of some old town whispering to other flamed representations of people. 'The word was passed amongst the souls he met and soon this knowledge spread. It created a dark imbalance, pulling those who listened into the shadows. They withdrew themselves from their lives and instead occupied a life in the darkness. We call them Outcast Shadows.'

Between the walking figures, Chris watched as one or two of them would peel from the main crowd and disappear into the flickering flames around the edge of the town. As the fire once again collapsed into a floating sea of flame, a series of twisted figures appeared from the surface.

'They became twisted and distorted creatures lurking in the shadows and evading the judgement.'

'Why?' Chris finally mustered enough sense to speak.

'Because they became tainted by fear. His words were enough to poison their intentions and actions with doubt. Why face the chance at Descending into darkness when a corrupted life could be lived, forever in the shadows, but always there on earth?'

'What did they become?' As the explanation sank in, Chris could start questioning what he was hearing.

'They became monsters, creatures of myth you would consider fiction or flights of fancy. They became labelled in your world as vampires, werewolves and other such dark demons. They are nothing more than decaying souls long past their time of judgement.'

'And the Councillor, the fourth one, what happened to him?'

The flames changed and returned to the interior of the Hall Of Souls And Scales.

'He returned to The Council after his time walking the earth, but they knew what he had done. They did the only thing they could in the face of his choices.'

'They judged him.' Chris declared.

'Indeed, and for his actions and corruption of the souls now in hiding there was only one choice.'

Chris watched, transfixed on the flame, as the fourth faceless Councillor stood beneath the three Chris knew.

'You are charged with creating imbalance amongst our world. Your feelings towards this Council's decision to offer a chance of Redemption has always been known.' Osiris' voice boomed. 'You had no right to corrupt those souls in a state of Redemption.'

'You had no right to put them back there in the first place,' was the angry reply. 'I did what I did to try to redress the imbalances *you* have created.'

'How dare you?'

'Do not sit there with your sanctimonious looks believing you are perfect. Your own decisions have had consequences. Do not think it has gone unnoticed that the souls who present themselves a second, third or fourth time more often than not Ascend towards the sun.'

'Their judgements are fair.' Osiris bellowed. 'Who are you

to say otherwise?'
'I level the same question at you.'

The air was tense as the four figures glared at one another inside the flaming hall. Chris unconsciously held his breath as he watched the proceedings.
'You say our judgements have affected the balance,' Osiris intoned, his voice filled with warning. 'Let it be shown that this council does not favour one fate over the other.'
'Lies.'
'Enough!' The white-haired Councillor declared and stood from her seat. 'We shall redress the balance. Your fate will be to join those souls you feel we have betrayed. Your fate will be Descent into eternal darkness.'

There was a pause as the fourth Councillor looked from one Councillor to the others.

His own seat sat empty between them, and his gaze seemed to settle on his vacant space.
'I accept this judgement.' He hissed menacingly and stepped up to the plinth of his seat. 'I will not take a descent into eternal darkness.'

As he spoke, the flamed apparition thrust out his hands into the base of the plinth, shattering it completely. The seat collapsed in a shower of sparks, resulting in the wreckage Chris had seen in the Great Hall.
'I do not go there to join them,' he continued as he walked away from The Council, his back turned to them. 'I shall become the Eternal Darkness, and in time I will redress the balance.'

With nothing else to say and nothing else to show, fire sparked and exploded into a flower of embers and flame. As everything returned to normality, the fire resumed a more natural appearance, and as Chris watched nothing else came from the fire, it was merely a campfire once again.

'What happened then?' Chris pressed as Azrael sat back away from the fire.

'Eternal Darkness was born,' Azrael sighed. 'His Descent brought new darkness into Sub-Terra, and with it, he became obsessed with righting the wrongs he felt The Council committed.'

'With the Shadow ones?'

'They did not come to his aid or answer his call. For all his intervention in their fates, they preferred a life away from judgement and remained in the shadows.' Azrael explained. 'But with his Dark Angel, Amber, the woman you saw in the Hall. With her he fights to claim the souls, he feels benefit nothing from judgement.'

'And that is where you, where we, fit in?'

'Indeed. We are charged with ensuring those in need of judgement do in fact face the council. We protect the unsure from the Shadows, and those on the cusp of one or the other are allowed impartial judgement. We fight to ensure fairness and seek to stop Eternal Darkness taking souls that by rights do not belong to him.'

'Just how do we do that?'

Looking up towards the blanket of stars, Azrael inhaled deeply.

'That is a lesson for tomorrow,' He murmured. 'For now, may I suggest some time to reflect on what you have learned and rest. We resume our training in the morning, and for the tests ahead you will need all the energy you can muster.'

'Sounds ominous.' Chris joked, but his remark was quickly rebutted by Azrael.

'More than you can imagine, Christian. What I teach you tomorrow you have experienced before, but to a much lesser degree. I will teach you how to see the unseen and harness our power to seek those souls in need of our intervention.'

The mood became suddenly sombre and heavy. 'But for now, rest. I trust you feel my words have answered at least some of your questions?'

Chris could only nod as he too turned his attention towards the stars.

Indeed Azrael had given him much to consider and as his eyes closed all he could be thankful for was that Ash had never had to face the choices as he was now. As his eyes closed and sleep washed over him Chris' thoughts wandered back through the memories he had suppressed, and before long he was back in a place he had tried to forget for so long.

The weather was cold but dry. Ash sat in the driver's seat of the patrol car, crewed with a younger patrol officer. Having worked together some months, they had quick fallen into a healthy routine. Ash was driving, and the shift had been an uneventful weekend night shift.

'Guess it'll be three am sleep if it stays like this?' Ash's partner yawned as he looked out of the passenger window.

Driving along the city streets, a handful of young students were huddled in a circle cheering as another spewed up on the pavement. A waterfall of brightly coloured sick cascaded across the sidewalk, and Ash could not help but smile.

'Typical Saturday night.'

'Yeah, she'll have a sore head in the morning.'

They continued along the routine patrols, watching the surrounding nightlife.

'Foxtrot Two?' A youthful voice blared from the radio mounted on the dashboard.

'Yeah, go ahead.' Ash's partner quickly answered, a clear eagerness still in his response.

'Just taking reports of a knife-point robbery on Poets Street, can you attend, please? Reports of three males, one with a knife, just threatened a taxi driver and made off with phone, money and car keys.'

Before the message finished, Ash dropped a gear on the patrol car, illuminated the lights outside and sped up the vehicle with ease.

'Know where you're going?' Ash's partner asked as he acknowledged their deployment on the computer mounted in front of him.

'Yeah, we're not a million miles away.' Ash replied, concentrating on weaving between the steady flow of cars on the city streets.

Chris knew he was in a dream when the scene changed. From seeing Ash and partner in the car receiving the call, the dreamscape altered to a small side street off the main road. As always, Chris was powerless to intervene and knew the dream would play its course as it always did.

The dimly lit street suddenly became disturbed by the cascading strobes of the approaching patrol car's lights. Dancing in a crazed pattern of red and blue on the wall, Ash negotiated the tight turn into the street and turned off the lights. Switching off the headlights, Ash edged the patrol car slowly along the dead-end street.

'Foxtrot Two on scene, where was the last sighting control?' Ash's partner quizzed the handler.

'Mapping puts you next street along, but there are alleys

all around, standby while we see if the phone has a tracker on it.'

Rolling to the end of the road, the car looked dwarfed by the tall walls of the buildings on either side. An extensive set of spiked gates stood proudly at the end of the road, barring their way any further. Beyond the gates was a loading bay to a shop on the adjacent street.

'I'd be amazed if they'd got over those,' Ash remarked, pulling the car to a stop in front of the gates.

'It's your turn to climb tonight,'

'Age before beauty,' Ash quipped and killed the engine on the car.

Once again the scene faded and changed to a view of a handful of uniformed officers gathered around one building a little further up the street.

The house was in a poor state of repair, bins overflowed with cans and spirit bottles and Chris could see Ash hammering loudly on the front door. The door buckled under Ash's powerful strikes, even so, there was no sign of life from inside the building.

'Police, open up.' Ash's voice bellowed through the letterbox. 'Open the door now, or it's going in.'

Ash's partner walked across, his phone held in his hand. 'The signal is close to here.' He announced and showed the screen to Ash.

'Not enough to put the door in,' Ash whispered. 'Any way to get it tied down?'

'No, it gives us a five-metre radius.'

'Damn.'

Ash walked to the window by the door and tugged at the battered frame. A small window inched a little with Ash's tug, and after a few seconds, the window popped open.

'Bingo!'

Reaching through the window, Ash pulled aside the

curtain on the other side and bathed the room beyond in torchlight. Panning the beam around Ash's light soon settled on a sleeping figure wrapped in a duvet.
'Wake up! Police.' Ash yelled through the window.

The young woman in bed stirred a little, slowly opening her eyes, which suddenly went wide in shock. Sitting upright in bed, the sheets fell aside exposing her naked body. Caught by surprise and more than a little embarrassed, Ash quickly switched off the torch and instructed her to come to the door.

The dream faded again as Ash and a handful of other officers searched the building. As Chris' view moved from the building, he watched as another officer sheepishly admired a battered phone on the floor, screen smashed but apparently the one they were looking for.
'Well, this is embarrassing,' Ash confessed as Chris moved away and the dream faded.

Chris dreaded what was to come. He knew while Ash was searching the streets, he was less than a mile away enjoying a night with friends.

Unbeknownst to him, at the time, this would be the last despatch for Ash as the sickening voice of the dispatcher came on the radio. There was nothing to see but pitch black darkness as the sound echoed in Chris' dream.
'Foxtrot Two, there's been another sighting of these offenders, can you travel back?'

Chris heard the engine but saw nothing.

Everything he knew of Ash's last hours, Chris learned from the police and coroner's report. Hearing the police car screeching around the streets, he knew the trio of bandits had been challenged by other officers and made off on foot into the twisting side streets.

Hearing the screech of tyres on tarmac, Chris knew Ash was drawing nearer to the end.

He dreaded what was to come as the images flashed in the darkness of his dream.

'Show us on scene.' Ash's voice declared as the world once again came into focus.

Ash bounded from the car, barely allowing it to settle before killing the engine. Springing along the street, Ash joined two other officers who pointed excitedly towards an open courtyard of an ornate building.

'We last saw him there,' a young female officer declared, pointing in towards the courtyard.

'Control confirm which one has the knife,'

'The one in red,' the dispatcher replied.

'That's the one we saw,' the young female officer declared, and Chris watched as Ash tensed.

The courtyard was dark with many places to hide. Cautiously Ash stepped through the gate and began panning around the yard with the torchlight. Ash released the first retention of the leg mounted pistol and inched into the darkness.

Listening intently, no sound caught Ash's attention. There was nothing but an eerie silence.

As Ash inched deeper into the shadows, a ragged voice blasted from the radio.

'He's running,' Ash stiffened, hand wrapping around the pistol grip. 'Down towards the Arboretum.'

Ash knew precisely where the other officer was and spun on the spot, running back towards the car.

Flicking the locks, Ash jumped into the driver's seat and gunned the engine. Screeching around the street, Ash threw the car around a tight bend and accelerated along a long sweeping bend in the road. As the road straightened out in front, Ash caught sight of the offender running and two other officers lagging a fair way behind.

Speeding down the street, Ash watched as the offender

in red bolted into the junction at the bottom of the road and turned out of sight. Throwing the police car around the intersection, Ash caught sight of him as he stepped out onto the path in front of the police car.

Slamming on the brakes, the back end of the police car skidded across the street, but Ash maintained enough control to stop safely.

Leaving the engine running, Ash exploded out of the driver's door and gave chase on foot of the offender in red.

A black baseball cap was pulled low on his head, and he paid no attention to Ash's commands to stop and stand still. Although the fleeing offender had a head start, Ash was not one to give up.

Propelling across the damp surface of the road, Ash closed the man down.

Crossing the broad road, Ash leapt up onto the sidewalk and saw the red-topped man was in reach.

Reaching out at the same time as maintaining momentum, Ash's fingertips grasped at the shoulder of the fleeing man's jacket. As the distance narrowed, Ash gripped the coat and jolted the man backwards.
'Stop! Police!'

The man still showed no concern and although Ash now gripped his jacket, the young man wriggled free, leaving Ash stood there, the discarded coat in hand.
What happened next, happened in a heartbeat.

There was no time for thought or consideration as the offender turned to face Ash.

Chris had seen this on the CCTV footage of Ash's last moments. He had seen the grainy image of the offender as he turned to face Ash. Cap lowered down his brow there was no face to see in the poor quality image from the camera. Ash, on the other hand, must have seen the killer's face and it would have been the last thing Ash had seen.

Dropping the coat, Ash shouted again, but the black-capped offender moved to turn away. Dropping both hands to his waistband, Ash had closed in to wrestle the man to the ground. As Ash went hands on, there was the slightest of movements from the offender as he turned to face back towards Ash.

The slightest shimmer of light showed on the camera, and this is what Chris saw now.

By the time the blade of the knife plunged deep into the crease of Ash's leg, the blade had pierced Ash's femoral artery less than a second passed.

Seeing Ash's ultimate moments in his dream as he had on the grainy CCTV, Chris watched the offender stagger backwards, the knife in hand. Ash stood frozen in place. It took a second for any reaction, but as the realisation of what was happening sank in, Ash's left leg buckled.

Dropping to the floor, Chris watched as Ash's killer faltered for a moment. Standing over the dying officer, the man seemed torn on whether to run or stay. As other officers burst around the corner, the killer decided and disappeared over the wall and into the darkness of the Arboretum.

Ash had bled out before the ambulance had arrived, surrounded by the familiar faces of colleagues and friends, there had been no hope of survival from the injury and catastrophic bleed.

Chris' dream changed again and became replaced with his first-person view. Chris had not been drinking that night, and the strobe of lights and hovering police chopper had caught his attention. Awash with curiosity, and knowing the crews on duty were his team, he had made his way towards the source of the commotion.

There had been no denying the looks of horror on his

friend's faces when he had arrived at the outer cordon.
'Chris, you can't be here.'

The voice was familiar. Peering over the crime scene tape flapping noisily in the wind, Chris was surprised to see his Captain walking up the hill towards him.
'What do you mean?' Chris knew something was wrong; he felt cold. 'Where's Ash?'
'Chris,' the look on the Captain's face told Chris what was happening.

Snapping the crime scene tape, Chris ran across the road and down towards the junction where Ash's patrol car sat abandoned.
'Chris please, I need to-' Chris barged past his Captain, unable to hear the other man's words.

Chris emerged at the junction and saw the inner cordon and officers gathered around the body lying under a white sheet on the road.
 The sidewalk had become stained with blood. CSI vans sat idling nearby, and the masked faces turned to look at Chris wide-eyed.
'Someone stop him.' The Captain bellowed as Chris sprinted towards the bloodstained sheet and corpse beneath it.

Chris remembered hands grabbing him and fighting against them. He knew he had hit more than one of them, burying frenzied fists into the faces of friends and people he had known for years. When finally enough of them had secured him in place, Chris had been forced against a nearby wall.
'Chris, please, calm down.' The Captain pleaded, and finally, Chris turned to look at him.
'Please, tell me it isn't...'

There was no use trying to beg for it to be different. No matter the pleading or praying, there was nothing that could change what had happened.

The Captain did the only thing he could and held out his hand. Nestled in his palm was the shield emblazoned with the four numbers that said everything to Chris. 'I'm sorry Chris, Ash is dead.'

The voice echoed, and the dream collapsed.

Waking quickly, Chris was overcome with emotion.

Trying desperately to cast aside the nightmarish retelling of Ash's death, he looked around at the smouldering fire. Azrael remained quiet and asleep. 'Curious they chose you,' a female voice whispered from the shadows beyond Azrael. 'So much emotion and turmoil.'

To Chris' surprise, Amber stepped into the dying light of the fire. Her soft face radiated beauty in the shimmering firelight.

'I intend to watch you with great interest future Reaper.'

Saying nothing else, she disappeared into the shadows of the night.

Chris was, once again, alone.

Chris woke to find Azrael pottering around the smouldering campfire. The flames had long since died and the dawn had yet to break.

'Nice of you to join me,' Azrael mocked as Chris stretched himself out on the rough floor.

'Why do I need to sleep if I'm well...'

'Dead?'

It seemed odd hearing the word spoken, but Chris nodded.

'Because you're used to it. You still occupy an existence, and that will drain you. We don't need to eat, but sleep allows us to process things we are exposed to and recover from the demands we place upon ourselves.'

'No food? I'm not sure I'm going to get used to that.'

Chris was joking but realised he had gone days, if not

more than a week, without even thinking of food.
'How do we work without food?'
'Lots of questions for such an early start,' Azrael dodged
the question and encouraged Chris to get up.

Chris brushed off his clothes and felt the chill of the
early morning air. He wished he had brought the hooded
robe with him, but still felt a strange sense of disdain
towards the tattered fabric.
'You're not actually cold, you know,' Azrael mocked as he
watched Chris cross his arms over his chest and rub his
hands against his biceps. 'It's all up here.'
'So what do I feel?' Chris snapped, more out of
embarrassment than anything else.
'Nothing,' Azrael chuckled. 'You think you do and so, to
keep you, connected to your life your head fills the void.'

Not wanting to concede, Chris thought to himself the
cold was not real and immediately the chill against his
skin disappeared.
'You see,' Azrael smiled seeing the change in his
demeanour. 'There's a lot you now experience that you are
entirely in control of. Come with me.'

Azrael walked away from the makeshift campsite they
had occupied and stepped towards the jagged edge of the
cliffs. Waiting for Chris to join him, he looked out across
the dark landscape. Although the sun was not yet peeking
above the horizon, the sky was lightening. The blackness
of night gave way to blue and finally a hue of brighter
light that warned of the impending sunrise.

Standing at Azrael's side, Chris could make out the
silhouettes of the rough landscape in front of them. Jagged
rocks jutted out, stretching as far as he could see before
they were once again swallowed by the darkness.
'Are you ready to learn something?'

As Chris turned to look at Azrael, his mentor did not

wait for an answer. Instead, lifting the hood of his cloak over his head, Azrael stepped forward and dropped over the edge of the cliff.

'No!' Chris screamed and tried to grab the fabric of Azrael's robes as he dropped over the cliff.

Filled with panic, Chris looked out across the edge of the rocks to look down.

He expected to see Azrael falling, if not already lying on the floor far below in a crumpled, lifeless mess. Instead, however, he saw nothing. The floor was too dark with night-time shadows to make out any details of Azrael's body.

'Azrael?' He bellowed down towards the ground.

Peering into the darkness, Chris strained to see anything.

'Perhaps you should trust in yourself a little and forget the things that bound you to the earth in your former life.' Azrael mocked as he stepped into view.

Although Chris appreciated that anything was possible since his arrival at Altum, he still could not fathom some things he had been shown. As Azrael looked up at him, stood impossibly on the face of the cliff side, Chris could not compute what he was seeing.

'I'm getting bored with seeing that dumbfounded look,' Azrael mocked. 'That said, you are getting quite good at it.'

Chris knew the look Azrael meant. Lips parted, mouth opening and closing like that of a floundering and dying fish, topped only with wide eyes and furrowed brow. It was a look he had perfected over the years. Hearing Azrael mock it reminded him of Ash's scorn. Too often Ash would chide his confused expression, highlighting all too often how embarrassing he looked.

'Join me,' Azrael offered and stepped further down along

the face of the stone.

'That's impossible.'

'Come now, after everything you've seen and learned, do you really believe that?'

Chris knew he was right. There was no denying the impossibility and implausibility of everything he had learned. Still, standing on the edge of the cliff, he could not conceive it being possible for him.

'Embrace what you are to become Christian,' Azrael's tone changed from one of playfulness to one of seriousness. 'The only way I can train you is for you to let go over your past life.'

Chris shuffled forward until the tips of his shoes hovered over nothing. Pebbles of crumbling stone tumbled towards the ground. Uncontrollably, his feet quivered with nerves as he steeled himself to take his leap of faith.

'Remove yourself from what you were.'

Chris wanted to listen, having seen the things done by Azrael, he wanted to join him on the cliff face.

'Let go of what you know. Trust in yourself.'

Torn and confused, Chris' mind told him to step, but his heart filled him with fear.

'Step from the ledge, have faith that the power of Altum will hold you. Let the Reaper inside you be free.'

Closing his eyes, Chris lifted his foot from the floor and held it out above the precipice. Pausing for just a moment, he allowed himself a few seconds of grace to settle his thoughts.

What if he was wrong? What if this was all some ridiculous dream or flight of fancy?

What if?

Without another thought, Chris released his weight from his back leg and stepped out.

'Trust,' Azrael hushed as Chris opened his eyes.

The world span quickly as gravity, or whatever force now bound him to the earth, pulled him downwards. Filled with fear he waited for the sickening feeling as he tumbled into the depths but it never came. Instead, he felt the solid ground beneath his feet as the world shifted ninety degrees and he stood on the face of the cliff looking down towards the floor.

'Your first step into becoming,' Azrael boomed and stepped towards him.

As the tip of the sun breached the distant horizon, the world was bathed in vibrant red. Casting a look upwards, Chris looked in wonder towards the sun that was now above him. Disorientated by his newfound position, he could not help but marvel at the beauty.

'Shall we begin?'

Returning his attention to Azrael, his heart sank as he saw Azrael spin around and draw his dagger from behind his back.

The morning was spent with Azrael and Chris attacking and parrying across the face of the cliffs. As the sun rose higher in the sky and passed through to the early afternoon, their training was relentless. Chris was tossed and tussled across the cliffs without chance to break or breathe. His body groaned against the exertion, but he fought back regardless.

With each minor victory, a nudge of his own blade against Azrael's skin or else a blow to send his opponent staggering backwards, Chris felt his resolve increase.

The world around saw nothing of their training. The few living souls that dared to meander the arid plains of the Atacama Desert could not see the two of them as they fought. To the living eye, there was nothing on the face of jagged stones. Perhaps the flutter of Azrael's cape may linger in the corner of their vision, but they would dismiss it as the flutter of wings from some unseen bird.

Those that existed on the plain between life and death were unseen by the living. That is, unless those with the power revealed themselves intending to take those from life to death.

All this Azrael explained to Chris as they fought throughout the day. Words interlaced with the clatter of weaponry as they fought hard and furiously until finally, with the day's sun once again descending towards the western horizon, Azrael raised his hand into the air. 'We are spent.' He declared flatly. 'A time to rest, perhaps?'

Spinning the long dagger in the air flamboyantly Azrael replaced it in the sheath at the base of his spine and stepped back up over the cliff edge.

Chris lowered his scaled scythes and followed Azrael up onto level ground. With perspective returned to normal, Chris could not deny he felt somewhat disorientated. Pressing his thumb and forefinger across the bridge of his nose, he steadied himself with a handful of deep breaths.

'You'll settle soon enough. The first time is always the most confusing for you.' Azrael offered, once again returning his voice to one of knowledge and kindness.

As the dizziness faded, Chris opened his eyes and looked towards his mentor.

Azrael stood still, his head turned towards an outcrop of stone towering above them on the far side of the open space where they had made camp. Chris watched as Azrael slipped his hand beneath his robe and once again removed the dagger from its holster.

'What is it,' Chris asked as he moved to stand beside Azrael.

'We are being watched.'

'By who?'

'Her.' Azrael hissed.

Chris followed his gaze and peered up towards the rocks but saw nothing.

'Who do you mean?' Chris pressed but suspected he knew the answer.

'The Dark Angel, Amber, she sits up there watching us.' Azrael pondered. 'And I am left wondering why.'

'What do you mean by that?'

'In times past she would have faced me. We have spent the years pitted against one another on more than one occasion. Yet now she sits in the shadows, watching. I am curious as to why.'

There was a hint of accusation in his voice, and suddenly Chris remembered the encounter in the night following his dream.

'We must leave, return to Altum and progress your preparations away from the prying eyes of Dark Angels and Eternal Darkness.'

Not waiting for Chris to agree, Azrael re-holstered his weapon and stalked across the dusty floor away from the charred remains of the campfire.

'Can you see the reason I have such an interest in Azrael's new pet?' The voice echoed from the dark centre of the smoke.

Since retreating into Sub-Terra, the banished Councillor had indeed become the essence of Eternal Darkness. Consumed by his hatred for The Enlightened Council, he had withdrawn himself inside Forca Tower. Decades of wallowing in anger and frustration had left him bitter and twisted. In time he had become nothing more than the hovering cloud of smoke from which his voice was the only thing left of his physical existence.

As Amber practised with a long spear, the essence that was Eternal Darkness hovered calmly. Ever watching his most trusted Dark Angel, he waited for her answer as Amber danced across the floor of the large room.

'Not really,' she confessed between strikes.

Expertly wielding the bound wooden stock of the spear, Amber sliced and thrust the pointed tip in all directions. Her graceful movements allowed her to bounce and leap majestically in every direction. Balancing the spear across her back and shoulders, she deftly spun the blade until, with the slightest shift of weight into her legs, she propelled herself upwards and somersaulted over in the air.

As she completed the leap, she thrust the head of the spear quickly downwards, burying it to the hilt in the stone floor. With the spear securely wedged in place, Amber shifted her weight and impressively balanced herself on the thin end of the weapon.

Body tight, core locked and perfectly balanced, Amber maintained her handstand.

Amber's concentration was intense. Viewing the world upside down, she levelled her gaze towards the Eternal Darkness. Closing her eyes slowly, she allowed herself to sense the tension in her body. Every muscle that twitched and flexed to keep her in the position she could feel. As her body quivered, she made her last move.

Flexing her elbows just enough to gain power, Amber launched herself up and over. Rotating in the air, she landed neatly on the floor, allowing her knees to swallow the impact from her landing. Slowly she stood herself straight and with the pride and grace of a professional gymnast dusted down her legs and turned to face her audience.

'Of course,' Amber mocked as she looked across at the cloud of smoke. 'Never any sign you approve.'

Between Amber and Eternal Darkness, there had always been a strange dynamic. With Sub-Terra, she was perhaps one of the few inhabitants who could remember his physical appearance. Now, as nothing more than the essence of darkness, she had grown to mock his chosen form. Amber had never understood how he had turned his back on everything to become a ghost.

'What would you have me do?' The voice retorted quickly. 'There is no need for me to be anything more than what I am.'

'Don't you miss the days when you were free to walk where you pleased rather than bound to a world of isolation?'

'My power is drawn from Sub-Terra, to realise it I had to become more than just a man. More than what I was.' There was a hint of reminiscence in his voice. 'You of all people know this.'

'I do,' Amber replied slowly, carefully delivering her words for fear of angering him. 'But it does not mean I fully understand it. Do you not miss the time when you had a name.'

'I have a name, I am Eternal Darkness. I am the very spirit of Sub-Terra, connected more than any soul has ever been.' His voice boomed and echoed around the hall.

'And in so doing you are forced to rely on me to emerge from the darkness and watch your enemies, recruit those souls which fall into your kingdom. If it were not for me, the ranks of Sub-Terra would be a portion of what they are now.'

Doing her best to remain calm, Amber voiced her opinion.

More than once she had experienced the wrath of Eternal Darkness. She had not climbed to the rank of Dark Angel without crossing him more than once. As he had slowly withdrawn from the form of a man to how he appeared now, his wrath had grown as much as his connection to the darkness.

'But who do they serve?' His voice was filled with menace. 'Do they serve the messenger or the master? I cannot deny you bring them here, but it is me who connects those souls to Sub-Terra. You are but the means, I am the end.'

Amber knew she had pushed too hard. It had not been her intention to upset her teacher, but there were things she did not understand about his obsession with Azrael's new student. Endless days he had forced her to watch from the shadows, observing the teachings of one Reaper to another.

'Tenebris,' she waited to see if there was a reaction to using his proper name before continuing. 'You've paid no attention to the Council's appointment beyond Azrael. Why now?'

Eternal Darkness, Tenebris as he had once been known, was silent for a moment. As Amber waited, she feared, by using his name, she had pushed too far. Staring towards the dark void at the epicentre of the smouldering smoke, she could not help but feel he was looking at her.

Prying the tip of the spear from between the stone of the floor, she admired the polished tip and waited for him to speak.

'You are perhaps the only person who calls me that anymore.' He murmured.

'There would be more if you emerged from this place.'

'My place is here,' Tenebris growled. 'There is no need for me out there, my place is here. Connected to the very heart of Sub-Terra.'

'Only because you make it this way.' Amber added delicately and stepped towards the floating cloud of smoke.

Stood before Tenebris' appearance as Eternal Darkness, Amber felt dwarfed by his presence. The dancing tendrils of thick smoke floated enchantingly all around as the void of black seemed to draw in everything around.

Peering into it Amber could make out nothing. Whatever sat at his core seemed to swallow everything. The light from the flickering flames could not pierce the void, it seemed devoid of presence and matter.

'It is the way I believe it must be.' Tenebris offered thoughtfully.

'What would ever bring you back from wherever it is you are now.'

Amber peered closer into the blackness, trying to fathom what lay beyond the glassy surface.

'Perhaps the time grows nearer that I will be forced to emerge from myself, but until then my Dark Angel, it is you who must be my eyes and ears. You are the hand of Eternal Darkness.'

'Yet you have me watch the Reapers?'

'Never one to let things lie, are you?'

'Like you said,' she offered a wry smile. 'You wouldn't want it any other way.'

'Indeed. Yet I must ask you to trust me in this matter for now.'

Tenebris held Amber in higher regard than she knew. There were many reasons he had remained in this form, not least of all was it allowed him to stay in control of his own powers. The day he had turned his back on The Enlightened Council, a seed had been planted inside him. The fire and brimstone of Sub-Terra had nurtured that seed, and it had grown. Tenebris had become consumed by it, ruled by it until he was no longer confident he could control it.

Stood at the spiked top of Force Tower he had looked across Sub-Terra and felt the fire burning within him. His skin had burned, his body had forged with the jagged bedrock. Where he stood, he had felt his skin fusing with stone, anchoring him in place. Not only was he becoming one with the Darkness, but he was becoming part of Sub-Terra.

It had been his only way to escape. With no physical form, he could not be swallowed into the ground, he could remain alive in his kingdom. It was not for any other reason than self-preservation that he had taken on his present form.

As he peered out of the dark void in the centre of his smoky apparition, he saw Amber gazing back at him.

Her soft skin had never ceased to hypnotise him. She had seen him in physical form; they had even shared a connection, which had been the reason he had kept her by his side. Tenebris, however, had never shared with her the proper reasons for his banishment into himself. Although he trusted her, perhaps in a way loved her, he knew one thing about those who lived in Sub-Terra.

There was always a desire to be more, a desire to become at one with the darkness, and if Amber knew his fear and weakness, he worried she may use it against him. 'It never fills me with confidence when you slip into silence.' Amber said, interrupting his train of thought. 'What are you thinking?'

'Nothing.' Tenebris answered, far more defensively than he had intended.

'Now I know you're lying. What is it about this new Reaper that intrigues you?'

'I see something in him that may help our cause.' Tenebris answered purposefully. 'Azrael would never normally have chosen him, yet we have set things in motion that brings him into the fold.'

'You've done a lot to ensure this,' Amber was teasing him for more information.

'I have my reasons.' Tenebris cut off her line of

questioning.

Amber knew she had angered him, pushed more than she should have, and the silence told her as much. Stepping back from the lingering cloud of smoke, she turned her attention away from the dark void and focussed on the weapon in her hand.

'I meant no disrespect,' she finally offered. 'I only wish to understand your obsession and what it means for us.'

'When the time is right, I will tell you.'

It was not the answer she had wanted, but Amber knew when she had pushed too far. Bowing her head, she accepted his explanation and excused herself from the chamber.

'I shall return to my watchful gaze.' Amber said as she disappeared out of the empty room.

Alone, Tenebris in his form as Eternal Darkness sat silent. Peering out through the window that was the void, he admired the interior of Force Tower. The veins of molten rock zigzagged all around. He felt that Sub-Terra was more a being than a place. The veins of magma were the blood, connecting every rock, every scarred inhabitant and every creature to him. He could attach himself and feel everything around him.

Only when he knew he was alone did Tenebris speak again. His voice was softer, calmer and more controlled. Talking to himself, he justified his reasons and vocalised his intentions for Azrael and Christian.

'In time, this newfound Reaper may offer me the chance to rebalance the scales. We will see if the snowball I have tossed into the hill will gather momentum or become nothing more than a mark in the snow.'

Azrael emerged from the door of the red building,

followed closely by Chris. Altum was once again dark and
bathed in the fantastic array of stars and shimmering
lights of every colour.
'What now?' Chris asked as the door closed behind him.
'Back inside.' Azrael replied with a coy smile.

Reaching past Chris, he grabbed the handle and
pushed the door open again. Filled with curiosity, Chris
stepped back in through the doorway and suddenly found
himself stood on the banks of the River Thames.

Chris had been here once before, and the memories
came flooding back as he looked towards the twilight
scenery.
'How?' Chris murmured as he walked towards the high
walls of the embankment.

'Altum is connected everywhere, through the Ianua we can travel anywhere on the planet that we are needed to go.' Azrael could see Chris was lost in thought and pushed no more on the explanation.

Chris walked to the waist-high wall which separated the path from the turbulent Thames below. To the right, the lights were alive and painting Tower Bridge in a cascade of bright light and enhanced shadows. Peering towards the bridge, Chris watched as a traditional red double-decker bus rolled across the bridge to the far side of the river.

'I've been here only once before,' he muttered. 'My parents brought me here as a teenager.'

Azrael listened but said nothing.

'I think it was the last holiday with my dad before he fell ill.' There was sadness to his voice. 'I doubt he could remember now.'

'Why is that?' Azrael finally asked, the melancholy silence becoming too uncomfortable.

'Alzheimer's,' Chris sighed. 'He saw the entire world through his life and now can barely remember what happened this morning.'

Chris was once again swallowed by his emotion. Azrael could sense it and allowed Chris his moment of silence. Looking around, Azrael admired the mix of old and new architecture. The Gherkin, all glass and steel, reached towards the twilight sky reflecting the slowly rolling clouds. A short distance along the same side of the Thames the Tower Of London stood proudly. All turrets and reinforced walls, the two buildings could not have been more opposite.

Admiring the lights and bustle of the evening, Azrael span slowly around and finally returned his attention back to Chris.

'Are you picking places I'm connected to for any reason?' Chris finally asked and tore his gaze from the rolling surface of the river.

'Very astute of you,' Azrael nodded approvingly as he spoke. 'You need an emotional connection for what I am about to teach you. It will drain you, and you'll need an anchor, and I knew this place would help give you that focus.'

'You knew my dad had Alzheimer's?'

Azrael felt uncomfortable for a moment and took a step back from Chris.

All around them well-dressed men and women walked past them, oblivious of the pair. It felt to Chris as if the wandering pedestrians did not know they were even there.

'I know everything about you, Chris,' Azrael confessed. 'I've watched you for a long time and need to know who it is I am training.'

'That feels perverse,' Chris interrupted. 'Like you've been waiting for me, that my life was somehow overshadowed and marked by all this.'

Chris did not feel angry, but his words were delivered with more bite than he had intended. Somehow he could understand Azrael's matter-of-fact explanation.

'You'll understand in time.'

'What life did you have before all of this Azrael?'

It was Azrael's turn to be on the back foot, and immediately Chris feared he had pushed too far. For all his attentive tutorship and stern guidance, Azrael was very much the epitome of death as Chris would expect. Azrael came across cold and emotionless, task-focused and disconnected from the world he was so intricately connected to.

'I can't remember much of it,' Azrael finally answered

slowly. 'I had a wife, a son, but I can't remember their faces anymore.'

'How long ago?' Chris asked as he stepped away from the embankment wall.

'Too long!'

Azrael's answer felt final, and as Chris looked to his mentor, he knew when enough was enough. Not wanting to test Azrael too far, he accepted the finality of his answer and changed his course of questioning.

'What am I hear to learn?'

'Soul Sight.' Azrael answered, and in a heartbeat, if either of them had one, the mood in the air changed.

The pair walked along the path towards Tower Bridge in silence. Chris took his place by Azrael's side and knew, in a matter of time, Azrael would elaborate on his answer. As they climbed the narrow steps up towards the road crossing the magnificent bridge, Azrael finally spoke.

'Souls Sight is the gift allowing Reapers to sense those in need of judgement. Those people, balancing on the edge of life and death, who need our intervention and protection.'

'Protection?'

'Dark Angels would seek to corrupt those on the brink with Dark Whispers to send them into the Shadows, or else take them if their souls appear balanced more towards a tainted fate of darkness.'

'There must be hundreds of thousands every day that need this.' Chris pressed as they reached the sidewalk.

'There are, and there are other Reapers that do the same as us, but there are fewer souls than you might expect.' Chris sighed. 'We tend, now, to focus on imbalances that draw attention from the Dark Angels and intervene where necessary.'

'What about those who are of no interest?'

'They can be presented for judgement by the Blind Guides,

judgment can be swift, and their fates remain their own.'

The more Chris heard, the more questions raced through his head. Altum, its purpose and existence seemed far more complicated than what he had seen so far. Every answer from Azrael appeared to add another term, another group of people intricately tied into the complex world he now found himself part of.

'So we only protect those souls that are what, vulnerable to this whisper thing?'

'Yes, that is my role and soon to be yours.' Azrael nodded. 'Other Reapers are tasked to other roles, but for us, we are there to intercept those that attract the gaze of Eternal Darkness and his twisted view on The Enlightened Council and their purpose.'

'I won't lie and say I understand all, or most, of what you're saying, but I guess it will start to make sense in time?'

'Perhaps!' Azrael chuckled. 'A lot of Altum you'll never have to be part of, and as a Reaper, your focus will be on the task The Council gives you.'

'Great,' Chris scoffed. 'Little cog in a gigantic machine once again.'

'Indeed.

Azrael stopped as they reached the first tall tower of the bridge and pushed through the door. Passing past the gathered people, they climbed their way up the tower until they emerged on a glass walkway above the road. Curiously and much to Chris' surprise, they found themselves almost alone on the glass viewing walkway.

Although the corridor of metal and glass was open, it felt claustrophobic and tight as they watched the meandering traffic rolling by obliviously beneath them.

'Are you ready?' Azrael finally asked as they looked down through the glass floor at the world below them.

'For what?'

'Your first taste of Soul Sight.'

'I suppose.'

Azrael grinned and focussed his attention on the sidewalk below them.

Chris watched Azrael intently as the older Reaper closed his eyes and took a long breath in. As he watched Azrael, Chris felt the air become tangible around them. Within the confines of the viewing platform, Chris could feel his skin tingling and a curious chill tickled along the inside of his spine.

'When you learn to focus yourself, you will see the world through eyes of death.'

Azrael's voice sounded unfamiliar, somehow distant and echoing as the words left his lips.

'There,' he suddenly declared and opened his eyes.

'What?' Chris jumped by Azrael's sudden movement.

'Here, down there in blue.' Chris dropped his attention down towards the pavement where Azrael now pointed. 'See her.'

'Yes.'

'No,' Azrael snapped. 'See her! Focus on her and see what I see.'

Chris' brow furrowed as he stared down at the woman who remained oblivious of the pair of eyes gazing at her intently from above.

She looked in her later forties, portly and hair in need of attention. The wind blowing along the Thames ruffled her hair, exposing the roots against her scalp that appeared silver against her dyed black hair. She wore a long mac coat against the cold and beige trousers.

'See her.' Azrael pressed.

Chris only saw the woman, nothing more. He took in her appearance but saw just a tired businesswoman stalking along the pavement towards some unknown destination.

'What do you mean?' Chris bit, frustrated.

'Close your eyes.' Azrael instructed and waited for Chris to follow his instruction.

Feeling ridiculous although nobody had paid them any attention, Chris obliged and closed his eyes.

'Breath, feel the air around you and hear everything.'

'It's soundproof glass.' Chris quipped.

'Listen! The world doesn't need your voice when you're seeking out souls.' Azrael barked angrily. 'Now listen, hear the world around you. Concentrate and feel.'

As Azrael watched, he saw Chris concentrate. Chris' posture changed as he calmed himself and wash away the embarrassment and followed Azrael's instructions.

'Think of your father.'

The thought caught Chris off guard, and he turned to look at Azrael, opening his eyes and forgetting the woman below.

'Focus,' Azrael snapped. 'Harness the emotion and focus on her below you, not me.'

Wanting to argue, Chris looked back to the woman and closed his eyes. Focussing on the sadness and regret, he felt towards his father, Chris felt the emotion swell inside him. Memories of London, of childhood and family times, washed over him and as it did so too did the odd feeling of electricity on his skin.

'Good.' Azrael whispered. 'Feel it grow, feel your connection to this world against your skin, you are part of it, at one with it.'

The feeling grew, and Chris' skin felt alive. Sounds filled his head, the footfalls of the people far below, the breathing of the three tourists at the far end of the walkway, the creaking of the suspension supports of the bridge. He could hear it all; he could *feel* it all as he concentrated.

'Now,' Azrael hushed. 'Open your eyes and see her.'

Tentatively, Chris opened his eyes and looked down at the woman.

The world was frozen in place, nothing moved, and the woman stood in mid-step on the pavement far below. Except now she looked different. The woman now appeared to be emitting a faint glow all around her. The light was tinted with red, and a corona of light hung brighter where her heart would be.

'What is this?' Chris gasped.

'What do you see?'

'Light, from her, red, her heart, not moving, still.' The words poured from him incoherently.

'She is to be judged, but her soul has been there before.' Azrael explained. 'She is not ready yet, her light is faint but her time draws near.'

'How do you know that?' Chris stared down as the world remained fixed in place and frozen beneath them.

'Let her go.' Azrael instructed, and instantly the world resumed its course and the red light from the woman faded to nothing.

'How did you?'

'Soul Sight in a snapshot in time, it does not need to be more than that to see the strength of the light and realise what state they are in.'

'But how do you know she wasn't ready? Nobody else down there had any glow to them.'

'That's because you only looked at her,' Azrael smirked. 'Everyone has a presence in Soul Sight, but I wanted you to see one who draws nearer.'

'What does everyone else look like?'

'Everyone has an essence. The light you saw was her soul,

and as it lives, it grows. When life draws to a close, we pick up on trails left behind as the soul escapes. You pick up the light much like the tail of a comet.'

'She wasn't leaving much.'

'And that is why it was not her time.' Azrael explained. 'As a soul grows it outgrows the confines of the body it occupies, the bigger the trail, the closer it is to leaving this level of life.'

'Are they all red?'

'Not all. Those in need of judgement, whose lives have not satisfied the natural alignment to light or dark, they are red. They are the ones we focus on. The brighter the colour, the more they need our protection.'

'Why not just tell her and let her fix things before her time is up?'

'We escort, we do not interfere.' Azrael snapped. 'They must be allowed to make their own choices or else become like Eternal Darkness and taint the process to our own will.'

Chris snatched his attention to Azrael. Filled with frustration and anger, he needed time, needed space from his imposing mentor.

'I need time to think.' He sighed.

'Walk among them, see them through whatever eyes you choose but remember this,' Azrael stepped closer to him. 'You are here to protect those at risk, not alter the balance of judgement. Do what you must so you can understand your place in all of this.'

Not wanting for a reply, Azrael turned and stalked off along the walkway, leaving Chris alone.

Azrael's voice echoed in his head. Meandering across Tower Bridge, Chris had no destination in mind and just allowed himself to walk. Although it was evening, the streets were still filled with people. Chris moved amongst them, unseen and unacknowledged by anyone around him.

Ahead of him, the neon sign caught his attention. As a light drizzle fell, the red, white and blue sign for the underground station seemed the right destination. Expertly moving between the flow of pedestrians, Chris arrived at the flight of steps leading beneath the damp streets. Moving quickly, he descended the steps and made his way towards one platform.

'Ticket?' A voice declared.

Chris looked up quickly to find a burly black woman in

her fifties gazing at him. It dawned on Chris he had no money, nothing material for the world he was now in, and felt suddenly self-conscious as the woman glared at him. 'Ticket?' She asked again, her voice firm and irritable.

An arm reached around Chris suddenly and handed the portly woman a small piece of plastic. Immediately the stern look on the woman's face broke, and she smiled, pushing a button to open a narrow gate leading into the platform.

The businessman that had flashed the plastic card stepped through the gate and Chris was left standing in front of the woman. The portly operator sat back down on a tall stool and returned her attention to a nail file that she ran across the fingers on her left hand.
'Excuse me,' Chris said, but she seemed not to hear him. 'Hello?'

Stepping up to the woman he waved a hand in front of her face but she showed no sign of having seen anything. 'She can't see you,' a hushed voice whispered in his ear. 'They can only see you when you want them to.'

Snatching himself around, Chris looked into the face of a gaunt man with pale skin and sunken eyes.
'How can you see me?' Chris asked as he looked at the stranger.

The man was in his late twenties, but his skin was pale and stretched. Something was unnerving about his appearance, and the beady sunken eyes seemed to dart around as if scanning every face in the surrounding crowd.
'Because little man,' the stranger's voice hissed. 'We are born of the same existence. We both live a life beyond life but not quite dead.'

The strange walked around Chris slowly and teased a thin finger across Chris' shoulders as he walked behind him.

'I've never seen a Reaper this close before,' Chris felt uncomfortable and stepped out of the man's reach. 'The power is yet to be grown in you, but I can sense it, taste it.'

The gaunt man stepped up to Chris and sniffed up loudly. Chris watched as a narrow tongue peeked over the man's thin lips and appeared to taste the air in front of Chris' face.

'What are you?' Chris stammered as he looked at the man.

'Look for yourself little Reaper, you'll see what I am if you truly look at me.'

Without another word, the man replaced his tongue into his mouth and turned away from Chris. Moving into the flow of people, he all but disappeared amongst the crowds as Chris struggled to watch him walk away.

'What the hell does that mean?' He whispered to himself and moved his way through the crowds in pursuit.

Zigzagging between the oblivious people, Chris fought to keep the back of the gaunt man's head in view. As a surge in the crowd blocked his view, Chris lost sight.

'See me with your Reaper eyes,' the hissing voice whispered from behind and Chris span on the spot.

The stranger was nowhere to be seen and as Chris turned slowly he once again caught sight of the gaunt man now stood on the far side of the crowd staring across at him.

'You do not know the power of your sight, do you?'

The voice sounded as if the man were by his side, loud enough to hear but only just above the chatter of the surrounding crowds. The gaunt man, the source of the voice, however, he remained on the far side of the crowd, standing motionless, staring.

'Trust yourself to see, see me as I am, and then you may understand.'

Chris glared across at the mysterious figure.
'How can you talk to me from there and sound like you are beside me?'
'Because I embrace the powers of my curse, I exist on a plain that allows me to be in many places at once.'
'So who are you?'
'I have no name anymore.'

Chris' mind pieced together what the gaunt stranger was saying. Closing his eyes, Chris focused on the feeling he had experienced on the glass walkway on Tower bridge. Holding in the emotion and torrents of feeling, he allowed himself to feel it again. The tickle of electricity again danced along his skin, and he knew it was time.

Opening his eyes slowly, the world looked different once again. Looking beyond the crowds, ignoring the shimmers of light and tails of coloured light, he peered towards the stranger.

What he saw was genuinely terrifying. The man remained in the same position, but his gaunt face and pale skin no longer looked back at him. Instead, a twisted face glared at him across the crowd. Stony grey in pallor and appearance, the man appeared to be made of stone. The twisted face glaring at him looked like a gargoyle. The sunken eyes seemed to glow as they stared across towards him.
'What are you?'
'I am an Outcast Shadow, one that chose my own fate away from the insipid Enlightened Council to live a life of freedom.'

As he spoke the Outcast Shadow's face crumbled and cracked. The movement of his mouth seemed to break and grind the outer layer of his face. A twisted smile appeared on his face as he acknowledged Chris' disgust and curiosity. The upturned lips became a crooked smile exposing a pair of razor-sharp fangs protruding from his mouth.

'Why seek me out, what do you want from me?'

Chris stalked between the crowds and across the space between him and the twisted appearance of the Outcast Shadow.

'In time my little Reaper,' he chuckled and in a cloud of dust was no more.

Chris sprinted the remaining distance and stopped short of where the gaunt man had been stood. There was nothing left to show anyone had been there. The thin cloud of dust had dissipated with the movement of the crowds and Chris was left standing alone against the far wall, looking around wildly.

'This is one messed up place,' he scoffed to himself and pressed his back against the tiled wall.

Watching the crowds, Chris felt suddenly overwhelmed and at a loss of everything around him. He had hoped that solace away from Azrael, and his instruction would do him good. Somehow he had believed by immersing himself among the living he would feel alive again, but he felt nothing of the sort.

Watching the meandering crowds as they filtered between the two platforms, he watched as they boarded the latest train to arrive at the platform. As people pushed and shoved their way into the packed carriages, Chris felt no connection to them. Chris felt cold, isolated and alone. 'What am I becoming?' He whispered and slid himself down to sit on the floor of the tube station.

Slouched on the floor, Chris remained there for a long time. Head pressed against his knees, he merely stared at the floor. Noting every detail on the tiled floor, every piece of chewing gum mashed between the tiles, every scuff of rubber. The irregularity and unpredictability of the debris distracted his attention enough.

When Chris finally returned his gaze to the station, he found it curiously empty.

Time had escaped him. Seated on the icy floor, he did not know how long he had been there, but it was long enough to realise the difference in his surroundings. The crowds had thinned, and while people meandered between the platforms, they did so in thin groups rather than bustling crowds.

'I need to go home,' Chris sighed as he stood up.

Not understanding where home was, Chris looked towards the illuminated information boards and planned for the arrival on the next tube train. Finding the right platform, Chris stepped away from the wall and followed the curved roofed tunnel until it opened out into the vast empty platform.

The platform was quiet now, only a handful of passengers loitered near the tracks. Casting a glance towards the LED message board, Chris realised he had some time until the next train arrived at the station.

Chris realised, as he looked at the blinking time on the display, just how long he had been sitting against the tiled wall. Wherever his mind had taken him had drowned out the world around him entirely. Whatever had happened in the *hours* he had been sitting there had wholly gone unnoticed.

'Excuse me,' a voice interrupted Chris' train of thought as he stood in the middle of the archway leading into the station.

Snapping back, Chris turned and took in the young man who looked up at him impatiently.

'Sorry.'

As Chris moved aside, the young man walked past. Something about him caught his attention, and he watched him walk towards the far end of the station.

Carrying a laptop bag and pile of papers tucked underneath one arm, the young man fiddled with a phone in his free hand as he put his belongings down on a bench. He stood only a little shorter than Chris, but his figure was much leaner and far younger. His dark skin and black hair hid his age, but Chris guessed him to be in his early thirties at the oldest, if not a little younger.

The man had caught his attention, but Chris could not fathom why. Something about the younger man's presence, his posture and his aura had utterly snatched Chris' attention.

Closing his eyes, Chris did the only thing which made sense. Having seen no reason for the man to demand his attention, Chris once again focussed his concentration on the electric feeling on his skin. Calming himself enough to know he was centred, Chris opened his eyes and saw the younger man in a different light.

The man was standing with his back to Chris and paid no attention to his intent stare. The same pearlescent light glowed from the centre of the man's back. Unlike the woman on the bridge, the man's light was a bright yellow, almost like the corona of the sun. The light remained tight around the man's body, no wisps of light stretching back away from him. It all appeared compact and close to his skin.

'Looks good, doesn't he?'

The voice was familiar, the same crackled voice who had spoken to him across the crowds. Chris spun around and saw the Outcast Shadow stood standing proudly on the platform. The clothes he had worn remained the same, but his skin had the same stony and cracked appearance as it had when Chris had seen his actual appearance.

'Who is he to you?' Chris asked as a wave of unease trickled through him.

'Nobody,' the Shadow snickered. 'Just another soul to feed on and add to the ranks of my people.'

'It isn't his time though,' Chris stammered. 'Is it?'

Chris cast a glance back towards the young man who had now sat himself down on the well-worn bench against the wall. His yellow light remained bright, but now something appeared different.

A single strand of light had danced like a twitching snake. It crept through the air away from the man and danced past Chris' face and across the platform towards the Shadow.

'What is this?'

Chris reached his hands towards the pulsating, twitching tendril, but his fingers passed through it harmlessly. While the edges were disturbed by his fingers, the core of light remained intact and unmoved.

It felt wrong, and Chris knew, by the perverse look on the Shadow's face, this was not right. Hypnotised by the dancing path of the tendril's tip, Chris watched as it made its way towards the Shadow's open palm.

'Stop it,' Chris barked. 'Stop it now.'

'Why should I, he is just another lifeless creature on this twisted earth? He's nothing to you.' The Shadow reached out with his fingers to greet the bright light. 'You have no reason to stop me. This man needs no judgement from your twisted Council, he needs no escort to the Great Halls.'

The light touched the Shadow's rough fingertip and slowly wrapped itself around his finger and down into his hand. The light moved like a snake, slowly, purposefully twisting itself over the rough grey skin.

Looking back towards the young man, Chris was surprised to find him now stood away from the bench and strolling across the platform towards him.

Unlike before, the man's face now looked blank. He still held the phone in his hand, but now it hung by his side in his loose grip. The man walked as if sleepwalking, slowly and laboured.

'What have you done to him?'

Chris looked to see the Shadow almost teasing the man forward as the strip of light from his aura wrapped further down his arm, almost sensually.

'His soul is now for me,' the Shadow grinned.

'Leave him alone.' Chris barked and stepped across to block the man's path to the Shadow.

The young man casually moved around Chris. His expression was blank, and he gave no sign he knew Chris was even there. Acting entirely on instinct, Chris knew there was something unnatural about what was happening. Raising his arm, he gripped the young man across the chest and stopped him in place.

The young black man rocked against Chris' barrier, and he struggled to hold him back.

'Let go of him.' Chris snarled and turned to look at the Shadow.

'Make me.'

The young black man cast a sideways glance at Chris, and in that look Chris knew what he needed to do. Although the man's body looked to be under control of the Shadow, his eyes told a different story. Fear burned in his eyes. In one look Chris heard the pleas for help as the man was powerless to resist.

'This must be what Azrael meant,' Chris whispered to himself thoughtfully.

Chris could not deny the sense of purpose he felt. Seeing the Shadow twisting this man's soul around his arm looked wrong and perverse. There had been nothing in Chris' Soul Sight showing this man's time was near. The light beaming from his corona had been bright and compact, unlike the woman on the bridge. Hers had been stretching out behind her, and Azrael had said her time was close. This man's had been nothing like hers.

Instinct kicked in.

Chris released his arm from the young man and leapt forward in one powerful move. The days of practice with Azrael told him what to do, and he knew where to strike. Punching through the air, he thrust out his leg and felt it land heavily in the Shadow's face.

Thrust back by the power of the blow the Shadow released his grip on the coiled light, and the young man stood dead in his tracks. Shaking his head as if to pull himself from a daydream, he focussed his attention in time to see the two men fighting.

Chris attacked, punches aimed towards the head and upper body of the Shadow. The first two landed firmly on the stone-like skin, but the third and fourth were deftly blocked, throwing him off balance. The Shadow returned from his own attacks. The two of them brawled across the platform, inching perilously close to the edge of the platform and the humming rails.

Other passengers scattered around the platform were oblivious to the fighting. The young man was the only one able to see the curious men as they fought. Chris attacked, then blocked. A strategically aimed kick swept out across his shins and sent him tumbling to the floor.

Landing roughly, Chris tried to use the momentum of his fall to right himself but fell hard from the platform and onto the rails below.

'No!' The young man shrieked as Chris tumbled onto the tracks.

The Shadow paid no attention to his prey's scream and jumped down to join Chris on the tracks.

Chris was at a disadvantage. The Shadow rained blow after blow down on him, and Chris did all he could to protect his face and head. The Shadow was in a frenzy, determined only to batter Chris against the mishmash of metal rails and concrete flooring.

One blow was mistimed, and Chris used it to his advantage. Breaking his guard for a second Chris timed his response to perfection and grabbed the Shadow's fist in his hand. Breaking the momentum of the attacks, the two men were locked in place, neither giving an advantage to the other.

With his free hand, Chris threw his own attack but found his own fist caught in the vice-like grip of his opponent. The two of them pushed against one another until they clambered to their knees and eventually rose up. 'Very much the trainee,' the Shadow snarled. 'Azrael would have bested me by now, but I could see you weren't up to his standard.'

Although he knew they were nothing more than taunts, Chris could not deny the frustration bubbling inside him at the Shadow's mocking. The frustration grew, but the two of them were locked, matched in strength and build they remained stood on the humming lines as a light appeared in the tunnel off behind them.
'Train,' the young men yelled as the station became filled with the rising noise of the approaching tube train.

Neither would give.

Chris held the tension in his arms and refused to give any advantage to the Shadow. Peering past him, Chris saw the rapidly approaching lights as the train barrelled down the lines towards them.

It was obvious neither of them would back down. Chris had no idea what would happen if the flat front of the metal train collided with him. His human instinct dictated that, although he was already beyond life, he did not want to find out what would happen.

Releasing the tension in his taught muscles for a split second, Chris feigned an advantage for the Shadow. Surprised by the sudden release from Chris, the Shadow pushed forward precisely as Chris had planned.

Switching his balance, Chris pulled the Shadow forward and buried his forehead hard and fast into the Shadow's face. The stone skin cracked and crunched beneath the massive blow, and immediately he released his grip on Chris.

The train was almost upon them as the front breached the mouth of the tunnel and careered down the platform towards them. Having broken free, Chris propelled himself upwards in a somersault and landed on the edge of the raised station.

'Got you.' The young man gasped and took hold of Chris' top to stop him from falling back onto the tracks.

As the young man pulled him away from the painted danger line on the platform floor, a grey hand reached up and gripped Chris' ankle.

The Shadow glared up at Chris, but there was no time. Flipping himself upwards and over in another spectacular acrobatic display, Chris pulled the Shadow up towards the platform and kicked out with his free foot. His kick landed on the Shadows jaw, snapping it grotesquely across both sides. The power of the kick launched the Shadow backwards in time for the train to reach their position.

The collision was far more dramatic than Chris had expected. The Shadow exploded in a cascade of jagged stone pieces, peppering the front of the train and walls of the station in every direction. The force of the exploding creature threw Chris and the young man tumbling backwards and falling to the platform floor.

The exploding stone did not go unnoticed. Although the fight had been unseen by the other passengers, the exploding rock created a reaction. The platform was filled with the screech of brakes as the train shuddered to a violent stop on the lines. People ran around panicked as Chris and the young man lay sprawled on the platform floor.

'What was that?' The young man asked.

Chris did not answer, his attention was fixed on the damage and debris from the shatter Shadow.

'Jay,' the young man continued as Chris finally moved his attention from the debris and to the young man. 'My name is Jay, I suppose I should say thank you.'

Curiously, Chris took the young man's outstretched hand and shook it firmly.

'I should go,' Chris finally declared and stood, dusting the remnants of the Shadow from his clothes.

'Wait,' Jay pleaded. 'I want to know more about what just happened.'

Chris stalked away towards the now crowded exit to the station.

'You don't want to know, kid,' Chris declared as he pushed past the panicking station staff and passengers.

The last thing he heard over the panicked voices and crackling radios was Jay shouting for him to wait.

Jay grabbed his belongings from the bench and hurriedly pushed his way past the crowd of people now gathered on the platform.

'Excuse me,' he apologised as he moved with haste. 'Excuse me.'

Emerging back on the main thoroughfare, he looked around desperately and eventually caught sight of Chris as he stalked up the escalator.

'Wait, please wait.'

Dodging by the other commuters, Jay finally caught up with Chris as he emerged out of the central station and back up onto the bustling London street. Reaching out, Jay grabbed Chris' shoulder and turned him around to face him.

'Please, wait a minute.' Jay pleaded, but Chris was having

none of it.

'Listen, kid, I'm grateful for your help, but you'd be better forgetting about it.'

'You can't expect me to forget what I've seen, do you?'

Chris could see the eagerness in the younger man's face. Wild eyes seemed bright against his dark skin. The lights of the massive advertisements screens towering above them glinted in Jay's eyes as he stared at him.

'Not here,' Chris finally sighed and turned to walk away.

Jay followed behind as Chris moved along the streets for some time. The evening had well and truly set in. The roads were no longer filled with suited businessmen and women, but instead, it was filled with tourists. Cameras flashed, and excited voices babbled all around as they passed the major tourist attractions along the route.

'Where are we going?' Jay finally asked as they passed along the front of St Paul's Cathedral and turned back towards the Thames.

Turning away from the main road, they entered the pedestrian-only slab path which lead towards Millennium Bridge. The buildings flanking either side of them were a mix of Classic Victorian architecture and angular modern structures. Passing along the steadily declining path, they finally arrived at the entrance to the impressive bridge.

Almost the opposite of the internationally recognisable Tower Bridge, the Millennium structure was modern and sleek. Either side of the bridge was a mix of metal and cables separating the walkers from the dark water of the Thames below. Although people meandered across the decked bridge, Chris positioned himself to the side of the bridge and walked down the steps towards the banks of the river.

Away from the crowds, the pair found themselves curiously alone beneath the bridge as a single boat chugged along the river in front of them.

'Who are you?' Jay asked as Chris sat himself down on a weathered bench looking out across the Thames.

'If you'd asked me that a few months ago, I could probably have answered.' Chris sighed.

'Curious answer,' Jay confessed as he fished around in the messenger bag slung across his body.

'Everything about me is curious.'

'I gathered that,' Jay quipped as he pulled a small wallet from the bag and held it out for Chris.

Taking the small leather wallet, Chris opened it slowly and found a plethora of identification cards inside. With Jay's help, he flicked through the centre card, which drew Chris' attention.

'I'm a freelance journalist,' Jay explained as he pointed to the card. 'I've written for most of the big print papers in London and featured online all around the world.'

'Impressive,' Chris replied, his voice betraying his sudden lack of enthusiasm. 'Certainly explains your insistence on trying to know what all that was about.'

'I've always had the knack of being in the right place at the right time. Seems tonight is another case of that.'

A wry smile was painted on Jay's face as he looked eagerly across at Chris. Whatever had happened weighed on Chris heavily. Jay had worked with people like him before and knew he would need to massage the situation to get Chris to open up to him.

'There's no story in me,' Chris sighed and handed the ID wallet back to Jay.

'You can't tell me that after I've seen a stone man get run over by a train!'

'Jay,' Chris barked and propelled himself from the bench. 'You are best not knowing about me and that thing, you saw.'

'Let me be the judge of that, please.'
'No!' Chris barked.

Jay knew he had pushed too hard and too fast. There was something in Chris' face that told him there was so much more to the man. Besides his unusual appearance, the sash kimono-style top and baggy trousers aside, his newfound interest carried a strange air of mystery. The look on Chris' face told him he was hiding something and what had happened at the station seemed utterly natural and normal to him.

'So,' Jay pressed delicately. 'Who are you?'
'My name is Chris Thomas, and that's all you really need to know.'

Jay sensed the conversation was over.
'It's been a pleasure meeting you Jay.' Chris continued. 'I appreciate your help back there, but it's best we go our separate ways.'

Chris held out his hand in a formal goodbye. As Jay took it, they shook hands, and Chris turned to walk away.
'If you want to talk,' Jay quickly added and held out a business card. 'I'm more than willing to listen. If it helps, I promise I wouldn't publish anything.'
'You'll forgive me for not believing a reporter.' Chris countered with a wry grin and took the card from Jay.
'All the same, the offer is there.'

Chris slipped the card into his pocket and walked away along the banks of the Thames.
'It's been an interesting encounter.' Chris shouted as he disappeared into a narrow alley leading back up towards the main streets.

Jay was awash with curiosity. There was indeed something about Chris that had caught his attention, not to mention the fantastical events he had witnessed on the platform. Jay could remember nothing about how he had stood on the platform looking at the man of stone. The last thing he had remembered was being on his phone sat on the bench.

After that, nothing, until he had felt Chris' arm across his chest. It was only when he had remembered things and what he remembered was almost beyond belief.
'I can see why you find him so curious.'

The voice was calm and alluring. Jay snatched himself back from his memories and turned to find the source of the voice. Soft and feminine, he was surprised to see a beautiful woman stood a little way behind him. Her untamed black hair was tied in a tight ponytail at the back of her head, but bushed out wildly beyond the band. Her face was slender, cheekbones sleek and angular.
'Who are you and how do you know him?'
'My name is Amber,' she declared confidently and walked purposefully towards him. 'I don't claim to know him very well, but he deserves your attention.'

Amber walked around him regally; her long legs betrayed the look of a stalking panther as she moved around Jay slowly. Jay was captivated by her natural beauty and the grace of her appearance.
'You seem to know something about him, why else would you say he is worth the attention?'
'Not as daft as you look,' Amber snickered. 'Can I offer you some advice?'
'Please do.'
'He told you his name, no?'
'Yeah.'
'Find out a little about him.' Amber teased as she traced her thin fingers across Jay's face and gazed at him. 'Start with Shasta.'
'Shasta?'

Releasing his face from her touch, Amber turned and

walked away, back towards Millennium Bridge. Amber offered him nothing else as she disappeared up the steps leaving Jay alone on the riverside.

'Well, this gets weirder and weirder.'

Feeling uncomfortably alone on the banks of the river, Jay did not loiter to be approached by anyone else. Sliding his wallet back into the bag, he tucked the papers once again beneath his arm and stalked back up towards the main streets and home. More than anything Jay needed to feel the safety of his apartment and have a very long, very strong drink.

*   *   *

Chris wandered the streets throughout the night. The people he passed changed as the night drew on until finally, he had had enough. Surrounded by groups of drunken people, the shouts and jeers became too much to handle.

'So how the hell do I get back from here?' Chris muttered as he returned to the open space at Piccadilly Circus.

Bathed in the bright light of the infamous advertisement screens, Chris was relieved to feel a familiar presence at his back. There was no need for him to turn around, he knew it was Azrael stood behind him.

'Have you been watching me or by chance arrive when I need you to?' Chris chuckled.

'Would it make you feel better if I said the latter?'

'Not really,' Chris confessed.

Turning around, Chris was surprised to find Azrael dressed entirely in the traditional look of death.

'I think it's time we returned to Altum,' Azrael offered. 'I have to say your performance at the tube station was quite something to behold. You did me proud.'

'Glad I didn't disappoint.'

Azrael reached into his cloak and removed a scabbard and blade similar to the one he wore at his back.

'It may have helped if you had carried one of these.'

Chris took the sheathed blade that Azrael held out for him and looked at it curiously. Retracting the blade partially, he saw that the metal was intricately etched with a distinct and ornate pattern. Under the cascading bright lights, the blade glinted and painted specks of light across his face.

'I take it this was a test?'

'Not the one I had hoped, but yes, facing an Outcast Shadow the way you did, told me you were ready.'

'I'm honoured.' Chris could not hide the strange sense of pride he felt.

'Let's get back, there's still more yet to be done.'

Carrying the weapon in his hand, Chris followed Azrael to a small door. The door looked to have been untouched for years, but as Azrael's hand gripped the handle, it opened freely. As soon as they stepped inside, the pair of them once again emerged through Ianua and back into Altum.

Unlike London, Altum was bathed in the bright light of the sun, which caused Chris to shield his eyes. Allowing the door to close behind him, he realised how beautiful the world around him looked. Although he had relished the chance to be among the living, it had reminded him how dirty and sordid; the world was.

One last thought entered his head as he walked away from the small red building. The journalist, Jay, had offered him the chance to talk and somehow Chris knew at some point he would need someone unlinked to Altum to talk to. Feeling the card in his pocket, he kept it from Azrael and saved it just in case he changed his mind.

Chris struggled to find any peace in Altum. It did not take long for Azrael to return to their routine and Chris to soon find himself practising for hours on end on parrying and attacking. Time passed by slowly as slowly Chris mastered his skills with the scythe and the inscribed dagger Azrael had handed him when they had returned. 'You seem preoccupied,' Azrael declared as he secured his own weapon in the sheath mounted at the small of his back. 'Care to share?'

'Not really.' Chris sighed and turned his back on Azrael.

Although Azrael's manner had softened a little, he still felt a deep-seated reservation towards him. There was always something about the Reaper that felt distant. The more Chris observed his mentor, the more he vowed never to forget his reasons for agreeing to all of this. Holding

Ash again was his reason for being at Altum. He knew Azrael had, at some point, held someone in such regard to walk the Reaper's path but that memory had long ago faded.

Eyes that had probably once been bright and full of life now seemed dull and grey. There was little of life left in Azrael's face, and it worried Chris deeply. He did not want to forget his purpose or become the shell of the man he had been.

'Why did you save the man at the station?' Azrael pressed as he watched Chris.

'You told me I would know when it was someone's time, it wasn't his.'

'How could you tell?'

'The light, the mist or whatever it is, wasn't the same as the woman on the bridge.' Chris slid his weapon behind his back and secured it in place as he spoke. 'It just felt right.'

'You trusted your instincts.'

'I suppose.'

'It was the right thing to do, Christian.' Azrael murmured and placed a hand on Chris' shoulder. 'You harnessed your Soul Sight and read the signs perfectly.'

'The Shadow though, why would he want to do that to someone not ready for death?'

'Because they feed off life,' Azrael began. 'The more a soul is alive, the more power they can consume.'

'They feed off people?'

'Yes. They corrupt the soul of their victim, which drags them into the rancour of damnation as an Outcast Shadow. To remain free from the call of our worlds, they must feed and by doing so they add more and more to their ranks.'

'They're like a disease, a virus.'

'They are the twisted things of nightmares.' Azrael explained. 'They have existed alongside the living for centuries, they've even become accepted in their culture to some extent.'

Chris released himself from Azrael's grip and turned to face his mentor.

'I've never heard of them.'

'Haven't you?'

A sly smirk painted itself across Azrael's face as he looked at Chris. The look unnerved him a little before he could press further, Azrael attacked.

It was a swift and calculated move, but Chris had sensed it. He had spent enough time with Azrael to realise the older man was up to something. Chris had detected the slow movement of Azrael's right shoulder as he twisted to wrap his fingers around the handle of his dagger. As Azrael's grip tightened, the muscles around his joint flexed enough for Chris to know what was happening.

As Azrael ripped the weapon free from the sheath and thrust it around and through the air, Chris was ready.

As the tip of the blade sliced through the air where Chris had been standing, he was already gone. Propelling himself upwards and backwards, Chris somersaulted away from the attack. As he landed, Chris thrust out both hands to his sides and suddenly, inexplicably and impossibly the pair of shortened scythes appeared in his hands.

'How?' He gasped as Azrael launched another attack.

The fight was fast, furious and deadly. Blades clattered and clashed with one another as the two men attacked and blocked against one another in a furious battle.

'You are finally in touch with whom you are becoming.' Azrael spat. 'Harness it, hold this moment and fight me.'

Taking full advantage of the surrounding environment, the pair fought and jumped in every direction. Chris' blades sliced perilously close to Azrael's face more than once, but the older man kept himself out of reach just enough. Returned attacks were equally close to connecting, but Chris kept himself just far enough out of reach to feel marginally in control in the fight.

'What did you mean?' Chris thrust the scythe in his left hand up and around as he growled. 'Humans know about the Shadows?'

Chris felt his grip on the scythe falter as Azrael twisted the blade of his dagger over and under. The weapon was ripped from Chris' grasp and span into the air.

'They have their own representations.' Azrael declared as he caught the released scythe and swung it around at Chris.

The scythe came to rest against Chris' throat as Azrael gripped him around the back of the neck and pulled him closer to the blade.

'Concede?'

Azrael loomed over Chris, but the younger man did not agree.

'Too confident,' Chris smirked. 'You've not won anything.'

Answering the look of confusion on Azrael's face, Chris casually tapped the tip of his second weapon against the back of his mentor's head. The look of surprise was priceless, and Chris let the moment sink in.

'Concede?' Chris retorted as he felt released from Azrael's grip.

Handing the weapon back, Azrael could not hide the look of pride on his face as he looked at Chris.

'You've come a long way,' Azrael swelled with pride.

Handing back the scythe, Chris was dumbfounded as

the weapon crumbled and disappeared in his hand along with the spare he held in his other.

'How did you do that?' Chris stammered, staring at his now empty hands.

'I didn't, you did.'

'I think you'll find I didn't.' Chris retorted quickly.

'That's what I have been teaching you, Christian. Everything up until now is giving you the skills and the tools to become the Reaper.' Azrael moved across to the edge of the plateau they had been training on and looked down at Altum as he spoke. 'Only when you have truly accepted will you be able to harness everything. What you have just done is prove to yourself that you can become.'

'But I do not know how I did that.'

'You do and when you realise that then you will be fully prepared.'

Ending the conversation, Azrael stepped up and over the edge of the plateau and descended back towards the central city. As he walked away, Chris ran to the side of the rock ledge as Azrael reached the bottom of the narrow stone steps to the ground below.

'Azrael,' he shouted.

Azrael stopped but did not turn to face Chris.

'What did you mean about the Shadows?'

'Think about the creatures you know of that live as they do. Things your cultures have accepted as flights of fancy.'

'I don't know what you mean.' He bellowed down.

'Mary Shelley had the right idea, so did Bram Stoker, and from there you have your answers.'

'Monsters?'

'Vampires, Werewolves, Zombies and the likes. They are all constructs and stories to excuse the fact that unjudged souls wander amongst the living.' Azrael looked up at Chris. 'They have shrouded themselves in their own mythology, which allows them to exist between the two worlds.'

'How much truth is there in those things?'

'Enough!' He mocked. 'Think about why every one of them is plagued with the story of infection. If you fall at the hands of these monsters what happens, according to the stories.'

'You turn.'

'And there it is. The truth behind the myths, Christian.' Azrael continued to walk away now as he spoke. 'For every fiction, there is at least a base of fact. The truth hides in plain sight and these creatures, the Outcast Shadows, are no exception. Until you are ready, you would do well to stay away from them.'

Azrael dropped to the path below and walked confidently back towards the main city.

'Can they hurt me?' Chris bellowed. 'Azrael, can they kill me?'

'I wouldn't advise you try and found out.'

Azrael's voice carried in the air but was faint as he left Chris behind.

Alone on the ridge, Chris turned his back from the city and looked out across the landscape. Filled with curiosity, he looked down towards his hands and wondered exactly how he had caused the scythes to appear in them.

There was nothing Chris could sense or feel that told him how he could repeat the gesture.

'I suppose it could be easier,' he scoffed and wafted his hands around lazily.

Chris felt ridiculous as he tried to manifest the weapons within his palms again. Twisting and rotating his wrists, he manoeuvred his fingers in any way he could, many combinations, to see if he could get a result.

'Oh look, I'm Spider-Man,' Chris chuckled as he mimicked

the infamous superhero's iconic pose.

Giving up on his attempts, Chris threw his head back and laughed at his failure. Alone on the uneven rocks, he could not deny he was disappointed, yet in a way it reminded him he was still, in some way, human in all of this.

Chris stemmed his laughter as the events on Millennium Bridge came flooding back. The young journalist had piqued his attention and now, realising he was still unsure of himself in all of this, Chris felt a desire to return to London and seek out the young man.

There was a lot that had happened in the underground station that the young man had seen. As if to rationalise his desire to have some connection to the living world, Chris convinced himself that he needed to understand what Jay had seen.

Chris just needed a connection, something to anchor him back to the land of the living, to keep him from becoming as Azrael appeared to him.

Lifeless, emotionless and lost.

Chris approached the Ianua building and paused in front of the massive door. Although he knew he was alone, Chris could not shift the feeling of being watched. Ignoring the icy shiver trickling down his spine, he opened the door and stepped over the threshold.

Feeling the familiar tug, Chris felt himself ripped from the floor and tumbling through the air until his feet once again met the ground.

Chris had intended to return to London, but curiously found himself surrounded by shadow and darkness. There was no sign it was night, no blanket of stars above his head or the twinkling of city lights anywhere around him. 'Where am I?' Chris muttered as he moved around slowly in the darkness.

His voice echoed around and there was the distant

sound of water trickling somewhere off in the distance. Walking cautiously, Chris stumbled as something limp was blocking his path and took his feet from beneath him.

Falling roughly to the floor, Chris rolled over and allowed his eyes to settle in the darkness and slowly the world around him took shape.

'Not where you wanted to be, is it?' Azrael whispered as he stepped from a deep shadow on the far side of the room.

'I don't know what you mean.' Chris quickly snapped. 'I don't know where I wanted to go.'

Azrael cocked his head, and Chris felt his mentor's gaze cut into him. Suddenly uncomfortable, Chris stood himself from the floor and looked across at Azrael.

'Do you know where you are?'

'Not a clue.' Chris replied shortly.

Azrael lifted his hands from his side and cupped them in front of him. Keeping his palms from touching Azrael span his hands slowly around until a spark of flame flickered in the space between his hands.

Watching the miraculous birthing of the flame, Chris watched, transfixed by the flickering fire as it slowly grew between Azrael's hands. Eventually, the ball of flame was the size of a tennis ball, and Azrael admired the bright flame as it hovered in the air in front of him.

'There are still a lot of things you do not know you are capable of yet Christian.' Azrael murmured, never lifting his gaze from the fire.

In one swift motion, Azrael launched the ball of flame up into the air. As the fire collided with the ceiling high above, the fire exploded and spread across the surface of the rock that made up the roof above them. Droplets of fire dripped down, but nothing touched either Chris or Azrael. With the fire spread, the cave in which they were stood was bathed in bright light.

'I know this place,' Chris mused as he dropped his gaze from the fiery ceiling.

It suddenly dawned on Chris what he had fallen over. His feet had caught against something soft in the darkness. Stretched across the floor, it had sent him tumbling to the ground, and Azrael's arrival had all but distracted him.

Slowly, filled with dread, Chris turned to look down at the floor and felt overcome with fear as he finally registered what he was looking at.

Dressed exactly as he remembered, Chris was looking at himself.

Leant back against the rough rock wall, he looked at peace. The cold had preserved his body, and a thin layer of ice had crystallised across the surface of his clothes and skin. Chris' eyes were closed, and for all intents and purposes, he looked asleep, all except the cold blue tinge to his lifeless skin.

'Why?'

'Why to bring me here,' Chris could not muster anger. 'Some sick way of reminding me what I did to end up here?'

Looking at his own body, Chris was overcome with guilt and disappointment. Although he seemed at peace, Chris knew the torment which had led him to this cave, knew the haunting shadows of Ash's death. What he was looking at was the remains of a man who had lost everything and given it all in.

'Why did you bring me here?' Chris growled and span to face Azrael.

A rage burned inside him that matched the dancing fire high above him. Stalking across the cave, Chris closed down Azrael in a handful of long strides. As he arrived,

Chris was surprised to find the pair of shortened scythes now held one in each hand.

'You mistake my intent Christian,' Azrael's expression remained calm an emotionless.

'Get over yourself for just a minute.' Chris barked, settling himself face-to-face with Azrael. 'You had a reason for making me look at that.'

Chris pointed back towards his own corpse in the cold cave behind him. Looking beyond Chris and to the body behind him, Azrael allowed a wry smile to creep across his face. The appearance of the grin did nothing to calm Chris. Instead, it fuelled the burning anger inside him.

'Wipe the smile off your face, you twisted devil.' Chris fought back the desire to pummel the scythes into Azrael. His hands trembled as he spat his words through gritted teeth. 'You've brought me here to show me exactly what hold you have over me, to tease me with my failure in life and the path I am now cursed to walk.'

'Hardly.'

'Hardly? Hardly? Is that all you can offer you sanctimonious asshole?'

Azrael moved with the swiftness of a stalking panther as he thrust both palms out and sent Chris stumbling backwards. Struggling to maintain his balance, Chris steadied himself and turned to face Azrael with his bodyweight dropped and prepared to attack.

'You are mistaken if you think *I* brought you here,'

It was the over-emphasis on the 'I' that stopped Chris from attacking.

Azrael stood calmly, almost prepared to accept whatever fury-filled onslaught his student offered, yet his words had halted the attack.

'What do you mean?' Chris remained poised, but his body language shifted from aggression to confusion, the muscles in his shoulder relaxed a little.

'Entering into the Ianua it feeds from the desires of the first to breach the threshold, I could no sooner have brought you here by following behind you than I could change the flow of a waterfall. The reason you stand in this cave Christian is that *you* brought us here.'

Azrael allowed his words to sink in. As the scythes disappeared from Chris' hands, he saw the other man visibly relax. The contorted face filled with anger and hatred softened, and as Chris stood up from his hunched attack posture, it was clear he no longer had the drive to attack.

'I've never wanted to come back here, it's the last place I would want to come.'

'Subconsciously you did, that's why we are here.'

'But there's no reason I would want to look at that.' Chris could no longer acknowledge his corpse behind him.

'Perhaps you knew you needed to understand the consequence of your actions in life and what it means in death.' Azrael answered softly. 'You will only ever be the one who will truly know why we came here.'

'I need to go.' Chris finally declared.

'I think you need to face what you came here to see.'

'I need to go.' Chris' voice quivered with bottled emotion.

'This isn't something you can run from Christian, face it now, and perhaps the journey from here will be easier.'

'I...NEED...TO...GO!'"

Chris' voice echoed loudly around the cave and before Azrael could protest any further Chris turned and walked towards the side of the cave. With a loud crackle that sounded like lightning, Chris disappeared, and Azrael was left alone in the cave.

Chris, on the other hand, emerged where he had initially intended. To his relief, the murky evening cityscape of London quickly materialised before him and he felt entirely free from the bleakness of the cave.

Brushing off the haunting memories of his own lifeless corpse, Chris took the time to take in his surroundings and drink in the urban landscape that surrounded him.

'I didn't expect to see you again,' the voice dragged Chris back from his admiring of the dusky city, and he turned to face Jay. 'How d'you know where to find me?'

'I don't actually know,' Chris answered and chuckled at Jay's raised eyebrow and confused look.

'So, what can I do for you?'

Chris couldn't help but chuckle, which again confused Jay all the more.

'It would probably sound wrong for me to say I don't know again.'

'Do you, people, drink?'

'No,' Chris smiled. 'But I have no objection if you want to drink.'

'It would be nice, I've been running around all day trying to script up an interview with the Home Secretary.'

'Lead the way then.'

As Chris followed Jay through the streets, he was overcome with a feeling of normality. Having looked at his frosted body, Chris still had no concept of time, no idea how long it had been since he had died in the empty cave. Although Altum, Azrael and The Council had accepted him, there had been something missing for him. Merely walking through the streets of London with Jay seemed to fill a little hole.

'This will do,' Jay announced as they walked towards the closed doors of a large Victorian building. 'Cat and Fiddle, been coming here since I started working at the newspaper. They do a good line of ciders...'

Jay cut himself short as he remembered his strange

companion would not be joining him in sampling the variety of hand-pressed and unique ciders.

'Looks quaint, I think it's been a while since I last stepped inside a pub.'

'You think it's been a while?' Jay asked as he pushed the door open and they both stepped into the impressive establishment.

As they took their seats at a small table on the far side of the pub, neither of them noticed Amber slide in through the slowly closing door. By the time the pair of them settled, Amber had all but melted into the shadows on the opposite side of the pub, unseen by either of them.

Once Jay had ordered his drink and carried it across from the bar without spilling a drop, the two of them sat down at the table. With a quick check to see they were not being listened to, Chris explained to the eager young Jay just precisely what he had witnessed in the tube station.

Jay all but hung on Chris' every word. The small pub was inconsequential and neither of them paid any attention to the other patrons around them. As Chris finished his attempt to explain, and in his own way process, what had happened to him there was a moment he thought Jay did not believe him.

'I suppose,' Jay finally said between swallowing a mouthful of the bubbling beer. 'If I hadn't seen what I did down in the underground, I'd write you off as a bit of a lunatic.'

'Believe me, I'm still coming to terms with all of this. Not all of it makes sense to me.'

'I don't expect it would come on man, you've just told me you've seen the one place everyone spends most of their life thinking about. You can answer the one question.'

'What would that be?'

'What happens when you die is there a life after death?'

'I can tell you there's something but quite what beyond that I don't know.'

The words hung in the air as the surrounding voices continued. Nobody was paying them any attention, save from the pair of dark eyes peering from the far corner as Amber sat patiently. Far enough away neither Jay nor Chris had noticed her.

'Why are you doing it though?'

'What do you mean?' Chris replied quickly, a little too fast.

'In all of what you've told me, there's something you've been holding back.' Jay paused for a moment, judging Chris' reaction. 'It's when you told me about the mountain and stopped yourself.'

'Mount Shasta,' Chris murmured thoughtfully. 'You're quite perceptive.'

'Gift of the job,' Jay grinned. 'Journalists have a way of seeing behind the masks most people try to wear and hide what they're really thinking.'

Chris tried his best to hold Jay's gaze confidently, but the curious look from the younger man seemed to penetrate his defences a little. Although Chris knew he was dead, knew there was no chemical imbalance to create emotion, there was still something deep in his soul that quivered when he thought of Ash. Jay was quite right that he had avoided Ash in the retelling of his situation. He had done it consciously and believed he had hidden it well enough.

Clearly, he had not.

'I don't mean to push you,' Jay finally said, sensing he had overstepped and was cautious not to watch Chris close him off.

Measuring his response, Chris looked around the pub for the first time. Taking in his surroundings, Chris admired the high beams and aged decor of the small pub. He could very well have been transported back fifty years to a quintessential English pub had it not been for the smartphones littering the tabletops and the occasional glances of people reading messages or notifications that popped up on the screens.

'That's one thing I don't miss,' Chris sighed as he turned back to look at Jay.

'What's that?'

'Being so connected to everyone, looking down at phones and screens every few minutes.'

'It can be a pain,' Jay glanced down at his own phone that lay face-up on the table. 'Necessary in this world though I'm afraid.'

Tapping the screen, Jay flicked through the notifications on his screen and paused as he read a message.

Chris noticed the change in the young man's face. The lines at the corner of his eyes softened a little at the corners of his mouth upturned just a little. Somehow his eyes grew brighter, and he caught himself as Chris stared at him across the table.

'Wife?'

'Pardon.'

'The message, your face lit up when you read it.'

'Girlfriend,' Jay replied, the smile painting itself obviously now across his face.

'How long have you been together?'

'Not long,' Jay switched off the screen and returned his attention to Chris.

'Savour every moment with her,' Chris sighed thoughtfully. 'You'll never know when things will be taken from you.'

An awkward silence descended between the two of them.

'Is that why you're here?' Jay finally disturbed the silence. 'For love?'

It was Chris' turn to be silenced. Sat opposite Jay, he strangely felt vulnerable and uncomfortable. Although he had searched out the young man, he had not known what direction their encounter would take. He had decided on what he would, and more importantly perhaps, would not tell Jay in all of this. Chris had decided Ash was something to be kept from his young friend, but now his feelings had apparently betrayed him.

'Yes,' Chris finally conceded. 'I'm here because of a series of poor decisions in life, and death it would appear. I ended up at Shasta because I lost someone and wanted to be with them again.'

'Where are they now?'

'I don't know. Beyond The Council, I couldn't say what these places are but yes,' Chris' voice trailed, the words catching in his throat as his eyes welled with tears. 'I have seen Ash, sometimes I wish I hadn't, but I have.'

'Surely that's your endgame though, the reason you do this?'

'Deep down, I think it's a dangling carrot to keep me in check. But yet, the hope of holding Ash again is the one reason I agreed to any of this madness.'

Chris fell silent and dropped his gaze to the table. As soon as he did, a shadow passed over the surface of the wooden table and blocked the light from the wide curtained windows looking out into the London street.

'Listen, mate, we're...' Chris began but stopped short as he looked up at the source of the shadow.

Stood beside the table, staring down emotionlessly was

Amber. Chris took a second to recognise her, but once he had, he was standing in a heartbeat. Casting the wooden chair out behind him, the pub fell into shocked silence as Chris turned to face off against Amber in the middle of the room.

All eyes in the room fell to the two of them as they glared at one another. Without releasing her gaze, Chris felt the weight of the two shortened scythes as they materialised in his palms. Wrapping his fingers around the warm wood, he tightened his grip and acknowledged their presence in his hands.

'Maybe you should listen before you make your decision,' Amber offered. 'I am not here to fight you.'

'Then why are you here?' Chris hissed.

'To offer you an alternative.' Amber raised both her hands and showed Chris she was unarmed.

'What alternative would that be?'

Amber circled around the room slowly, Chris kept his gaze locked on her all the while. Amber came to a stop beside Jay and dropped herself down to speak to him, never releasing her stare from Chris.

'It's probably best if you take yourself out of the way my dear, I expect this is about to get messy, and I'd hate for you to get hurt.'

Jay looked from Amber to Chris, who offered a curt nod of agreement. Jay scooped up his phone and bag and dashed to the far side of the room.

'All of you,' Chris said firmly. 'Leave now.'

Although Chris' voice was firm and commanding, the patrons of the pub were transfixed on the interaction between Chris and Amber. Snatching his gaze from Amber for a split second, he turned to look at a burly middle-aged man and glared at him menacingly.

'I suggest you all leave,' Chris snarled. 'NOW!'

The middle-aged man held his ground for a moment, but the ferocity of Chris' words and the unmoving glare soon readjusted his perception.

'Come on fellas, let's leave 'em to it.'

As the pub emptied, Jay remained pressed against the bar, staring at the two of them intently.

'You too Jay,' Chris said firmly, not releasing his gaze from Amber. 'This is something you don't need to see.'

'Be a good little pet and do as he tells you.' Amber mocked, her voice raised and condescending.

'Go!' Chris barked and dropped his bodyweight down to his knees and lowered himself into an attack position.

As the door closed silently behind Jay as he left the pub, the two of them were finally alone. The only noise came from a leaking tap somewhere behind the bar. Everything else was eerily silent.

'Care to listen?' Amber asked as she picked up a glass of something from the table and sniffed the contents before placing it back on the table. 'I don't miss much of this, looking at your face, I see you do.'

'Enough games just get to the point.'

'I can see why Azrael has taken a shine to you, very much his protégé.'

'I'm nothing like him,' Chris barked far too quickly.

'Trouble in the family, dear?' Amber smirked. 'You're more like him than you think, of course, you have your motivation for being here while Azrael just knows nothing different now.'

'Motivation?'

'Your love. I can smell it on your skin as you stand there. Your heart may have stopped beating, but love lasts beyond life, my dear.'

'What was your offer?' Chris did not like the feeling Amber was eliciting in him and changed the subject.

'Direct and to the point, I like it.' Amber sauntered around the room until she arrived face to face with Chris. 'Care to hear my offer, little Reaper?'

'Get it over with.'

'Sub Terra is not a place of damnation if you will help redress the imbalances created by the fearful Enlightened Council. You have only been sold one half of the coin and made your decision based on biased facts and partial truths.'

'And I suppose you have something to offer from your side of the coin?'

'Very much so,' Amber whispered. 'Eternal Darkness is nothing to be feared, if embraced it can provide you limitless opportunities, one being the reclaiming of your lost love's soul.'

Amber allowed her words to hang in the air for a moment. She could see the conflict in Chris' expression and knew it was not the time to push.

Chris could not deny the appeal. Azrael and The Council had only offered him the promise of Ash once he had served them as long as they demanded. Here, in the vast and empty pub, Amber was offering him a compromise without the same level of undecided commitment.

Looking at her though, Chris knew there was deceit in her words.

There was more that remained unsaid that masked the truth of her words. It was an instinct, something he had learned in life, but he could see something more behind Amber's cold and calculating stare.

'I'll pass.' Chris finally answered, his voice croaking barely above a whisper.

'Not the most convincing answer, Chris,' Amber offered. 'I don't need your answer now. This isn't about a quick win for me. Take your time and come to your decision in your own time. You know where to find me when you make sense of all of this.'

Casually, almost dismissively, Amber turned and walked towards the door.

The two scythes in Chris' hands disappeared as she stepped away, and what happened next caught them both by surprise.

Neither had heard nor seen the new arrival in the empty pub. Materialising from nowhere, Azrael stepped into the room dressed in his traditional garb. The heavy cloak and hood were draped over his body, the deep shadows of the hood obscured his face. As Amber reached the door, Azrael casually and effortlessly threw his dagger through the air.

As the blade embedded in the wood where her hand was about to be both Chris and Amber turned to face Azrael.

'You would do well to leave Christian alone.' Azrael's voice echoed from the empty hood. 'This is not a time or place for your lies and games.'

'Ever the protector of the weak.' Amber scoffed.

'He isn't weak,' Azrael snarled.

'Time will tell.'

As the words left her mouth, Amber pressed herself back against the door and propelled herself forward through the air across the room. Azrael, prepared for the attack, did the same and they met in mid-air above where Chris stood in astonishment at the prowess and power of their simultaneous attacks.

Chris felt the air whoosh past his face as Amber and Azrael collided in mid-air. Neither of them held more force than the other and instead of the two falling to the ground together, a strange and unexpected shock wave threw them apart. Both of them were propelled like poled magnets.

Azrael landed first, his cloak rippling like disturbed water as he rotated on the spot and folded back his hood almost casually. As the veil dropped limply to rest against his back, a full-sized scythe materialised in his hands.

Amber dropped to the ground far rougher than Azrael. As she landed, she allowed her weight to drop low and thrust out her right leg straight out to her side. Pressing one palm hard into the floor, Amber raised her free hand up and behind her and smile as her own spear appeared in her vice-like grip as she glared across at Azrael.

'We've danced around this for far too long, Reaper,' Amber snarled. 'I suppose it was inevitable.'

'I'm not here to fight,' Azrael answered calmly. 'Leave Christian, leave his companion, and we will say no more of this.'

Standing up slowly, Amber's movements were graceful and feline. Her body, clad in the black and grey figure-hugging outfit, looked powerful and imposing. As Amber brought the spear around from behind her back, she levelled the tip towards Azrael threateningly.

'Your puppy can make his own choices, but you cannot trap him into your world of lies and deceit.'

'I obey the will of The Council, nothing more, nothing less.'

Chris eyed Azrael curiously. There was something different in the older Reaper's face. Chris watched as Azrael closed his eyes and drew in a long breath. As he watched, Chris saw Azrael's face go tight and then relax. Only after he had expelled all the air from his deep intake of breath did he open his eyes again and turned to look at Chris.

'Whatever happens, you must remember what you have agreed to do, the role you have accepted as your own Christian.'

'What do you mean whatever happens?'

'Old Azrael here knows that in times such as these, where imbalanced souls face one another, there is always finality to it.'

'I accept that.' Azrael said calmly and returned his attention to Amber. 'Perhaps it is better if you too leave us be Christian.'

'I'm not going anywhere.'

Chris stepped towards the two of them but was

stopped by Azrael's raised hand.

'In the eyes of honour there can only ever be one against one, this allows the balance to be maintained. This is our fight, this is our choice.'

'That's right, little pup, sit back and watch the demise of your mentor.'

Amber attacked first. The massive spear thrust through the air towards Azrael as she threw herself up and over in the air. Having expected the attack, Azrael braced himself and sliced the curved blade of the scythe up in front of his body to deflect the powerful attack.

Chris could only stand back and watch as Amber and Azrael fought in the centre of the room. Each parry and attack sent one or the other of the opponents tumbling backwards, and before long the tables and chairs had been cast aside, most in pieces scattered around the room.

At last, Amber gained enough purchase during one of her attacks, and she could propel Azrael up and through the air backwards.

Chris watched in surprise as Azrael's body smashed through the large pub window, sending glass showering in every direction. The people meandering on the street outside screamed and jumped back as the cloaked figure slammed hard onto the pavement outside.

Amber was relentless and followed Azrael through the shattered pane. Perching on the windowsill, she dropped to the pavement and thrust the spear down hard towards Azrael.

Sensing the attack, Azrael barely dodged his head to the side as the tip of the spear sank into the tarmac almost to the hilt with the handle. Fighting to pull the weapon back, Amber shifted her weight onto her back leg, and Azrael chose his moment to attack.

Swinging his legs around he caught Amber just right

and sent her tumbling to the floor roughly. The sharp gasp told him he had winded her, and he took every advantage of his immediate dominance. Gripping the handle of the scythe on the floor, Azrael swiped it through the air and watched in dismay as Amber performed a perfectly timed flip taking her out of the blade's reach.

As the scythe sliced harmlessly through the air, the two of them righted themselves and continued their attacks.

As Chris reached the window, he saw Amber launched backwards into a parked car. The force and power of Azrael's attack sent the vehicle shuddering backwards a good ten feet as Amber's body slammed heavily into the passenger side of the car. The side windows shattered in a cascade of safety glass and the chassis was buckled and bent as Amber pushed herself off the side of the damaged car.

'We can go at this for all eternity, Azrael.' She spat as she launched a flurry of punches in his direction.

Choosing not to answer, Azrael changed his manner of attack and launched himself towards Amber.

Discarding the scythe, Azrael attacked the slender woman in a flurry of punches and kicks. Between them, as Chris could see it through the shattered window, they were equally matched. Each time one of them would land a solid blow, the other would quickly counter with their own.

Their fight continued out amongst the streets. People scattered in every direction to avoid being caught up in the melee. As they moved along the road, tossing one another into parked vehicles and walls along the way, the dense clouds allowed heavy raindrops to fall.

It was not long before the pavement was slick with rain and Azrael's cloak had become soaked and now hung limply, tugging at his legs and torso.

Chris noted the police car screeching down the street long before Azrael or Amber did. The furious cacophony of sounds as the two fought did a lot to drown out the sound of approaching sirens. As the car skidded to a stop along the street, Chris watched as two well-armed officers leapt from the vehicle.

'Leave them,' Chris bellowed as the two officers sprinted down the street and past the broken window. 'You won't be able to stop them!'

The two officers paid no attention to Chris as he scrambled over the shards of broken glass to join them on the street. Watching closely, he saw the two officers approach the fighters and level their weapons.

Punches and kicks flew between Azrael and Amber, and they appeared to take no notice of the commands blurted by the armed officers. Azrael's punch connected hard with Amber's face and sent her sprawling backwards onto the pavement.

'Police, stand still, stand still now!'

Azrael cast a glance across at the officers and the weapons they pointed towards him.

'This isn't your fight,' Azrael warned as he returned his attention to Amber who righted herself from the floor.

'I said stand still,' the officer repeated gruffly.

Amber moved with impossible speed. Her attack was not levelled at Azrael but at the two officers now shouting instructions at them. In the blink of an eye, Amber propelled herself through the air, closed the gap between her and the two men. Gripping one weapon in each hand, she tore them from the men's grasps and before they could realise what was happening she had moved to stand a little off to the side of the farthest police officer.

'What the-' one of them stammered as he looked at his now empty hands comically.

'He said this was not your fight.' Amber barked and thrust the butt of the weapons through the air in a full arc.

As the plastic stocks connected with the heads of the two officers, the power of the blow sent them tumbling to the floor. Both landed heavily, one on top of the other, knocked unconscious by the furious attack by Amber. Caring nothing for the weapons, she dropped them to the floor and turned her attention back to Azrael.
'What say we show your little pup exactly what we can do?'

Amber launched herself up and over and landed proudly on the tall wall of the pub building. Looking above him, Chris could see the height of her jump and watched as Azrael leapt through the air to join her. Poised and stood on the side of the building, the two of them allowed their weapons to re-materialise in their grasps before once again resuming their barrage of parries and attacks on the face of the building.

As the two of them fought, climbing ever higher up the front of the Georgian building, Chris noticed one onlooker holding his phone towards the fighting pair.

Stalking through the crowds, Chris snatched the phone from the grip of the young man.
'Oi, what do you think you are doing?'

Chris ignored the protest and prepared to delete the video. As his eyes fell to the screen, he realised that the video was showing nothing of what was happening on the side of the building. Curiously Chris raised the screen to point at Azrael and Amber as they fought and on the screen, it showed nothing.

Everything was as it should be, the strained stone walls, the glass glinting in the early evening sun, the water stains on the face of pale stone from a leaking gutter. Everything was there except the two spectral creatures that fought furiously, impossibly stood on the side of the building.

'How is that possible?' Chris gasped as he focussed on the two fighters and back to the screen.

'Tell me about it, I've been trying to film it since they came out the pub.' The man spoke with a thick, Cockney twang. 'Mind if I have me phone back?'

Dumbfounded Chris allowed the phone to be taken from his grasp and stepped away from the man. When he finally returned his attention to Azrael and Amber, it was in time to see them leap from the face of the pub frontage and onto the sleek glass facade of the neighbouring office block.

Their fight raged as furious as ever as they climbed ever high up the face of the glass high rise building.

'Any idea what it's all about, mate?' The phone man asked Chris as he stared upwards.

'I have an idea,' Chris answered noncommittally. 'Suppose I should help.'

Without waiting for a reply, Chris ran towards the glass office block and threw himself up onto the smooth glass surface. As the young man stared up incredulously at what he had just seen, he once again raised his camera phone towards Chris but was not surprised to find the screen showed nobody on the face of the tall glass building.

'Bloody 'ell, some proper weird stuff today.'

Leaving the gathered crowds behind, Chris sprinted up the side of the building to try to reach Amber and Azrael, who had already passed a third of the way up the massive structure.

The fight continued onwards and upwards along the face of the glass office building. As Chris sprinted along the smooth surface, his senses adjusted to the distorted perspective. Although his eyes told him the world was in fact sideways, the floor below behind him and the sky ahead of him, he continued upwards.

Reaching the pinnacle of the ornate glass structure, Azrael and Amber remained furiously engaged in battle. The spear and scythe thrust and parried around and towards each other with all but a handful of attacks from both sides missing their mark.

'Stop!' Chris bellowed as he sprinted up the building, but neither of them paid him any attention.

The wind was deafening and whipped around them as they fought. Azrael's cloak billowed in every direction as he ducked and dived to jostle a position of power over Amber.

Azrael was worrying. Every attack, the thrust or swiping arc of the scythe seemed predicted and expected by Amber. Only once or twice did the blade of his weapon pass close enough to cause Amber any concern. Every other time he watched in disbelief as she nudged or blocked each attack precisely.

Sweat was beading on Azrael's forehead as he furiously defended himself against Amber but knew he was bested. Her movements were swift as she hugged her body to the glass and propelled herself behind and around Azrael.

Before he could react, Azrael felt the bite of metal against his dead flesh. Although he was dead, the essence and power flowing along the invisible veins of the metal blade caused a reaction against his flesh. The cursed metal of Amber's spear sliced through his skin and the wound burned like fire.

Pulling himself away from the attack, Azrael turned to face Amber and backed away towards the narrow pinnacle of the building.

'The power of Sub-Terra is undeniable, Reaper,' Amber growled as she span her spear and brought it to rest across her shoulder. 'Eternal Darkness has trained me, nurtured me to be his right hand.'

Cursing against the searing pain, Azrael offered her no reply. Instead, he dropped his attention to the wound on his right arm and tore the fabric free to expose it.

Jagged pale flesh looked charred and burned, tendrils of smoke inched out of the injury as Azrael tapped out the glowing embers.

'The fires of Sub-Terra flow through my blade. Even you can feel the power of my world.'

'You're not the only one.'

Azrael adjusted his grip on the scythe and spun the heavy weapon in front of him. As the speed increased, the long blade glowed a pale blue. As the light grew, the blade made a glowing circle of light as Azrael increased the speed of the spinning scythes.

'It will change nothing,' Amber spat and lunged forward.

Thrusting the spear towards the rotating weapon, the blades met and a shower of sparks erupted at the point of contact. Amber thrust, span and thrust again as Azrael fought back with the curved blade to keep her at bay.

'Stay back.' Azrael snarled as Chris finally reached them. 'This is not your fight.'

Amber's blade sliced across Azrael's back, leaving another jagged burning wound. Wincing again a second, third and fourth attack left more burning injuries across Azrael's, leg, torso, arm and face.

'Azrael, no.' Chris screamed as Amber's next attack sliced cleanly across the back of his hand.

Azrael's natural reaction against the attack was to open his hand, before he could think the scythe fell free from his grip and tumbled to the floor many floors below.

'It is over.' Amber growled as she levelled her weapon at Azrael's throat.

Chris watched as Amber moved closer to Azrael. Expertly, she moved her hands along the long shaft of the spear while always keeping the sizzling tip hovering just above Azrael's dead flesh.

Out the corner of his eye Azrael sensed Chris' movement. With Amber entirely focussed on him, she missed the miniature weapons materialising in Chris' hands. When they had settled in his grip, Azrael made eye contact with him.

So much was said in a single locked glance between the

two of them. The slightest of movements in his head told Chris not to attack. The sternness of Azrael's glare locked him in position, and Chris could only watch what happened next.

'The world is not simple Christian, you must embrace your powers and your promise to keep the balance.'

'Your last words?' Amber hissed. 'We both know there can only be one outcome of this.'

'I know,' Azrael agreed and returned his gaze to Amber. 'But the outcome may be delivered differently than you would like.'

'Meaning what?'

Before either Chris or Amber could react, Azrael made his move. Gripping the wooden shaft of Amber's spear, he looked from her to Chris and offered him a knowing look. 'Make the right choices Christian.'

Wrapping his fingers around the wood, Azrael could feel the power in his grasp. The flow of energy within the spear was tangible, the heat was noticeable against his skin and he could feel the rhythmic throb almost like a heartbeat in his palm.

Sensing it for just a second, he felt Amber's grip fighting against him at first as he feigned attempting to pull the spear away from his neck. As the balance of push-pull adjusted, Azrael looked deep into her eyes.

Their faces were close and when he spoke his voice was barely above a whisper. His ultimate words caught Amber completely by surprise.

'My end is by my own hands, not yours.'

Before Amber could do anything she felt the shift in direction as Azrael stopping pushing the spear away from him and instead yanked it abruptly towards himself.

'No!' Chris shrieked as Azrael closed his eyes and prepared himself.

The world seemed to move in slow motion as Chris tried to lunge forward to stop Azrael. There was no chance of him intervening, Azrael's action was fast and caught both Amber and Chris by surprise.

As the tip of the blade pierced the skin in the hollow of his neck Azrael's eyes remained closed but the look of surprise and pain could not be hidden.

Scrunching his eyes tighter, the lines on his face became deeper as he thrust the blade of the spear deep into his own neck. When the tip of the blade erupted through the skin at the back of his head, the skin was already burning and the smell of charred flesh was harsh in the air.

Azrael's hands fell limply from the wooden shaft and his weight slumped against the weapon, dragging Amber down to her knees with his lifeless corpse suspended on the end of her weapon.

As they landed on the glass, Amber allowed the spear to drop and Azrael's head came to rest against her shoulder.

Stood to one side, Chris was confused by the sudden change in Amber's demeanour. Supporting Azrael's lifeless form against her shoulder, she slowly, almost caringly, pulled the blade free from his throat. When the weapon was free, she allowed it to disappear and curiously supported the back of Azrael's head as it rested on her shoulder.

'You have died a warrior, I cannot take that away from you.' Amber hushed. 'If you had seen through the fog of The Council's deceit then perhaps we could have been allies instead of this.'

Amber traced her fingers through his dark hair before she lifted her attention and looked across at Chris. 'Honour him.' She said finally and moved to one side allowing Azrael's body to tumble away from her.

No longer secured to the vertical glass wall of the building, gravity took hold of Azrael. As Amber released him, his body lurched and dropped heavily from the glass side of the building.

Chris wanted to avenge Azrael. His own fire burned inside him but there was nothing he could do. His own weapons had disappeared from his grip and he watched as Azrael's body tumbled through the air just out of arm's reach.

'Revenge,' was all he could say as he turned away from Amber and launched himself off the face of the building.

The weightlessness was a curious feeling. As he left the glass frontage of the office building, he tumbled through the air and felt his centre of gravity shift uncomfortably in the pit of his stomach. Tucking his arms down by his side, he streamlined his profile and flew through the air with sickening speed in pursuit of Azrael's body.

As the floor grew ever closer ahead of them, Chris pressed his body tight until Azrael was within reach. Tumbling backwards, Azrael's arms and legs whipped along with the fabric of his cloak. His eyes remained closed and as they fell towards the pavement below, Chris wrapped his fingers around the tattered fabric of Azrael's clothes.

Walking into the Great Hall, it was deathly silent.

Chris' footfalls echoed around the cavernous room deafeningly. Walking towards the three remaining platform seats, Chris felt the eyes of the Council members boring into him.

'Present yourself before The Council.'

As Chris moved out into the open space beneath the platforms, he struggled to raise his gaze towards the councillors. As the silence settled, the echoing voice disappearing to nothing, Chris heard the flapping of feathers.

Turning, he watched as the green-robed woman landed delicately on the marble floor. Her tied black hair ruffled as her wings folded down and disappeared from view. There was something regal and majestic about the way she carried herself. Although she held Azrael's body in her arms, the weight of his corpse seemed as light as a feather in her grip.

'Lay him before The Council.' Osiris declared as Malpas strolled to the base of the three platforms.

An altar raised itself from the marble floor as she approached. Reaching the edge of the flat table, she laid Azrael on the cold stone and bowed her head in respect at the fallen Reaper.

'His body lies at the feet of this Council because of your actions,' Osiris boomed as the three platforms slowly lowered to the ground. 'His soul is spent because of your connection to the world of the living, and for that, you must answer to us.'

Filled with shame Chris stood rooted to the spot, unable to move. Each of The Council members stepped from their seats and walked towards the altar and Azrael's body.

'Christian,' Osiris declared firmly. 'Join us.'

Reluctantly, Chris shuffled himself across the distance to the body and took his place alongside the cold stone. Malpas stood silently to his side while the Councillors positioned themselves on the opposite side, all their eyes lowered to Azrael.

'Do you know why he lies before you, spent and empty?'

'No,' Chris' voice caught in his throat.

'Balance!' One of the female Councillors interjected, with his eyes, transfixed on Azrael Chris did not see which had spoken.

'In times of genuine conflict, when darkness faces light, there must always be finality. It has long been avoided to keep the balance between Ascent and Descent.' Osiris explained slowly. 'That is why agents of Altum and Sub-Terra do not come into contact unless there is no other choice. This battle was inevitable, yet it was not time for it to pass.'

'What do you mean inevitable?'

'There can only ever be one true Reaper as the ancient coven demands. Others may aid him, but only one may possess the full power to bring the unjudged into our Halls.'

'And Azrael was the one,' Chris whispered. 'What happens now?'

'The inevitability came from the fact Azrael presented you to The Enlightened Council. He presented you to replace him, yet your behaviour and obsession with life has shown his choice to be ill-informed, and you are not, in fact, ready to take up that mantle.'

Chris snatched his gaze up from the body to look at Osiris. The old man's face was hard to read, but the sternness of his gaze caught Chris by surprise. Holding himself, Chris locked gazes with Osiris and held firm. 'Can you fault me for wanting a connection?' Chris worked hard to keep his voice calm. 'You pull me from my life and place me here with an ultimatum, how was I supposed to react.'

'We took you from nothing, you took *yourself* from life.'

The blunt declaration stung, and Chris was caught off-guard.

'Azrael saw something in you, nurtured that and in time you would replace him, giving him the end to his Reaper's Journey.'

'It can still be that way.'

'You are not ready.' Osiris bit venomously. 'The fact Azrael lies here proves that you were not ready.'

'How was I supposed to know any of this?' The anger boiled over as Chris slammed his hands onto the marble altar. 'You bring me here, tease me with Ash and then demand I serve you indefinitely. You let Azrael school me in the ways of Reapers, but all it shows me is that the man that once was Azrael had become hollow.'

'He was a servant to the Great Hall, the balance of order-'

'He was lost. You condemned him to this, and he forgot why he was here. He had forgotten whatever carrot you had dangled before him as you did with Ash for me.'

It was Osiris' turn to be surprised. Chris' face was contorted with frustration; his knuckles were white as he pushed his fists into the solid surface beneath.

'Azrael was never here by force.'

'Only because you let him forget his reason. I returned to them lest I not forget the life I left behind.' Chris could not have stopped if he had wanted. Everything he said came from all he had seen of Azrael and Altum. 'Can you fault me for wanting to remember the reason why and be more than a hollow, empty servant of death?'

Chris sensed Malpas move to his side and quickly turned to face her.

Fuelled by frustration and bottled anger, Chris thrust both arms out to his side and felt the weight of his weapons as they materialised in his hands.

Malpas was quick to respond. Her wings unfolded with surprising speed and quickly pulled her up and away from Chris, taking her out of reach of his weapons.

'Enough!' Osiris bellowed, but Chris was not listening.

Had his heart been beating, Chris would have heard nothing but the *thump-thump* loud in his ears. As it was, stood in the Great Hall, his attention was fixed on Malpas who glared down at him. The slow flapping of her wings kept Malpas out of reach yet frustratingly close, which only fuelled Chris' frustration.

'Christian.' Osiris repeated and waited for a reaction.

'What?'

'Respect these Halls and respect your fallen mentor and stow your weapons. This is not the place.' Osiris tempered his voice a little and was relieved to see Chris react.

Turning his attention back to the altar and Councillors, Chris agreed and allowed the scythes to fade from his grip. As the weight disappeared from his palms, so too did it from his body. Chris uncontrollably slumped forward to lean against the altar once more.

'Now is not the time. For now, we mourn the loss of Azrael, and then we will decide what we are to do with the legacy he left in you.'

Malpas allowed herself to return to the floor and as her wings folded behind her back, she stepped to Chris' side. Leaning in close, she whispered to him so only he could hear.

'You have made your choices, right or wrong, and now we must all live with the consequences.' Her words hurt to hear. 'You were right to seek a connection to life. It is too easy to forget what we all once had.'

Chris stiffened as he felt her fingertips grazed the back of his hand that rested on the altar. It was unexpected, and the softness of her voice caught him entirely by surprise. Twisting to look at her, he saw the same poker-faced expression, yet her eyes told him something else.

As the Councillors returned to their grieving, Chris felt oddly warmed by the softness offered by Malpas. Where she had seemed the stern and unforgiving guard, he saw something different in her look. As he was about to speak, she stealthily removed her fingers from his hand and returned her gaze to the fallen Reaper.

Time passed slowly, and the remaining time in The Great Hall that day was spent in silence. Neither Osiris nor the other Councillors said anything to Chris.

When he was finally dismissed from the stone altar, it

was merely a gaze that told him to leave. Dropping his head in respect, he stepped away from the gathering and walked with a heavy heart back out into the open air of the Pantheon and the bright light that bathed Altum.

Leaving the Hall Of Souls And Scales behind, Chris made his way to his sanctuary on the far side of Altum and was relieved as he stepped through the door. As the door shut Chris could not contain his guilt and grief anymore. His knees buckled, and he fell roughly to the floor.

Slumping back against the wall, he buried his head in his hands and wept.

It was an odd feeling. Alone in the training room, Chris could not quite fathom what he was feeling. Undeniably he was awash with guilt at having caused Azrael's death, but there was also an insatiable sense of loss. For all his sternness and unshaken devotion to his responsibilities, Azrael had fathered him in a way since arriving at Altum.

There had been something more than mentorship, as Osiris had put it: Azrael had seen something in Chris that had allowed him to present him to The Council. The time they had spent together had changed Chris in so many ways, yet Azrael had always nurtured him in a way that made it all feel right.

Chris knew there were things he did not understand, the more delicate details of everything that kept Altum in motion, but that would come.

Wiping the dry tears from his face, Chris stood himself and walked to the display where Azrael's dagger sat proudly.

The bright light pouring in through the full window glinted on the blade. With trembling fingers, Chris reached for the weapon and lifted it from the stand. Balancing it in his hand, he held the dagger to the light and twisted the blade slowly, admiring the intricate carving along its length.

'It is yours now.' The voice made him jump, and he turned, hoping to see Azrael stood behind him.

The room was empty, but he knew he had heard the voice.

'Your Reaper's Journey begins now, Christian. Do right by me, by The Council and by Altum, and perhaps in time we will meet again.'

Azrael's voice faded into silence, and as Chris stood, bathed in the bright light, the sorrow and sadness faded away. Alone in the training room, Chris suddenly felt filled with a sense of pride and purpose.

'Until that day,' Chris spoke to the empty room. 'Until then, I will do you proud.'

Amber crashed to the floor. The pain seared through her right side where her own spear had been violently thrust into her flesh. The acrid smoke billowed from the jagged wound as she clutched herself against the heat. 'Fool,' Tenebris' voice boomed from the centre of the hovering smoke.

Amber's weapon had emerged from the smoke and grazed along her side, thrown by some unseen hand behind the veil of smoke. The shaft now vibrated slowly as the blade had embedded itself almost to the hilt in the far wall of Force Tower. On her knees, Amber bit back her anger as she stared at her weapon.

'I made my approach to the new Reaper as you commanded, hoping to convince him to hear us.'

'I told you to work in stealth and in secret.' Tenebris

growled. 'Not bumble into the path of Azrael and cross swords when the time was not right.'

'His end was inevitable, it was from the moment he recruited the pup into The Order.'

'But now was not the time. All you have done is cement this Christian into blind obedience for the corrupt council.'

Amber turned her gaze towards the hovering smoke in time to see the dark centre expand. Although the corona at the centre of the smoke was dark, there was something more mysterious held within. As Amber watched, a shadowy black silhouette could be clearly seen against the dark background walking towards her.

Whatever it was appeared human. Somehow, outlined against an almost black background, the dark figure seemed darker, blacker as if it was sucking every inch of light from the world around it.

Amber had seen the physical manifestation of Tenebris only twice before. As she watched his onyx-black silhouette walk fluidly towards her, she was filled with dread. Reaching the edge of the smoky cloud, Tenebris appeared to pause for a moment before stepping over the edge of the smoke.

Appearing in the real world Amber could see the detail of his physical presence. Tenebris emerged as a living shadow, somehow darker than night, blacker than anything humanly possible. He moved with fluidity, and the edges of his appearance seemed to shimmer on the dim light of Sub-Terra. He had no features, no face, just the vaguely recognisable outline of a man but nothing that could be said to be features or details.

'I did what I thought was best.' Amber stammered as Tenebris flowed towards her.

'You should never have touched the mortal,' Tenebris hissed as he stalked past Amber and retrieved the spear from the wall. 'It was clear to see his connection to the living world was something that needed careful consideration. The Council even acknowledged this by teasing him with his lost love.'

'He appeared to want to listen when I spoke to him, there was hesitation in him.' Amber quickly retorted. 'There is hope.'

Spinning the spear lazily in the air, Tenebris levelled the tip at Amber's neck and forced her to stand. Wincing against the pain in her ribs, Amber stood as the razor-sharp tip of her own weapon teetered beneath her chin. 'There *was* hope, my dear Amber. Whatever hope there was has now gone.'

'If it was inevitable, why should Azrael's end not have come to pass when it did?'

'Because right now The Council will keep their newfound student at arm's length. They know his emotional imbalance will be a risk to their expectation of order. With this, you have introduced an unknown.'

'Their options will be limited.'

Amber moved quickly, catching Tenebris by surprise. Had there been any visible eyes on his featureless face, they would have gone wide as Amber ripped the spear from his grasp. Twisting the momentum of the surprise attack, Amber rotated and drew the spear around with ferocious speed until the sharpened blade came to rest next to Tenebris' head.

'You lose no skills, even with injury, my dear Amber.'

'Like I said,' Amber snatched the spear away from Tenebris and rested the end on the uneven floor. 'Their options will be limited.'

'Explain.'

'They can choose to replace their new Reaper, but that would come at a cost, Azrael has already poured a lot into the pup.' Amber spoke confidently, ensuring she had her master's attention with what she was saying. 'They will bench him and continue his training until they feel he is ready.'

'And both of those mean someone must take up the mantle of Reaper until either Christian is exiled or prepared.'

'There are limited choices.'

'But it still means we are no closer to our goal of toppling the corrupt Council and allowing Sub-Terra to once again be filled with the souls it deserves.'

'Then perhaps our efforts should be more overt and less secret moves in the shadows.'

Amber allowed her suggestion to hang in the air for a moment.

Tenebris seemed surprised by her words and moved around her slowly. Passing close to her, Amber felt the air between them chill. Tenebris' form appeared to pull the light, feeling and warmth from all that surrounded him. His very presence was something akin to a literal black hole, devoid of passion and emotion.

'We have survived with less than half the souls we should have been granted from the great and Enlightened Council,' Tenebris all but spat the name. 'To rise against them and force them from their elevated thrones would be futile and offer them the reason to dismiss the balance entirely. No, we must be more cautious.'

'If I may?'

Amber's voice seemed to quiver, tainted by the nervousness with what she was about to say.

'When have I ever suppressed your thoughts? Of any souls within Sub-Terra, yours has earned the right to speak your mind.'

Although she had been given, Amber paused for a

moment before she spoke.

'Would all this have not been easier had you not allowed yourself to descend from The Council? A seat amongst the fearful would have at least allowed you to have sway.'

'Hardly an answer to our problems now.' Tenebris fought to hold back his bubbling frustration.

'Yes, but a point nonetheless.' Amber smirked at having reminded Tenebris of the consequences of his actions.

'However, it may give us an advantage on an alternative path.'

'Go on.' Tenebris' interests were piqued.

'The Outcast Shadows have never pledged allegiance to either side, preferring to live disfigured and tormented amongst the living. Could we not consider a parlay with them to help destabilise The Council and bring natural deliberation to Ascent or Descent?'

Tenebris paused in his movements and stood motionless in the space between Amber and the cloud of smoke.

'The Shadows have nothing to gain from allegiance to either side.'

'But their numbers would swell our ranks to be a force worthy of notice, enough perhaps to remove The Council.'

Amber felt she was baiting the line enough. Although featureless, she could see the change in posture and appearance as Tenebris weighed up her suggestion. She dared not push. Even without words, Amber knew she had baited enough and any decision now would have to come from Tenebris himself.

'How would you suggest we parlay with the Shadows, what can we give them in return for their souls?'

'Freedom.' Amber quickly countered. 'With The Council removed any souls that remained unwilling to Ascend or Descend would be given to them, food to their dwindling darkness.'

'Imbalance would follow.' Tenebris added thoughtfully.

It was now time for Amber to offer her last idea. Like a conspiring ghoul, she moved to Tenebris' side to whisper where his ear would be.

'As their numbers swell, we would feed on the darkest, take them from the Shadows and bring them into the Darkness. In time our numbers would swell beyond anything we could dream and at last Sub-Terra will be a power to be feared.'

Tenebris inhaled slowly. Walking away from Amber, he moved to a massive opening in the wall of Force Tower and looked at his world below.

The burning fires raged, deformed souls meandered the walkways far below, but Sub-Terra seemed empty to him.

'Sub-Terra has always lived in the Council's shadow's fear.' He snarled. 'Who are they to deny this world what it rightly deserves?'

'The streets should be swollen with souls, yet all we see is this.' Amber pointed down to the world below.

'My world should be filled for no other reason than fairness. Who are they to defy the balance, to deny the rightful passage of those who deserve their Descent into this world?'

Tenebris was filled with rage. Somehow his appearance grew even darker as she stood himself tall as he stood in front of the opening.

'Make your approaches to the Shadows, see what appetite there is for unity.'

Knowing her work was done, Amber bowed her head enough and stepped away from Tenebris. Only when she was gone, when he knew he was alone, Tenebris allowed himself to relax.

Leaning his arm against the edge of the window opening, he peered out across Sub-Terra.

'Too long have I watched my world suffer, too long have I been deprived the souls that are rightfully mine.' Tenebris rested his head against his arm. 'The Shadows cannot be trusted but they will offer a means to an end and when we are done, when The Council topples then I shall return the world to order. Ascent or Descent and nothing in-between. No return for redemption, no hiding in defiance, just one or the other. As it should be.'

With his plans made, Tenebris turned from the window and walked back towards his sanctuary within the cloud of smoke. Casting one last look behind him, checking that Amber had gone, he stepped into the dark iris and faded completely from view. As the opening closed, he could see Forca Tower disappearing behind him and was once again happy in the safety of his isolation.

Amber, on the other hand, had heard everything Tenebris had said. Concealed behind the wall on the far side of the tower, she could not help but smile.

She had nurtured a small flame that promised to become a raging fire. All they needed now was fuel, and with her master's blessing, she would get it from the Outcast Shadows.

'A means to an end indeed,' she sniggered as she left the tower room and set about her task.

'How much does your human know?' Malpas asked as she walked through into the large training room.

Chris had been sat cross-legged facing away from the door. Since arriving back, he had barely moved and instead sat staring out of the glass at the world outside. He had heard Malpas enter the room but chosen not to speak until he had to.

Sighing he released the tension from his muscles and dropped his hands to the floor. Turning slowly he faced Malpas to answer her.

'My human?' Keeping his frustration in check was hard. 'Would you mean Jay?'

'His name is hardly relevant, my dear.'

'To you, perhaps not,' Chris quickly retorted. 'But for those of us who have respect for life still, then names indeed are important.'

Knowing the argument was likely to go round, Malpas offered a nonchalant shrug and nodded at Chris.

'Ok,' she sighed heavily. 'How much does your, does Jay know?'

There was an accusation in the question. It laced the words, and Chris could all but feel the stern gaze from Malpas as she waited for an answer.

'Enough.'

'You really don't understand any of this, do you?' Malpas snapped. 'The world below should have no knowledge of this. By telling him you have exposed him to our world but also made him a creature of interest to all sides.'

'All sides?'

'Reapers, Ascendants, Descendants and Outcast Shadows. A soul which is consciously aware of fates beyond death appeal to all sides.' She sauntered towards Chris as he stood up slowly. 'So your little stunt may have put him in more danger than you realise.'

Hoping to frighten Chris, Malpas watched as he took in what she was saying.

The look on his face suddenly changed, and he shifted his gaze to look at her.

'You're saying she will be more interested in him?'

'Amber?'

'Yes,' Chris snarled. 'She will have an interest in him now he is aware of all of this?'

'I would think it was obvious considering how she found her way to you so easily.'

'Good!' Chris barked and stalked to the dagger on the plinth. 'At least I know a way I can find her now.'

Chris snatched up the etched dagger from its place and stalked across the room towards the door. Passing alongside Malpas, he was surprised when her hand gripped his wrist.

'The Council would prefer you to remain within Altum while they decide the path forward for you.'

Chris felt the tightness of her grip on his skin and stood rooted to the spot. His attention was fixed on the door ahead of him, and for a moment he remained transfixed in his position. Feeling the weight of the dagger in his hand, he mulled over his options for a few seconds, before turning to look at Malpas.

They were close, their faces almost touching as Chris turned to look at her. Her hazel eyes looked bright, catching the light cascading through the window. Although her face was stern, there was warmth behind her eyes that caught him by surprise. Her jet-black hair was tied tight behind her head, accentuating her features and full lips.

Distracted more than he should be, Chris cast aside the thought and pulled his hand free from her solid grip. 'Now Azrael is gone it makes sense I assume his position,' Chris said confidently. 'After all, it is what he was training me for.'

Stepping towards the door, he was frozen by the light chuckle from Malpas. Filled with frustration, he snapped his head around to look at her. Her mouth was upturned on one side, and she looked across at him as if weighing up the comments of a petulant child. Her dismissive and almost mocking look frustrated him.

'What?' He snapped.

'Your actions have hardly bathed you in glory or filled The Council with confidence in you.' She measured her words as she closed the gap between them. 'What makes you think they will even trust you with his mantle?'

'Because Azrael had faith, I could do it.'

'He's been wrong before.'

Her comment hit him like a brick wall, and he could not hide the hurt look on his face. Taking a step backwards, Chris felt suddenly shaken.

Malpas allowed those feelings to linger. She could see his resolve shaken and watched as Chris tried to take in what she had said. As his eyes moved from side-to-side, she finally allowed herself to speak again.

'Your fate has yet to be decided, but your actions here and now will ultimately feed into their decisions.' Her tone was softer, almost caring. 'It would be best for your future here, to remain here and heed the mentorship of those of us who have endured lifetimes in Altum now Azrael is gone.

'People like who?'

'Me for one. There will be others who would seek to fill the gaps left behind in Azrael's passing.'

'You would all seek to contain me here while The Council decides my fate? Go on with the training in the vain hope they decide to keep me here.' Chris' voice rose.

'You have your reasons to remain here, we all do, and you need to remember this.'

'Held in place by a carrot on a stick.' He bellowed. 'Offering me just enough for obedience while she remains free to wonder where she wants, the one who killed Azrael.'

'This is entirely your doing.' The softness had evaporated from her voice. 'You made your choice, and now you live with the consequences, you brought yourself here nobody else.'

'Enough!' Chris growled through clenched teeth. 'You're right, it was my choice that brought me here, had Azrael torn from his rightful place, but you can think again if I am going to sit back and wait.'

'What will you do?' Malpas interrupted as Chris reached

the door.

'If she is drawn to Jay, then I will watch and wait until she comes back.'

'And then?'

'Then I'll kill her.'

'Azrael tried what makes you think you could succeed where he failed?'

'That's not something to worry about now.' Chris pulled the door open. 'I can't sit here wallowing in self-pity and regret knowing she is out there doing whatever damage she can. I need to make amends for what I've done with or without The Council's blessing.'

As Chris stepped through the door, Malpas shouted for him to stop.

'What?' He snapped.

'Take this,' she offered and tossed a piece of fabric across to Chris.

Catching the light material, Chris looked at it curiously. 'You don't strike me as the traditional robe type, maybe this will be a hybrid for you.'

After turning it over, Chris realised, it was a sleepless hood made of the same feather-light black material Azrael's full robes had been made of. Slipping his head through the hole, he pulled the hood around the back of his neck and allowed the fabric to sit on his shoulders.

'It will conceal you when you need it to.' Malpas offered, once again her voice softening and the half-smile appearing to warm her face. 'Just remember one thing.'

'What's that?'

'You wear the hood, but you are not a Reaper. Perhaps it will save you in the end.'

Not wanting to push further, he took Malpas' offer of words and the black hood as her consent to leave. Offering only a thankful nod, a subtle tip of his head, Chris stepped out through the door and allowed it to close behind him.

The sun was setting in the distance, and Altum was bathed in a growing red glow from the sinking sun. Although time passed differently, Chris could not deny the cascade of colours soaking the city gave it a heavenly feel. Looking out across at the shimmering dome of the Hall Of Souls And Scales. Immersed in the sunlight, Chris felt himself feeling resentment towards the Hall and The Council seated within.

Walking towards the Ianua, Chris passed nobody on his journey. Looking back as he meandered along the quiet streets, he was convinced he could see the outline of Malpas stood on the hilltop behind him. Although her words had been laced with understandable anger, there was something in the way she had spoken to him that had disarmed him.

'Christian!' The voice was commanding and stern, without turning he knew who it belonged to.

Stopping to stand in front of the closed door to the Ianua, Chris took a deep breath before he answered.

'Osiris.' Chris kept his voice respectful and calm.

'Malpas was tasked with keeping you in Altum, where do you think you are going?'

'Really want me to answer?'

'You are forbidden to leave Altum until The Council have decided your place amongst us.'

Chris turned to face Osiris, who stood alone in the middle of the street. His long flowing robes glistened in the light of the setting sun. The lines on his aged face seemed thicker and darker as he looked across at Chris.

'The choices being what?'

'You will continue to train as Azrael's replacement until such a time as The Council considers you worthy to assume his mantle or else...' Osiris' voice faded.

'Or else what? What other option would there be?'

Osiris looked uncomfortable, unwilling to answer Chris' question for a moment.

'Well?' Chris pressed.

'You would be judged, your fate most likely to walk the earth in another life to prove your worth.'

'And there is your answer,' Chris snapped. 'You would gladly hold me here with the option of submission or expulsion, and if that were the option I would lose my Ash, and I cannot let you have that.'

'Your fate is not through The Ianua, it is here in Altum.'

'I will choose my own fate this day, Osiris.' Chris replied confidently. 'This is not out of defiance for your traditions, but out of respect for Azrael. I acknowledge the mistakes I have made and the cost it has had. The honourable thing to do is right those wrongs.'

'That is not your choice to make.'

'It is more my choice than yours. When it is done, I will either return to you for whatever judgement The Council sees fit to deliver or else not return at all.'

Chris wrapped his hand around the handle and pushed open the door of The Ianua.

'I cannot support what you are choosing to do.'

'It wouldn't change anything, I've decided.'

'However,' Osiris continued softly. 'I will not stop you, go forth on this path, and if the fates see fit, then we will see each other again Christian.'

'I'll take that.' Chris said and stepped into the darkness of the small building, leaving Osiris alone in the street behind him.

The door to the apartment was battered and scratched.

An outline of the old numbers could be seen on the stained wood, but the brass numerals had long since disappeared. Stepping to the door, Chris removed the hood, and his head appeared from the darkened shroud.

Checking the hallway was empty, Chris raised his hand and rapped his knuckles on the massive fire door. 'Who's there?' A familiar voice mumbled from behind the door.

'Open the door.' Chris replied flatly, knowing Jay would be peering through the scratched spy hole in the middle of the door.

Waiting, Chris finally heard the locks and chains unfastened on the door, and eventually it opened enough to allow Jay to peer through the cracked door.

'Oh, it's you.' Jay's tone changed, and he quickly opened the door, allowing Chris to enter the apartment.

Stepping over the threshold, Chris was taken aback by the interior of the apartment. The first thing which caught his eye was the large window on the far side of the open plan room. The view was spectacular and showed the Thames and in the distance the London Eye and familiar outline of Big Ben.

The apartment itself did not match the battered hallway. The decor was minimalist and modern, sleek and angles and lines giving it very much the bachelor pad appearance.

'Better inside than out,' Chris declared as he walked through the spacious lounge and towards the expansive window. 'Wasn't expecting this when you opened the door.'

'I put my touch inside, can't do much about outside.'

'I like it.'

Jay moved behind the island in the kitchen and poured himself a glass of water from the sink. Swallowing down the entire glass, he wiped his mouth with the back of his hand and replaced the glass on the worktop.

Looking across at Chris, he was surprised to see how powerful and imposing he looked. Silhouetted by the bright landscape outside, Chris looked tall and broad. The folded hood hung limply against his bag, and his shortly cropped hair seemed uniformly cut, the skin visible at the fade going halfway up the back of his head.

'I'm sure you didn't come here to talk interior decoration,' Jay announced. 'Especially considering what your friends did to the Queen's Head.'

'Queen's Head?'

'The pub!'

Chris had rested his left arm against the glass and was

looking down at the street below. Seeing the meandering bodies many levels below he was surprised how insignificant it all seemed. Concentrating he allowed his body to relax and with enough concentration he could see the lifelines of the people walking the streets.

Without focussing on any individual, Chris scanned the world with Soul Sight. The intricate feathering lines of light tracing around and behind the people were intricately woven. From his vantage point, the lanes of their movement looked like veins along the streets.

Hypnotised by the chaotic pattern, Chris was ignorant of Jay's questions. Lost, instead, in the admiration of the random beauty below.

'Why did you come back?'

Jay's voice finally brought Chris back. As the Soul Lines faded, he slowly turned to look at Jay.

'Say again?'

'Why did you come back? After everything that happened in the streets, I expected never to see you again.'

'I wouldn't be here if they had their way,' Chris mumbled as he stepped away from the window. 'Was there any fallout from Azrael and, her?'

'You could say that.'

Jay picked up the remote from the side and turned on the larger TV mounted on the wall in the lounge. The channel was already set on the news, and the repeated news article had just begun again.

A middle-aged woman stood on the right side of a police cordon, a frenzy of activity behind her as officers in forensic suits moved around the debris in the road. Her broad London accent was clear in her voice as she spoke towards the camera.

'...reports were received early this morning of an explosion at an East London pub. Shortly after the first call, reports came in of a mass fight in the street. During the altercation, two armed officers have been hospitalised, and the offenders are yet to be located. Sources from near to the scene report having seen explosions, and there appears to be structural damage to the adjacent buildings.'

The camera panned around slowly, taking in the destruction at the front of the old public house. Shattered and dented cars littered the street and as the camera crawled, the trail of destruction led across to, and up the side of, the glass-fronted office block.

'...the Metropolitan Police are yet to release a statement, but rumours are circling of a possible terror link but as yet nothing from official sources. We will, of course, keep you up-to-date with any developments...'

The television sound switched off, and Jay tossed the remote onto the sofa on the far side of the room.

'The city is quite panicked, everyone looking over their shoulders at any sight or sound that is in the least bit suspicious.' Jay sighed. 'It's been a long few days.'

Chris took a second to appreciate what had been said. 'Hold on, few days?'

'Yeah, you disappeared two days ago with your friend in your arms, and the woman just walked away.'

'Amber,' Chris snarled. 'Have you seen her since?'

A look of confusion appeared on Jay's face.

'Isn't she from your world?'

'No,' he spat. 'She's from somewhere else, but I would very much like to see her again.'

'You and them both.' Jay point towards the muted television. 'They've released sketches of your friend and her as part of their enquiries, both of them wanted for questioning.'

'Good luck with that.' Chris mocked. 'Azrael is dead and she, well, who knows where she is.'

Jay stood thoughtfully for a moment, his attention passing between Chris and the television. The young black man looked perplexed and finally returned his attention to his guest.

'Why does this bring you back to my door then?'

'Pardon?'

'After the violence, I've seen in two of the times we've met, I have to say being around you is inherently dangerous. That, and I don't suppose you came for a follow-up check on how I was.' Jay's astuteness caught Chris by surprise. 'That and a supernatural creature like you hardly needs to be knocking on my door, so there must be a reason.'

Chris paused for a moment. In all he had confessed about Altum and the complex world he now inhabited, he had never had an end game. If anything Jay had been an outlet, but it had become apparent by dragging Jay into his world he had exposed him. Chris had exposed him, not only to the hidden truths but also the dangers.

'I want her.' Chris hissed.

'And how am I supposed to help you?' Jay quizzed, his voice remaining calm. 'Until a week ago, I did not know any of this existed. Hell, had I not seen what I did in the underground and at the pub, I may have just cast you off as another crazy trying to sell me a story.'

'You're more useful than you think.'

'That sounds equally ominous and terrifying at the same time.' Jay quipped. 'Care to elaborate, or don't I want to know?'

Chris moved around the apartment slowly and came to stand in front of the wall-mounted television. Staring at the picture, he saw the muted news report giving some updated on an ongoing crisis in some far off country.

The pictures stirred no emotion in him as he saw scores

of bodies in a war-torn country. The faces of mourning children filled the screen, but nothing touched at his feelings. Chris knew he should feel something yet, looking at the images, he felt utterly empty.

'I need to apologise,' Chris sighed and turned from the television.

'For what?'

'Back in Altum, I've been told that by confiding in you, exposing you to the truths of the other world, that I've put you at risk.'

'No shit!' Jay snapped. 'I'd call an exploding pub and some crazy ass fight on a train line pretty risky.'

'You've got a point.' Chris chuckled. 'But I mean more than that. They were events that unfolded before you, but from what I'm told things are different now.'

'Meaning what exactly?'

A look of concern appeared on Jay's face as his brow furrowed and his eyes fixed on Chris.

'Meaning what?'

'It's said that those who are Outcast and those who have Descended will now seek you out. By me exposing my world to you, I have somehow attracted them to you.'

'But somehow I don't think you've come to apologise and make things better have you?'

Chris averted his gaze from Jay. Surprisingly, Chris felt the guilt as the young man looked across at him. It perplexed him that sadness wasn't something he could feel, but guilt was.

'Not exactly,' Chris confessed.

'Care to elaborate?'

'I need to find Amber, I'm sure you understand why.'

'Your friend?'

'Yes,' a lump formed in Chris' throat for a second. 'He was my mentor, and because of my decisions to trust you, to talk to you, she killed him.'

'It was hardly your fault if I remember rightly, he offered her the fight.' Jay attempted to mediate, but Chris' answer came quickly.

'He did that to protect me, it was entirely my fault he was forced to make that choice.'

For the first time, Jay could see a shadow of remorse on Chris' face. Something in his eyes that told him there was far more beneath the exterior Chris portrayed.

'You can't blame yourself, we all make our own choices in life.'

'This isn't life,' Chris growled, his voice low and filled with rage. 'This is death, I am death.'

'So what do you plan on doing?'

'With your help, I want to draw her out and avenge Azrael's death. Bring about her demise and prove my worth to The Council and maybe honour Azrael enough.'

'I can't say the idea sits comfortably with me,' Jay began.

'I didn't expect it to...' Jay raised his hand and cut Chris short.

'But as I see it there are two choices. The first is to cast you aside and go about my normal life in the hope they leave me alone. The second is to agree to let you use me and hope you stop them before they get to me and do whatever they do to me.'

'I'll leave you to make a choice.'

Chris excused himself and moved towards the door. As his gloved hand gripped the handle, he was stopped by Jay's voice behind him.

'My chances are much better with a guardian angel on my shoulder.' Jay offered quickly as Chris held the door.

Turning slowly, Chris fixed his gaze on Jay, his expression blank and emotionless.

'There's one thing I have learned in all of this so far Jay,' he paused for a moment. 'I am no angel, no guardian, I am merely an agent of death. I am a Reaper.

'Then I'm happy to have a Reaper watching over me.'

'I suppose we should come up with a plan,' Chris smirked and released his grip on the door.

Days passed, and Chris occupied the shadows. He suspected his attempts to disguise himself amongst the bustling streets of London was nothing more than show, and had Amber been looking he would be all too easy to see. The hood did enough to keep him from the view of the living. Although he skulked as much as he could, the disguise appeared to mask him from the attention of the everyday folk around him. Occasionally Chris would see someone take a second glance towards him, but nobody ever made eye contact with him.

It was as if he were just not there, invisible as he meandered along with everyone else.

As the third night rolled in, Chris allowed Jay to settle before he removed the hood and appeared from the shadows in the kitchen.

'Jeez,' Jay gasped as Chris appeared abruptly. 'You could at least give me some warning, don't think I'll ever get used to that.'

Chris smoothed the hood against his back and could not hide the wry smile on his face.

'I'm still getting used to how much this works,' Chris confessed as he lifted himself onto the worktop. 'But I'll try to remember next time.'

'Please do.' Jay chuckled as he slumped down on the sofa.

Sipping from a bottle, Jay enjoyed the cold beer and allowed himself to relax a little before he paid any attention to Chris.

Night had settled in, and the apartment was dimly lit by a small lamp against the far wall. Jay always preferred to keep the lights low in the room so he could take in the impressive view of London out of the window.

As the night was clear, no remnants of smog or clouds, the entire city looked peaceful and picture-perfect.

'I guess there's been no sign of your woman?' Jay asked as he took a long swig from the bottle.

'Nothing.' Chris grumbled, the seriousness returning to his expression. 'Another day to try tomorrow.'

'Has there been anything?'

'Some bits but nothing of note.'

Jay sat up on the chair and perched himself on the edge, his interest piqued by Chris' answer.

'Go on.' He pressed casually.

Reluctantly, Chris dropped from his seat on the countertop and walked to the expansive window. Standing in front of the glass, he peered down again at the movements of the world below. Appreciating the view with normal eyes, resisting the urge to Soul Sight, Chris watched for a moment before he answered.

'When you entered the underground, there was another of

those creatures like last time.'

'The gargoyle thing?'

'Indeed.' Chris nodded. 'There was another stalking you as you walked onto the platform.'

Jay tried to recollect his journey on the underground, but nothing stood out to him. It had been like every other commute, uneventful and filled with faceless people. 'I remember nothing.'

'You wouldn't, I dealt with it while you were preoccupied with the blonde woman from your office.'

Thankful for the dim light, Jay felt his cheeks blush a little as Chris explained what had happened.

*   *   *

People were all but crushing to fit on the escalator leading down to the platforms. Three or four levels below the ground, the air was stifling. Even though hundreds of people were crammed into the tight corridors and platforms of the underground, the atmosphere was surprisingly quiet.

Snaking through the crowds effortlessly, Chris chuckled at how self-absorbed the world seemed to him. Most people were glued to the screens of their smartphones or else deep in conversation on hands-free sets, barely paying any attention to one another.

Chris had not noticed the diminutive stature of the small man that stalked close behind Jay a few metres ahead of him. It was not until the little man loitered at the entrance to the platform, allowing people to push past him that Chris first took note.

Shrouded in an oversized coat that covered far too much of his shape and appearance, Chris watched as the small man observed Jay's movements intently.

Moving out of the flow of people, Chris kept Jay in sight, the young blonde woman feigning amusement at some outlandish comment he had made no doubt. Pressing himself against the wall, Chris adjusted his hood to ensure he was hidden and concentrated on his Soul Sight.

As the world became filled with tethered lines of light from the surrounding bodies, Chris focussed his sight on the loitering man.

Concentrating hard to drown out the interference from the other lifelines, Chris could finally focus on the man.

There was no aura of light around the shrunken man. No tendrils of light floating away from him, instead there was nothing but darkness and shadow. Right then Chris knew what he was looking at. The Outcast Shadow seemed utterly devoid of life, and everything around him seemed tainted by the darkness.

Chris wasted no time in making his move.

Sliding between a pair of oblivious businessmen, Chris slipped his arm around the neck of the Outcast Shadow and dragged him through an open service door and out of the main flow of commuters. Caught completely by surprise, the small man struggled but allowed himself to be pulled into the brightly lit corridor.

As they passed through the open door, Chris slammed it shut with his foot, and as he pushed the man away from him, Chris summoned one of his scythes into his free hand.

Preparing for a fight, the small man ripped off his coat and tossed it away behind him. The jacket had indeed been hiding something as the small man's flesh was covered in grey fur. His body seemed mutated and disfigured, and the first thing Chris associated with his appearance was that of a werewolf.

'Reaper,' the *thing* growled, his accent distinctly Russian. 'Leave me be you a putrid agent of death.'

'I am not here for a fight.' Chris quickly interjected and raised his empty hand out towards the man.

'The weapon in your other hand would say otherwise.' The Russian hissed. 'Have you come to drag me before your masters and send my soul for judgement?'

'From what I've seen, you have no soul left.' Chris sneered. 'But no, I am not here for that today.'

'Then speak your reasons and be done.'

Chris was uncomfortable, the tension in the air was tangible and matched the smell of electricity from the power lines of the underground network.

'I am seeking Amber, the one who walks from darkness.'

'Why would I have any connection to her?' The man grumbled as a train rocked the surrounding walls. 'She would seek to tame my soul as much as you would.'

'She took something from me, and I am seeking her out so she can answer for it.'

'So it is true?'

Chris was disturbed by the sudden change in the other man's demeanour. Where he had been poised and prepared for the attack, he now appeared to relax. A broad grin painted itself on his face, and he seemed like a scheming golem staring back at him.

'The worlds truly are out of balance,' he mumbled thoughtfully.

'Get to the point, demon,' Chris snarled. 'You can either tell me where to find her or not.'

The man looked as if he was considering Chris' request for a moment. A sudden change in his stance was the only warning Chris got before the man attacked.

'The Reaper's are falling,' the man bellowed as he propelled himself across the gap between them, his clawed fingers pointed towards Chris.

Chris moved with speed and grace. Bringing the small scythe slicing up and around as the furred man attacked. The blade tore the man in half with ease. The tempered metal sliced through flesh, muscle and bone as a knife would pass through butter. The undead Shadow was no more, as his body disintegrated in a cloud of smouldering ash.

'Not while I've still got things to balance out,' Chris hissed as the cloud of dust fell lifelessly to the surrounding floor.

Spinning the weapon in his hands, he allowed it to disappear. Paying no more attention to the ash; he opened the door and returned to the flow of people.

Emerging from the narrow service corridor, Chris replaced the hood on his head and merged into the background once again. As the next train rolled into the station, Chris caught sight of Jay once again. Nothing had changed. The blonde woman seemed equally amused by whatever he was saying, and Chris was relieved to see his interaction in the tunnel had gone entirely unnoticed.

*   *   *

Chris watched as Jay swallowed down the rest of his drink and sank back into his seat. He had taken in everything Chris had said and tried to process the implications of what it meant.

'All that seriously happened, and I was literally a handful of steps away from you?' Jay's voice was filled with disbelief.

'Yes,' he replied flatly. 'But it told me nothing, other than everyone has an interest in you. Exactly as they said they would.'

Chris slammed his hand against the glass and pressed

his forehead against his forearm. Slowly exhaling, his breath did not cloud the glass as it should, and the glass gave no reflection of him being stood there.

'Surely it's just a matter of time before she comes.'

'I don't know,' he sighed, feeling the weight of impossibility weighing down on him. 'What if she never comes, what if her own people have done to her what they were planning to do with me?'

'What were they going to do with you?'

Jay walked past Chris and retrieved another bottle from the fridge. Grabbing a second, he walked back and held the frosty bottle out for Chris to take.

'I can't taste anything,' Chris said, declining the drink.

'Humour me,' Jay said as he pushed the bottle into Chris' hand. 'I'd feel better if the dead guy in the corner looked like he belonged here.'

Taking the bottle, Chris turned his back on the window and leaned against the metal frame to watch Jay. Popping the lid, Jay took another swig as he returned to the sofa. Sliding back down, the atmosphere in the apartment mellowed a little as Chris popped the cap from his own bottle.

Placing the cold bottle against his lips, he felt nothing. Chris heard, more than felt, the liquid tumbling down his throat but felt no physical sensation. The action of drinking, however, made him feel at ease. Although it was an empty notion, there was something about it that broke the tension in his body and allowed him to relax just a little leant against the window.

'Try again tomorrow then?' Jay asked as he smirked at Chris as he downed the beer. 'There's more in the fridge if you want them.'

'I'd better not waste your stock.'

'There's plenty more!' Jay replied with a wry smile.

Jay awoke alone in the apartment; the dawn light cascaded through the panoramic window and bathed down on him as he lay on the sofa.
'Chris?' He yawned as he sat up. 'You still here?'
    Chris was still in the room but with his hood folded neatly over his head he was invisible to the living. Stood in the far corner of the room, he watched the young journalist ready himself for work. Occasionally Chris would notice a sideways glance in his direction, which told him the other man knew he was still there.
'Right, you hovering ghost,' Jay chuckled. 'If you fancy taking a walk, I'll be heading to the office now.'
    Grabbing the large mug of coffee from the worktop, Jay sauntered towards the door and stepped out of the apartment.

Chris remained inside the apartment and waited. Moving towards the window, he peered down toward the street and waited for Jay to appear. A few moments after leaving the apartment Jay appeared on the pavement below looking around the quiet street. It was too early for there to be much in the way of people or traffic, and as Chris watched, it was easy to follow Jay's path.

Watching Jay with Soul Sight, he remained in his vantage position for as long as he dared. As Jay's shimmering lifeline disappeared, Chris made his move.

It was a move he had perfected under Azrael's tutelage in the Atacama Desert, and he had been waiting to use it. Concentrating, positioning himself on the plain between life and death, Chris took a handful of steps back away from the window and braced himself. When Chris felt ready, he sprinted across the room, and as he reached the glass window, he dived through it.

The glass did not shatter; it did not show Chris having even touched it. Instead, he passed through the glass and emerged outside in the open air. Tumbling head over end, Chris somersaulted twice before he righted himself to land perfectly on the ground below.

The only indication detectable of his appearance was from a handful of leaves that moved with no signs of wind or breeze.

Marvelling at his achievement, Chris could not suppress his smile as he rose to stand fully erect. 'Impressive,'

Chris recognised the voice instantly and his body tensed. Turning slowly on the spot, he knew who he should see before him.

'You have a nerve,' Chris hissed as she came into view.

Clad in the familiar catsuit of black material, Amber stood tall and proud. Her pale brown skin looked healthy and glowing in the bright morning sun, and her wild black hair was pinned back tightly to her head. In one hand she held the long spear she had used to kill Azrael.

'A nerve for what?' Amber smirked. 'I'm sure it's you who has been seeking me out.'

'Quite right.' Chris snarled.

Chris summoned his own weapons into his hands, and as he felt their weight within his palm, he brought both scythes around in front of him. Checking the pressure in his hands, he spun the blades around expertly before he pointed the tips of both weapons across towards Amber.

'My offer still stands. Surely the behaviour of The Council has shown you that your little world is not what Azrael would have had you believe.'

'Your offer?' Chris spat. 'Delivered gracefully by killing Azrael, convincing me that your cause is honourable, I think not.'

'Azrael's death was his own doing.'

'By your hand, your weapon.'

'Not entirely by my hand, he ended his existence.'

'Forced upon him by you.' Chris argued, his voice filled with boiling rage.

'Oh get over yourself Christian.' Amber suddenly bellowed. 'This battle is less about you and more about an injustice centuries old. Your meagre appearance on the board has simply forced my hand sooner than I would have hoped.'

'Doesn't change the fact you killed him.'

'And that,' Amber hissed. 'Is when you show no understanding of our customs, our world, any of it.'

'Enough talk.'

'Azrael's choice to die came when he engaged me in combat. The rule always stands that the representatives of Ascent and Descent may only face one another with one certainty.'

'And what is that?'

'Finality.' Amber paused for effect. 'In such a fight between Reapers and Dark Angels, the balance must always be honoured, and an end must come to one or another.'

'It should have been you!' Chris growled. 'It should have been you.'

'I think you'll find that fate was supposed to be yours. Your dear Azrael protected you from an untimely end by sacrificing himself to save you.' Amber let her words sink in, reading the change of expression on Chris' face before she continued. 'So if anyone, it should have been *you*.'

The words hit Chris like a concrete wall. For a moment he could not comprehend what Amber was saying.

'So now what?' Amber interrupted his train of thought. 'How do you wish to move beyond this moment?'

'There is only one choice as I see it.' Chris hissed through gritted teeth.

'I see many paths, nothing is as absolute as it would seem when fuelled by anger.'

'Anger changes nothing; there is just one choice I can make in all of this. It is the only reason I came back.'

Amber knew where Chris was headed. The look of pure contempt and hatred in his eyes told her all she needed to know. Testing the spear in her hands, she prepared herself for the inevitable.

'It's a shame you will never understand your true potential. If only you would see the world through a less tainted perception. Then, perhaps, you could help to bring balance to an imperfect system overseen by a trio of fearful relics.'

'I will be no part of your guise to overthrow The Council and their order.'

'Their order?' Amber laughed. 'Their order in a world of chaos? I think not. Their fearful denial of what is the rightful path of many.'

'Enough words.'

'Is this really your choice?' Amber admired the blade of her weapon. 'Are you, Christian, the fledgling Reaper, prepared to seek battle with a Dark Angel knowing full well the only outcome will be that one of us should perish?'

'Yes.'

There was no pause for thought in Chris' answer. His words were resolute, his posture matching his determined words as he shifted into a ready stance.

'Then,' Amber replied dismissively. 'It shall be done.'

Amber offered Chris a curt nod of the head and levelled her gaze towards him intently.

'However, London has seen enough of our world.'

Amber ran at Chris, suddenly catching him completely by surprise. As she wrapped her arms around Chris' neck and upper body, he felt tugged from where he had been stood. A strange sensation washed over him as he felt like he had been sucked beneath the waves of a turbulent sea. Falling and rolling uncontrollably. All the while Amber's body was pressed against his, and he could feel her jaw resting against his neck.

When they landed, they did so with such force that the two of them were torn from one another. Chris tumbled roughly to the floor and was glad to find his landing on the floor softened by something. Amber, on the other hand, was more familiar with the process of teleportation and landed squarely on both feet, upright and confident.

Chris rolled twice before he came to a grinding, sliding halt on the soft floor. Righting himself, Chris dusted off the white powder that was stuck to his body. Looking around it took a few seconds for him to realise that the white powder was in fact snow and the absence of cold against his skin had thrown him.

'A more fitting setting for your end, I think,' Amber waved her free hand theatrically, bringing Chris' attention to their surroundings.

It felt familiar, the tall trees climbing up towards a grey and heavy sky filled with rolling snow clouds. Flakes of snow fluttered lazily from the sky sporadically, adding to the isolation of the mountainside.

'Where are we?' Chris asked as he stood.

'Do you not recognise your own resting place?'

'Mount Shasta?'

'Indeed, a fitting place, don't you think?'

Chris chose not to answer. Instead, he launched his attack and pounced across at Amber.

His attack was quickly thwarted by her perfectly aimed spear. The metal tip of her weapon deflected Chris' scythes easily, sending him sprawling off-balance into the snow once again. Face covered, he spat out what had tumbled into his mouth and rolled onto his back to look up at Amber.

'This will be an easy fight,' Amber mocked. 'Just another wannabe Reaper fighting for a wrong they think is right.'

Amber struck again, the spear slicing through the air and burying in the snow where Chris' head had been. He had sensed the movement, the twitch of the muscles in her shoulder, just in time and propelled himself aside as the blow landed. Fed from the momentum of his move Chris rolled out of her reach and struggled back to his feet.

'Enough talk.' Chris yelled.

Chris was fuelled by fear and hatred, a dangerous combination. His attacks were powerful but poorly aimed and equally ineffective as Amber brushed them aside effortlessly. Chris thundered forward, blow after blow, attack after attack raining down on Amber. Each time she would shift her body or slice the wooden shaft of her spear just enough to cast each of the blows aside.

Amber smiled.

Chris' brow furrowed and his eyes narrowed as he thrust the scythe in one hand up and around while twisting the second through the air at waist height. Sensing the movement, Amber knocked aside the higher of the attacks and propelled herself in a backflip up and over the second attack. Landing on the snow, she followed through the momentum of her jump by spinning her weight around, sending a kick squarely at the side of Chris' head.

He had no time to react as the kick slammed heavily into the side of his head, sending him again sprawling to the floor.

'Your end is the only certainty, how long it takes is completely up to you.'

Amber refrained from attacking again, watching Chris with curiosity.

Every attack he had launched had been easily cast aside, his weapons had never even near being a threat to her, yet there he was getting up once again. Amber could not deny his tenacity; his drive to face her and avenge what he believed was her responsibility for Azrael's death.

Rising once again to his feet, Chris dusted himself off and buried the blade of each scythe into the ground beside him.

'Surrendering to your end?' Amber smirked, but Chris did not answer.

Drifting purposefully, Chris slid his fingers beneath the hem of his hood and pulled it up over his head. The deep shadow swallowed his face and features, leaving only the black void where his head should have been.

Taking a moment, Chris composed himself before reaching down to retrieve his pair of weapons. Eventually, he spoke, his voice echoing in the glade of tall trees on the mountainside.

'If I fall, I fall as a Reaper.' Chris announced confidently, more confidently than he actually felt. 'In honour of my friend and my mentor.'

'Then it shall be done.'

Their fight raged furiously along. To Amber's surprise, Chris was filled with a new sense of purpose and his attacks slowly became more focused and precise. More than once the jagged edge of his weapon would slice the air close to her body, forcing her to make a hasty retreat.

Each time Chris gained any sort of advantage over his opponent, it was short-lived.

Part of him suspected Amber was toying with him, somehow drawing him in only to knock him aside and retake whatever ground he had gained.

They no longer exchange quips or remarks, both of them concentrated on keeping their own attacks and defences in place.

Chris feigned an attack in one direction and when he saw he had drawn Amber in, he quickly altered his course.

Twisting his body, he dropped low and simultaneously sliced the scythe up through the air.

It was the first time his weapon had made contact, and it did not disappoint. The blade sank through the material of Amber's clothing and dug into her flesh. Her skin separated either side of the blade, but no blood trickled from the wound. Grasping at the injury, Amber stagger backwards and put distance between the pair of them. 'Lucky shot,' she howled through gritted teeth. 'It won't be repeated.'

Chris had no time to revel in his luck, or skill, as Amber returned with her own foray with the spear. Thrusting the long weapon out towards Chris, he was surprised how quickly she could dance the weapon up, over and around in the air. Moving with unbelievable speed, Amber rained down attack after attack, pressing Chris deeper into the woods.

Disorientated by the trunks of the towering trees, Chris felt his back slam roughly against the solid base of one tree. Surprised, he moved himself to the side as the blade of Amber's spear dug into the trunk where his chest had been.

Yanking her weapon free from the wood, Amber squealed in frustration and returned her attention to Chris. 'You are delaying the inevitable,' Amber tried to sound calm, but the tension in her voice gave her frustration away.
'Each moment is a victory then,' Chris retorted as he stepped around the full trunk, putting it between him and Amber.

Buying time, he circled slowly around the wide trunk, keeping it between them so he could catch his breath and think.
'Enough cowardice and games.' Amber spat as she rotated

around the trunk slowly.

Out of the corner of his eye, Chris caught sight of a plume of smoke billowing lazily towards the sky. Casting his attention momentarily towards it, he traced the faint outline of a building through the trees in the distance.

There was no logic to his choice, but it made sense. Scooping the snow against the flat blades of the scythes, Chris flicked as much as he could towards Amber and made his dash.

What he intended to do once he arrived at the wooden hut in the depths of the mountain woods was anyone's guess. Having no more of a plan than *RUN*, Chris shoulder barged past Amber and sent her sprawling to the floor.

Hearing her land roughly on the floor, Chris sprinted with all his speed down the gradual slope towards the billowing smoke and the picturesque cabin. His progress was hampered by the deep snow, but he continued on regardless. Zigzagging between the trees, Chris allowed gravity to drag him down the slope faster.

Amber's voice carried in the air behind him, but he could not make out her words as she fought to put distance between them. All Chris needed was time to think, time to devise some way he could overpower Amber. Compared to his unskilled bumbling, she was a finely trained warrior, and he knew she had been right when she had called his successful attack as mere luck. 'Think, think.' He panted as he sprinted down the hill.

Chris could see the distinctive features of the log cabin now. A light burned inside and the silhouette of a man could be seen through the window. The cabin was a picture-perfect representation of what he would expect buried deep in the mountains. A sanctuary of solitude against a white backdrop of peace and serenity.

But all that was about to change.

Chris was caught unawares as Amber launched herself through the air and landed on his shoulders. Using the trees to propel her she had all but flown down the mountainside in pursuit of Chris and now sent him sprawling to the floor releasing his grip on both his weapons.

Chris rolled thirty feet in the snow as the two scythes flew in opposite directions. Disorientated and confused, Chris paid no attention to where they landed as he tried to understand what had just happened. Once again entombed in a layer of snow, he rolled over and looked up in surprise to see Amber staking across the barren ground towards him.

'How?' he gasped but did not wait for an answer.

His eyes went wide in horror as Amber flicked the spear into a reverse grip and launched it through the air towards him. Releasing her hand from the shaft, the weapon span in the air as it was propelled at Chris.

This time he could not avoid the attack and felt this chest tighten as the blade sank into his flesh and embedded itself in the left side of his chest. Thrown back to the floor by the power of the spear, Chris watched as Amber hurried herself to tower over him.

Wrapping both her hands around the shaft of the spear, she pressed her weight onto the weapon and pinned Chris to the floor. From her position above him, she leered down at him, her eyes filled with venom.

'And here you are, exactly where you should be.'

Leaning down on the spear, she twisted the blade deeper into his flesh, and Chris felt a burning pain deep inside him.

'Can you feel it?' Amber sneered. 'The fires of Sub Terra burns within it and now, within you.'

Chris could not deny the searing pain burning inside his chest. It felt like molten lava flowing between his ribs and behind his breastbone. Writhing on the floor, Chris clutched at the spear, desperate to pull it free.

With surprising ease, Amber lifted Chris from the floor, keeping him pierced on the blade. Feeling his weight tugging on the metal, Chris gripped the wooden shaft to save from being skewered by the weapon. Spinning him around like an impaled rag-doll Amber rotated him around before flicking him off the end sending him flying.

Chris slammed into the wall of the cabin and slumped down to the floor. The impact of him hitting the wall disturbed the layer of snow on the sloped roof and sent into tumbling down on top of him.

The wound to his chest still burned despite the jagged blade having been torn free from his chest. Whatever cursed power possessed the metal remained inside him, and he could feel a pulse of searing heat spreading from the jagged gash.

'Who's there?' A gruff voice bellowed into the air as the startled occupant of the house stumbled into the darkness. 'Stop messing or else I'll happily shoot you. Show yourself.'

Chris' voice caught in his throat, and he could offer the man no answer or warning.

Stalking through the snow, Amber bore down upon him.

'Hey you,' the gruff voice commanded as he stepped across the porch.

Looking across, Chris saw the man level a shotgun at Amber. Unaware of Chris slumped against the wall, the man took aim and offered another warning.

The man was every inch the typical mountain dweller. Clad in a chequered shirt, a long grizzly beard adorning his face and a tight woollen hat pulled onto his head, he was every part the stereotype Chris would have expected.

Hip-mounting the long-barrelled shotgun, he wrapped a twisted finger around the twin triggers and took up the slack.

'Final warning, this place is private property. I have every right to defend it any way I see necessary.'

Amber finally looked at the man. She quickly cast aside the threat he posed with the shotgun and continued on towards Chris.

A single shot rang out, the sound sending a flock of nesting birds scattering into the air.

'That's a warning, the next won't miss.' The man declared and levelled the sights in line with his eyes for a more accurate shot.

At the sound of the shot, Amber stopped dead in her tracks. Chris sat just out of reach and the man a little further with his weapon aimed at her from the veranda above her.

'I wouldn't do that if I were you,' Amber warned but did not look at him as she spoke. Her attention remained on Chris.

'You're in no position to give orders, Missy.'

'Really?' She offered Chris a knowing smile. 'I'll be back for you.'

Turning to face the old man, Amber levelled the spear towards him menacingly.

'Go back inside, this is nothing to do with you.'

'You're on my land, little lady, I suggest you remember that and get yourself back to where you came from.'

'Not likely.'

Amber moved around the side of the cabin and stood at the base of the stairs leading up to the raised porch. All the while, the gruff man kept the gun levelled at her. As she walked, Chris crawled from his position to see what was happening.

'I won't warn you again.' The man repeated.

'You've already said that,' Amber replied dismissively as she slowly ascended the stairs. 'That's the funny thing about you people, never willing to do what needs to be done, always offering warnings and ultimatums.'

'You've got a nerve, stop where you are.'

'I don't think I will.'

Amber reached the top of the steps and saw Chris stagger around the side of the building to see.

It was all the audience she needed.

Still grasping the spear, Amber swiped it diagonally through the air as she stepped onto the veranda. The man never knew what happened as the blade sliced through his torso from the hip up to his shoulder.

He was dead before his body could register anything.

The natural twitch of his dying brain locked his finger on the trigger and the second round from the shotgun exploded in Amber's face. Propelled backwards by the blast, she tumbled back down the stairs as Chris watched on in horror and disbelief.

The man's body remained standing for a second before the top part separated from the lower. Blood dripped and puddle as the two severed halves of the dead man crashed to the wooden floor.

'What have you done?' Chris screamed. 'Why? He had nothing to do with this.'

Amber stood slowly, one hand holding the left side of her face. As she turned herself to look at Chris, he could not help but gasp at what he saw.

The entire left side of Amber's face had gone. Tattered and charred flesh hung limply where his cheek, eye socket and jaw should have been. Her feminine features were

now wholly disfigured, and whatever beauty Chris had
noted had not been replaced with a disfigured appearance
of torn flesh and missing features.

Amber's vicious wound did not bleed or show any other signs of more profound injury other than the significant portion of her face being absent. The features that should have been there were now a mass of torn and tattered skin that was repulsive to look at.

'This needs to stop now,' Chris bellowed as he scooped up one of his scythes from the snow.

Only being able to find the one weapon, he held it firm in his right hand and limped across the snow towards the base of the steps where Amber stood. Removing her hand from her face, it was easy to read the expression on the undamaged part of her face. The remaining brow furrowed and her eye narrowed as Chris stepped closer. 'Enough of this!' Amber screamed and launched herself at Chris.

Wrapping her hands around his waist, she wrestled him back against the support struts for the veranda. Chris slammed his elbows down in a flurry of blows, and although each impact hit home, it did nothing to loosen her grip on him.

Amber pressed herself against his midriff and kicked up with her right leg. The heel of her foot slammed hard into his face, sending a jolt of pain searing down the right side of his body.

With Chris reeling and slightly disorientated, Amber adjusted her grip around his waist and used her surprising strength to toss him back out across the ground in front of the cabin.

The power behind Amber's grip on him was astonishing to Chris as he flew roughly through the air. Sprawling once again on the snowy floor, Amber did not let up. No sooner had he landed did Chris feel her hands grip on his clothes and once again lift him upwards. Feeling himself being manhandled like a mere rag, Chris was once again thrown upwards.

Chris smashed into the front door of the cabin that the gruff man had left ajar. Tumbling into the room, his momentum was stopped by a large wooden rocking chair that splintered into a dozen pieces as it cushioned his landing. Doing his best to orientate himself, Chris looked around frantically but took in little detail of the interior of the log cabin.

Amber was standing in the doorway in a heartbeat. Filling the narrow frame, she stepped into the room and into the dancing firelight from the open fire on the far side of the room. The flickering flames caused the shadows on her injured face to move as if the tattered flesh was wafting in an unfelt breeze sickeningly.

'You will not walk away from this,' Amber spat as she

bore down on him. 'You entered into combat, and you will fall by my hand, fall as your bastard mentor did.'

Amber's words reignited the fire inside him, and as Chris tried to right himself, she was on him again.

This time as Amber leant down, Chris thrust his fist up towards her chin in a powerful uppercut. His knuckle met with the remaining two-thirds of her jaw, and the power of the blow tossed Amber's head back violently, sending her staggering backwards.

Chris took advantage of her unbalance and launched himself up, throwing another two punches as he moved. The first slammed hard into Amber's collarbone and the second sank into the void where her face had been on the left side. Feeling his fist make contact with the exposed bone Chris recoiled quickly giving Amber enough time to return his attack.

Her own blows were less powerful but faster. Her agility and flexibility allowed her to rain six or seven solid kicks and punches on him before Chris could do enough to pull himself out of her reach. The two of them continued back and forth until finally, Amber landed a solid kick in his stomach, sending him stumbling backwards.

Chris tumbled backwards over a coffee table in front of the fire and felt the sold hearth of the fire behind him. No sooner had he steadied himself than a snake of flames whipped around in front of his face as the hood that enveloped his head was engulfed by fire.

Ripping the burning fabric from his head, Chris tossed it aside and batted away the smouldering embers that settled on his hair and face.

'Still clinging to the hope you are human,' Amber scoffed. 'The fire cannot even touch you, and yet you panic like a child.'

'I'd rather feel a little human than end up a twisted bitch like you.'

'That's why you'll never beat me. I accepted long ago who and what I was.'

'Well good for you,' Chris spat and launched another series of attacks.

They moved around the wide living area of the cabin, crashing into and through various items of furniture. Neither of them noticed the fire from Chris' discarded hood take hold and spread across the long sofa and up a massive wall hanging around the fireplace. By the time they noticed, the fire had already swallowed an entire wall and had already snaked its way along the beams high in the roof above them.

Shadows became elongated and had they been able to feel it, the heat would have been tremendous as the fire spread. With neither being able to gain an advantage over the other, they were pulled apart as a burning beam came tumbling to the floor and landed in a cascade of sparks and flying embers.

Jumping back in opposite directions, the pair stared at each other over the burning beam.

Chris saw Amber move, but the giant flames obscured what she was doing. Peering over the dancing flames, Chris tried to see what she was up to but could make out nothing.

The first he knew was when she threw herself through the wall of fire, both arms stretched out towards him. It took a second to realise why it was only as the light of the fire shimmered on the blade that he realised she was once again wielding the spear.

The jagged edge of the metal blade dug into his right cheek, and once again he felt the fiery pain as it gouged a rip along the line of his cheekbone and to the corner of his mouth.

Giving Chris no time to register the pain, Amber was on him again as she landed on the stable floor. Driving the spear forward again, he felt another sting as it ripped across the length of his back from shoulder to waist.

Knees buckling with pain, Chris dropped to the floor, his body alive with the burning sensation that seemed to come from every part of his battered body.

Chris was done.

He knew it, and Amber knew it as she walked around him, holding the tip of her spear against the underside of his chin. Using the blade to tile his head upwards, Chris watched as she moved to stand in front of him.

'I told you it was inevitable.' She said, shouting above the crackle of the raging fire around them. 'You challenged me as a Reaper, as the inadequate and unprepared successor to Azrael, and now you are on your knees before me.'

'I won't beg!' Chris declared defiantly.

'Good, it would make no difference if you did; there is no other end to this than what must be done.'

'Get on with it then,' Chris replied and raised his chin off the icy blade. 'I've done enough to make Azrael proud.'

The light of the fire seemed to distort for a second, but Chris' gaze was locked on Amber.

'Any last words?' Amber asked as she drew the spear back and prepared herself to strike.

'Whatever happens, my second death will hopefully prove my worth.'

'I don't think so.' Amber grinned and thrust the spear forward.

Chris heard the weapon slicing through the air, the crackle of flames seemed drowned out behind him, and he waited for the end.

It did not come.

With his eyes closed, Chris sensed a dark shadow cast over him and as he opened his eyes, he was shocked to see something other than the burning cabin around him. Stood in front of him, her jet-black feathered wings spread wide on either side of her was Malpas. Held, almost delicately, between her hands was the tip of Amber's spear, only an inch from Chris' face.

'You cannot interfere, it is written he must...' Amber bellowed but was cut short as Malpas ripped the weapon from her grip.

Spinning the long shaft around, Malpas slammed the wide handle hard into Amber's side, sending her flying across the room.

'There will be no end to this today.' Malpas bellowed, her voice loud and confident.

'You cannot defy tradition.' Amber screamed as she righted herself. 'His end is mine.'

'It is not.' Malpas replied flatly. 'His end is not yet, and when it is, I suspect it will not be at your hand.'

Amber was enraged. Furious at Malpas' intervention, she screamed as she sprinted across the room, but her attack was once again cut short by a second blow from her own weapon.

'He...is...mine.'

'No, you Dark Angel of Eternal Darkness. It is time for you to heal your wounds and leave this fight for another encounter.'

'I will not go until you honour the traditions of battle.'

The broad smile that appeared on Malpas' face both angered and confused Amber.

'There are no traditions in the battles between Dark Angels and the uninitiated. Chris is but another soul that can be plucked from you grasp.'

'He is a Reaper.' Amber shrieked.

'On whose say?'

Malpas glanced at Chris, who looked up at her confused. A sudden wave of embarrassment washed over him as he realised what she was saying.

'He entered combat as a Reaper.'

'Misguided beliefs do not make something fact Amber, we both know this.' Malpas chose her words and tone carefully. 'Take your weapon and return to Sub Terra. A time will come when you will face him again, but only when he is ready and only when he is what you already believe him to be.'

'Deceit and lies, a game to break him free from his bond to me.'

Malpas had been calm long enough. Folding her wings down against her back, she moved with sickening speed. Before either Chris or Amber could understand what she had done, Amber found herself poised at the tip of her own weapon, pressed against her throat as it had been on Chris', not moments before.

'Christian may not be able to best you, but we both know a battle between us would be on far more even ground.' Malpas warned. 'In your current state, I am confident we both know who would walk away the victor.'

'You will pay for this.'

'Perhaps. But until that time comes, I believe your master is calling.'

Malpas moved swiftly, raising her free hand into the air as she thrust her palm out and connected with Amber's chest. As her hand touched, Amber felt pushed with such force and power that she was powerless to resist.

As Chris watched on, he saw Malpas thrust her hand towards Amber, but as it touched, he watched the Dark Angel evaporate in a shower of black fire that exploded in a flurry of black and blue.

With Amber gone, Malpas turned to look at Chris on the burning floor, his face and body battered and torn from his fight with Amber.

'It is time for you to return to Altum, I believe it is time for your judgement.'

Unable to protest, his body swallowed by the burning fire and pain, Chris slumped into Malpas' arms and slipped into a dark unconsciousness.

'What have you done?' Tenebris bellowed as Amber staggered into the vast room at the top of Forca Tower.

Still nursing the vicious wound to her face, Amber was caught by surprise with Tenebris' tone. Stopping dead at the top of the staircase, she looked towards the hovering cloud of smoke where the voice lived.

'I did my duty as your Angel.' She answered hesitantly.

'By facing Azrael's protégé?'

His words hung in the air for a moment as Amber tried to plan her answer.

'He offered me engagement in, what was I supposed to do?' She worked hard to keep her tone respectful and calm.

'You should have declined.'

'What and turned away from conflict?' Amber was about

to say more but cut herself short.

'Interesting you had more to say but chose not to,' Tenebris teased. 'Perhaps you were referring to my choice to remain here in the Dark Realm and not engage in these games myself.'

'Perhaps.' Amber retorted a little too quickly.

'Speak your mind.'

'I'd rather not.'

'You've never been one to hold back, do me the respect of doing the same now.'

Amber was reluctant, she knew Tenebris' temper too well, and his voice told her he was holding back his fury. Having wrapped a bandage around the injured side of her face, Amber tentatively approached the cloud of smoke but maintained a safe distance.

'The fact you choose to dwell in the Dark Realm does not concern me,' she began diplomatically. 'What does concern me is the fact you see it fit to send me out yet scorn me when I make my own decisions on how I think things should be done.'

'You forget your place.'

'Only as much as you do!' Amber kept her tone level. 'You sit in your refuge, yet it is me who wanders the land of the living, fighting your battles on the ground while you remain safe in your overseeing sanctuary.'

'It is not my time to walk the earth again, not yet.'

'So you have said for a long time now and have I ever questioned you?'

It was Tenebris' turn to be caught off-guard.

'You haven't.'

'So the same should be afforded to me, I think.'

'But you forget I, above all, having sat amongst The Council have seen the greater scheme of things which have been and are yet to come.'

'You have this luxury,' Amber quickly countered. 'Us working on the ground do not have the foresight you do. Without a full understanding, how can you not expect us not to act on instinct and what we think is right?'

Tenebris fell silent, and Amber waited for her master to continue. She had always been able, to be honest, and open with him, but this felt different. By killing Azrael, she sensed she had pushed too far, tested his limits to breaking point, and the best thing to do right then was wait to see what he had to say.

Allowing Tenebris his time, Amber walked to the broad window, allowing her to look over Sub Terra. Gazing at the gap in the jagged red stone, she could see the burning fires in the streets below. The disfigured demons that occupied the city walked around below, paying the spiked tower no attention.

Amber loved the view she always had.

Perched on her vantage point always reminded her of the power she really held. The right hand of Eternal Darkness, she had the entire city to command if needed. With no face or physical presence, Amber was the face and voice of Tenebris and Darkness itself.

Peering down, Amber could not put her finger on the moment where everything had aligned for her. What exactly it was which had brought him to Tenebris' side and saved her from disfigured damnation.

'You know your own worth to me.' Tenebris said, his voice seeming closer than it had been.

Not wanting to turn, she knew the swirling cloud of smoke had moved across the room to hover behind her. Amber could feel his presence behind her as she looked out across Sub Terra.

'It cannot be overstated the need for patience in the grand scheme of things, Amber.' Tenebris whispered to her, his words feeling as if they touched her neck. 'Your move against Azrael can be...forgiven.'

'I'm not asking for forgiveness,' Amber snapped and turned to face the cloud of smoke confidently. 'I live by my decisions, and however, you see best to deal with it, I will accept without question.'

'Regardless if you are asking for it or not, I give you my forgiveness for his death.' Tenebris' voice was firm, and Amber listened intently. 'What I must now ask of you is to leave the fledgeling Reaper alone from this time on.'

'They manipulated me to secure his freedom from my blade.'

'Rightly so considering your haste to face him.'

'He challenged me; I did not seek him out.'

'They did nothing wrong by the rules of combat. He is no Reaper, he is not ready, and deep down you knew that.'

'I...'

Suddenly Amber was acutely aware how exposed she was before Tenebris. To lie would serve no other point than to enrage her master. Unable to hold the gaze she knew came from the dark corona of the cloud, she turned away to look back out across the city.

'You knew!' It was a statement, not a question. 'Would a Reaper be so easily overpowered by even my most skilled Dark Angel?'

'Probably not.' Amber conceded quietly.

'Then the appearance of Malpas was nothing more than an intervention of The Council which makes amends for your removal of Azrael from their ranks.'

'How so?'

'If they had disowned or discounted him, then they would have allowed him to perish at your hand. By sending, or allowing Malpas to intervene, we at least know the fledgeling Reaper remains a candidate in their eyes.'

'Why is it so important that he remains?'

'Because he is my snowball in the mountain.' Tenebris answered thoughtfully. 'The time will come when the seeds you have sewn will take hold or else we will await the next candidate who replaces him.'

'Your patience astounds me in all of this,' Amber answered thoughtfully. 'You would happily wait centuries to seek the balance you have been denied, wouldn't you?'

'There is no point in rushing.'

Amber turned to once again face Tenebris and touched her hand towards the wispy tendrils of smoke around the edge. Toying the smoke between her fingers, Amber contemplated it.

'Your face will heal,' Tenebris offered to break the awkward silence.

'I'm sure it will. Mortal weapons leave a mark but nothing I cannot handle.'

'Your face should be devoid of imperfections.' Tenebris cooed, the sudden softness in his voice catching Amber by surprise. 'Would you allow me to remove the scars when you are healed?'

Subconsciously, Amber traced her fingers across the surface of the neatly wrapped bandage. Her fingers pressed where skin and bone should be and still found no resistance. Tenebris was right in the fact her face would heal, but the tattered flesh would remain scarred as a reminder. There was only so much that could be remedied beyond death.

'I would wear the scars as a reminder as I always have.' Amber answered defiantly.

'Some things will never change,' Tenebris mused. 'I would have it no other way and honour your choice.'

Amber half-smiled, the side of her face exposed from the bandage upturned, giving her face a softer look.

'My Dark Angel, you trust I foresee a shift in our path in the future.' Tenebris offered. 'Our time will soon arrive when we can address The Council and their biased, broken system that denies the fair judgement and Descent of souls that are rightfully ours.'

'I trust you,' Amber whispered.

'I never doubted it. The fledgeling reaper represents a junction in the path. His choice will either serve us or deny us, but the seeds are sewn and soon, when the time is right, we will rise again to what we should be.'

Amber spent the rest of the evening alone with her thoughts, looking out across Sub Terra. The injury to her face felt curious as the skin knitted together beneath the bandage. It would not be long before her bones would have returned and the skin although pitted and scarred would have formed again, giving features once again to her face.

As Tenebris left her alone with her thoughts, Amber could not deny the longevity of her master's plan caused her concern. That said, though, she trusted Tenebris implicitly. Whatever method he had set in motion would be something she could do little to influence or alter.

The future was not set and as he had said more than once, Christian was far more instrumental than she had ever understood.

A voice whispered, the words barely audible above the sound of an ocean lapping against the shore. Chris could not fathom what was happening. He longed to hear the words spoken by the hushed voice.

Straining to hear, Chris could make out very little of what was being said. It was more than just a word or two; it was as if whoever spoke was telling him something. 'I can't hear you,' Chris tried to say, but no words would come from his mouth.

In fact, the more he thought about it, Chris could feel nothing of himself.
'Where am I?'

His own voice echoed through the space which surrounded him, but he had not said them. Chris had not felt his lips move or the muscles in his jaw allow the words to form. The voice echoing around him was his own, but it had not come from him.

What's going on?'

Again Chris' voice surrounded him, but nothing responded. The hushed voice still whispered the same pattern of words, but Chris could still not make them out. 'Can you hear me?'

Panic set in as Chris tried to make sense of what was happening. Forcing himself to think, he tried to move any part of his body he could, but he felt as if there was nothing there.

'Chris?'

The voice was all too familiar and stunned him for a moment.

'Ash?'

'Can you come to me?' The response came too quickly for it to be a reaction to his question.

'I can't see you, where are you?' Chris pressed.

'Where are we?' Again the answer was too fast to be a response to his question.

'Stop playing games, whoever you are.' Chris yelled.

'Is that you whispering?' Ash's voice asked.

The constant whispering voice remained in the background, as did the sound wave lapping waves against an unseen shore. Pushing beyond the background sounds, Chris tried to pinpoint the source of Ash's voice.

'Follow my voice Ash, I'm here, I'm here.'

'Where are you?'

Frustration set in, and Chris struggled to find Ash and himself in the darkness. With nothing to centre him, nothing to help orientate himself, there was only black and confusion.

'Come to me.' An unfamiliar voice interrupted, and immediately all other sounds stopped. 'Come to me, and we shall see what fate awaits you, Christian.'

Not waiting for an answer, the darkness lifted. As the light slowly increased, the outlines of features all around him came into focus.

The first thing Chris noticed was the silhouette of three figures standing a little way ahead of him. As the darkness lifted, he slowly felt the presence of his own body, as if the dark had been numbing every part of him.

'Who are you?' Chris asked as he looked down to see the outline of his hands and fingers awash with curiosity.

'You know the answer, you've seen this process once before from the outside.'

Chris' head swam as he tried to make sense of what was being said to him. The voice who spoke to him was female and familiar, everything that materialised around him felt oddly familiar yet unknown at the same time. It was as if a fog hung over his memories, refusing to lift no matter how hard he tried.

'Where's Ash?' Chris suddenly remembered Ash's lingering voice he heard a few moments before.

'Ash is here,' a second voice answered.

'Everything from your life is here.' The first voice continued. 'It is time for us to see the value of your life and offer your judgement.'

Chris' mind raced for a moment.

'No!' His voice was high-pitched and panicked. 'This isn't what needs to happen.'

'The Council is decided,' the first voice interrupted. 'Your fate is to be decided like any other soul.'

'But I am a Reaper,' Chris pleaded. 'I mean, I can be a Reaper. If I can finish my training, then I can follow in Azrael's example.'

'Azrael would be here were it not for you.' The first woman snapped. 'You cannot adhere to the rules and expectations of The Council and our way of life which has led to this judgement.'

'But I am not ready!'

'That is clear in your actions. A ready candidate would not stumble blindly into the world of the living at the cost of your mentor and almost yourself.'

'You are not ready to rank amongst the Reapers, to serve this Council or sit amongst us.' The second woman sighed.

The Hall Of Souls And Scales finally came into focus. Rising behind the three councillors were the trio of seats and lined behind them was an audience of shadows and silhouettes. The facial features of his audience were utterly distorted, save for one.

Save for Ash, who stared across at Chris from behind The Council.

Seeing Ash's face teased a new fire inside Chris as he made eye contact with his love. Feeling the intensity from Ash fed the fire as Chris turned his attention back to The Council filled with new purpose.

'And you, Osiris.' Chris directed his attention towards him. 'You've remained quiet, which seems uncharacteristic for you.'

'There is little I need to say,' Osiris replied calmly. 'This is not my judgement, it is yours.'

'Seems that The Council has already decided.' Chris retorted, his words filled with accusation. 'You stand my past before me like an expectant audience, haunt me with the voices of my life yet speak of all the things I have failed to do in service to you.'

'Your tone,' the first woman warned. 'It is not one this council will tolerate or accept.'

'If I may be so bold,' Chris interrupted with a wave of his hand. 'You bring me here to face your judgement yet scorn me when I speak my mind as I feel it needs to be said. I respect this council, your ways and all that Altum stands for, but I will not sit idly by as a loyal subject for fear of reprisals in your judgement of me. That is not what this is about.'

'How dare you!'

'I dare because, for all his flaws, all his undying loyalty to you, Azrael taught me the value of a Reaper and his duties.' Chris moved towards The Council but found his movement blocked by some unseen barrier. 'If you wish for me to lay my life before you so you can choose my fate, then you'll bloody well listen to what I have to say.'

Malpas appeared to the side of The Council, her wings no longer visible and her body clad in the green attire of her ceremonial robes. She approached Osiris respectfully, offering a curt bow before approaching the centre councillor to whisper in his ear.

Chris waited patiently. He felt enraged and put out at the interruption and eyed Malpas furiously as she whispered to Osiris. When she had finished speaking, she offered Chris a swift glance and nod before she turned her back and disappeared behind the ghostly shadows that watched from behind The Council.

'The Council needs time to deliberate.' Osiris declared suddenly. 'You are dismissed.'

'I beg your pardon?' Chris stammered incredulously.

'We do not need to hear more, enough of your life has been seen to make a suitable judgement.'

'I am not done,' Chris bellowed, but a raise of Osiris' hand silenced him.

'You would do well to take this time to make your preparations.' Osiris said firmly. 'You will be recalled to the Great Hall when our deliberation is done, but until then...'

Osiris did not finish his sentence. Instead, he beckoned

forward one member of the gathering observing the proceedings.

Ash stepped from the crowd and walked towards The Council.

'You will have your time in the company of the one you love, a gift for the brief service you have given us.' Osiris offered an open hand towards Chris which led Ash towards him. 'It is not a common practice however instead of your service perhaps this will soften the blow.'

As Ash stepped towards him, Chris could no longer feel his resentment and anger for The Council and their traditions. Ash's pale blue eyes and soft skin shimmering in the light was all that stole his attention. Taking his hand, Ash led Chris along the width of the Great Hall and out through the doors into the hallway beyond the hall.

'How is this possible?' Chris stammered as the doors closed behind them.

'I don't know,' Ash answered softly as Chris brought them to a stop just beyond the doors.

'I need you,' Chris whispered.

Holding Ash's hand, Chris felt suddenly as if everything was alright again. The tender touch of skin was all he had needed for so long, and suddenly the consequences of everything he had done seemed immaterial to what he had then.

'I've missed you,' Chris stuttered, his eyes filling with tears.

'So have I,' Ash said and touched Chris' cheek tenderly. 'From the moment I lost you, I have longed to hold you again.'

Chris sobbed, he had missed the tender touch of his love for too long, and now he was overcome with emotion. 'What will become of this, of us?' Chris struggled to form the words as his lip quivered and throat tightened.

'That does not matter,' Ash sighed. 'What matters now is that we are both here, together for the first time in a long time.'

'Neither of us should be here.'

'That's true, especially you.'

Chris averted his gaze, guilt suddenly filling him at his choice in the cave of Mount Shasta.

'I didn't know what to do.'

Holding Chris' chin softly, Ash raised his face, so their eyes met.

'What's done is done. Let's not waste this time dwelling on the past, instead, let is just be here now.'

Their lips met, and everything faded away. For the first time in a very long time, Chris finally felt content.

'It is time,' Ash whispered, moving back from Chris' embrace. 'They need you back.'

There was pain and sorrow in Ash's face, something hanging heavy behind those pale blue eyes.
'What is it?' Chris asked he reached out and tenderly stroked Ash's cheek. 'What do you know that I don't?'

Ash could not look at him and stepped away uncomfortably. Turning away from Chris, the silence and atmosphere were uncomfortable. As Chris reached out to turn Ash around to face him, their hands met. Ash remained steadfast, back facing Chris, and clasped his hand for a moment.
'If they send you back, you will go with no memory of this,' Ash sighed heavily. No memory of me or what we have.'

'Is that what they will do? Send me back for a chance at redemption?'

'Better than the alternative.'

'Descent wouldn't be so bad,' Chris tried to sound convincing. 'At least I would remember you.'

'Tortured by me, you mean.' Ash countered quickly. 'Condemned to a life where you know you have no chance to see me again, so close but yet so far from one another.'

'You'd prefer I forget you and return?'

'For your sake, it would be the easier option.'

Chris forced Ash to turn and face him. Their gaze locked and Ash suppressed the tears falling.

'And your sake?' Chris cooed. 'What would be better for you?'

'You not being here.' Ash snapped angrily. 'I'm sorry, I didn't mean it like...'

Chris released his grip and took and step back from Ash. Once again he swam in the guilt at his choices in life and death. All he had ever wanted was to be back with Ash, yet all he had done was cause more pain.

'You're right,' Chris' voice was barely above a whisper. 'By doing what I thought was right, I have made things so much worse.'

Ash felt uncomfortable as Chris' gaze dropped to the floor. Head lowered, Chris looked broken and half the man he was. Shoulders sunk, brow furrowed, he looked beaten. To Ash, it seemed as if Chris had finally given up.

'I saw you that night, you know.' Ash confessed. 'When you arrived where my body lay on the floor, I could see you.'

'How?'

Ash bolted, and the world around them disappeared in a flash of bright light. Snatched back from his melancholy, Chris looked around confused until a familiar setting appeared around him.

'I don't want to be back here.' Chris coughed. 'I've spent enough time stuck in this moment I would rather be anywhere else.'

'But you need to see it from a different light, Chris.'

Ash's hand lingered in the air as if setting all the pieces in place.

Chris came into view. His Captain stood by his side with Ash's covered corpse beneath a pale sheet on the road a short way behind them. They spoke, but the sound was muted. It didn't matter as Chris knew all too well what was being said.

'At first, I didn't know what had happened.' Ash began. 'I remember feeling the pain and then suddenly nothing. I had my eyes closed so tight when the pain hit and when I opened them I was still standing there in the street.'

The view changed, Ash was now stood above the covered body facing away from it. Hunched over, Ash held just above the waistline, nursing the injury the murderer had caused.

'I saw nothing, but then again I didn't know what was happening.' The emotion was building in Ash, the words becoming tarnished with a slight quiver. 'When I turned around, the first thing I saw was you.'

Chris saw Ash's ghostly form turn and see Chris stood with the Captain. The pain on Ash's face washed away in an instant, replaced with a broad and loving smile. Ash ran across to Chris with one bloodied hand outstretched to touch him.

'I couldn't touch you,' Ash's ghost tumbled through Chris. 'You couldn't see me and I think right then I knew I was dead.'

The word hung in the air uncomfortably. Chris watched as Ash's ghost turned around, looking perplexed before a look of realisation appeared. Ash looked around frantically and screamed and shout.

'I screamed your name for what felt like an age, but all you did was stare at my bloodstained shield in your hand.'

Precisely as Ash's words described, Chris saw himself teary eyed holding the bloodied shield in his palm.

'I've still got it,' Chris sighed. 'Well, I still had it. When I was, you know.'

'I know,' Ash said warmly. 'I never cared for the new apartment, too small but I was there with you.'

Chris eyed Ash curiously.

'How if you Ascended?'

'In here,' Ash tapped just above Chris' now dead heart.

'Our connection, our love, it allowed me to see you when it was needed.'

'I never knew.' Chris choked.

'There's one more thing I need you to see.'

The world moved in reverse at an uncomfortably fast speed. Chris struggled to watch everything happening but could make out the occasional detail.

Chris saw himself arrive, saw the others arrive before him.

The scene thinned out, the forensic examiners repacked their equipment and disappeared, and suddenly the night air was filled with the flash of red and blue lights.

'You're going to make me watch?' Chris gasped.

Ash lifted from the floor and walked backwards towards the idling police car and got back in. The car sped backwards up the street and suddenly time froze.

'Can you see?' Ash asked, pointing towards the police car.

Awash with curiosity Chris walked across the road to the frozen vehicle. He could see the two officers sat in the car, Ash wide-eyed staring intently as if searching for someone out of the windscreen.

'What is it you want me to see?'

'Look beyond me Chris, look beyond the car, the lights and everything.'

Allowing Chris to explore it took him a few long seconds to see what Ash was trying to show him.

'Now you see.'

'Now I see.'

In a flash of light, the scenery faded, but the last thing to etch into Chris' vision was a single face hidden in the shadows of an alley on the far side of the road.

Chris knew the face, there was no way he could ever forget it.

Amber stood in the shadows of a dark alley, her body consumed by darkness but her face pierced the camouflage as the strobe of the police lights caught her soft face. There she stood, intently watching and waiting.

'Why was she there?' Chris snarled, not moving his eyes from the spot where Amber had been standing but had long since disappeared.

'There are still things you do not know about this world, but I believe she *whispered* to my killer.'

'Meaning what?'

'Meaning I think she is the reason I died alone that night.'

'Why show me this now, Ash?'

'Because you needed to know,' Ash hushed. 'Before you face your judgement, you deserved to know everything.'

'But there is nothing I can do about it.'

'I didn't want you to.'

The hallway of the Hall of Souls And Scales reappeared around them, and Chris physically jumped when he saw Malpas standing by his side.

'They want you back,' she said flatly and beckoned Chris towards the door.

'Just remember,' Ash murmured. 'I will always be there no matter where they send you.'

Ash pointed to Chris' chest, and oddly he felt warmth in the empty cavity of his chest.

'I love you,' he blurted, tears rolling down his cheeks.

'As do I, my sweet, as do I.'

Chris could not look at Ash, it hurt too much. Quickly he turned and followed Malpas back into the Great Hall.

'Are you ready, have you done what was needed to face your judgement?'

There was a unique softness and caring tone to Malpas' words as she walked with towards the centre of the room.

Chris noticed The Council had returned to their ivory towers and now towered above them, each occupying their ornate raised seat. All three pairs of eyes watched him intently as he walked as confidently as he could to stand before them.

'I don't know if anyone is ever ready,' Chris confessed. 'But no matter what I can say, I'm here now so that will have to do.'

Offering only a curt nod, Malpas stopped in her tracks, and Chris moved to a circle of light on the floor alone.

Stepping into the circle, Chris felt himself bathed in bright light. Allowing his eyes to adjust, he slowly lifted his head to look up towards The Council.

'Christian Thomas,' Osiris' voice echoed around the vast room. 'You stand before us to face judgement by the three members of The Enlightened Council. Is there anything you would wish to add before we pass our judgement?'

Chris thought for a moment and then slowly offered his answer.

'There isn't anything I can say to affect your decision.' He said calmly. 'It is your right to make your judgement, and I accept whatever it is you choose to do with me.'

Straightening his clothes, Chris stood tall and waited for his judgement.

'Tradition dictates that those not fit for Ascension should step out from the circle of light in which you stand and to that end,' Osiris was clearly pausing for dramatic effect and relishing in the theatricality of it all. 'That end this Council requests you step out of the light.'

Although Chris had expected it, there was something about being told he would not Ascend which hurt. Doing his best to hide his disappointment, and also to steady the fluttering fear bubbling in the pit of his stomach, he stepped out of the light obediently.

He was cast into darkness, the ring of light extinguishing immediately as he stepped out of it.

'A soul that falls from Ascent will face the possibility of darkness in Descent, you find yourself now stood in the darkness, do you not?'

'I do.' Chris answered quietly.

Chris took his time to look at each of the councillors. Osiris stood as he addressed him while the two other members peered down at him from their seats.

'How does the darkness find you?' Osiris asked, but Chris did not know how to answer, or even if he should. 'Is there no representative of Eternal Darkness to claim this soul?'

The words echoed, and Chris prayed not to hear the sneer of Amber from the shadows.

There was no answer.

'Then Descent and Darkness do not call you this day.'

'Redemption then?' Chris exhaled.

Osiris looked down at him, his eyes filled with intensity, and Chris struggled to hold his gaze.

It was the longest time he had ever experienced before Osiris spoke again. Chris looked around desperately to see

Ash for one last time, but he found no audience peering at him anymore.

He was alone.

Facing the end of his life to return to another and there was nobody else with him.

'Your fate has been decided,' Osiris finally declared, voice booming loudly.

The floor rumbled at his feet, and Chris was overcome with concern.

'Will it hurt?' He blurted, but Osiris did not answer.

The floor shook, and Chris struggled to keep his balance.

'Christian Thomas, your fate will not differ from all others who have walked a path like yours.' Osiris declared.

Something caught his attention, a hole in the floor growing slowly wider just in front of him. Chris peered and for a moment saw something shimmer in the darkness below him.

'Your path is to be that of...'

A column emerged from the dark hole in the floor and sat on top were two things Chris immediately recognised. Chris looked from the pair of scythes mounted atop the stone column and up to Osiris.

'...a Reaper.'

Chris was astounded by Osiris' poker face; even now there was no emotion in the old man's look.

'Do you accept to finish your training at the mentorship of Malpas and resume your journey to replace Azrael?' Osiris asked as Chris reached out towards the scythes.

'Without a doubt I do.' Chris declared confidently.

Grasping the two weapons, he lifted them from the altar and held them out in front of him.

'Your journey is just begun Christian Thomas, Reaper of The Enlightened Council and protected soul of Altum.'

Chris swelled with pride.

After everything he had seen, done and experienced, he knew the truth of Osiris' words.

This was indeed the beginning of the next part of his journey.

TO BE CONTINUED

ENJOY THIS BOOK? YOU CAN MAKE A HUGE DIFFERENCE...

Reviews are the most powerful tool in helping me build trust in my stories and creativity. When it comes to getting attention for my books, there is nothing better than an honest word from someone who has entered my world and enjoyed the story I have told.

At the moment I don't have the power behind me to advertise on billboards or in newspapers (trust me, I'm working on it) but I do have something the big advertising agencies don't have and that's YOU!

An honest review shared, no matter how short, catches the attention of other readers and help give my books validity.

If you have enjoyed this book I would be more grateful than you can imagine if you would spend just a few moments leaving a review on the book's Amazon Page.

Thank you so very much for your time and I look forward to inviting you back for another adventure soon.

ABOUT THE AUTHOR

Tobey Alexander, the author of Timothy Scott and many other stories has his online home at www.tobeyalexander.com. You can connect with him on Facebook at www.Facebook.com/TobeyAlexanderAuthor or else on Instagram at www.instagram.com/tobey_alexander_author and should you want to contact him via email at TobeyAlexanderAuthor@GMail.com it would make his day to hear your thoughts on his adventures.

ALSO BY TOBEY ALEXANDER

Have your read them all?

In the Magdon Series

Origins Of The Magdon: Five Novelette Anthology

In 1911 a teenage Archibald Skevington travels to Vercovicium, a Roman Fort on the border of Scotland, to satisfy his interest in history. An accidental discovery of a subterranean crypt thrusts him onto a path that will consume his life. Following Archy's adventures from five key events in his life he uncovers a terrifying monster, forgotten from history, that slumbers in the darkness. What secrets lay in the shadows and how far will some go to see it unleashed upon the earth?

FREE to download

Into The Dark

Picking up decades after Archy's death, an unsuspecting family are dragged into the same world of the fabled mythical creature. When his wife is kidnapped and held to ransom, Gabe and his two children must research their long-dead ancestor's obsession if they hope to save her.

The family must come together as a secret cult hell-bent on resurrecting the beast holds everything they hold dear on a knife's edge. When the time comes, they must make an impossible choice, save the one they love or save the world?

Available now

From The Dark

With his family shaken by their encounter with the Magdon and cultist Veks, Gabe once again finds himself in their crosshairs. Dragged once again into a world of secrets, Gabe and his daughter must seek the help of others allied to the protection of humanity. Despite their actions, the world remains at risk as the Veks have discovered a new way to recall the beast from the shadows.

Dragging you once again into a world of shadows and monsters, Gabe and his allies must search through their family history and seek help from a most unexpected ally in this twisting mystery adventure.

Available now

In the Timothy Scott Adventure Series

Timothy Scott: Shadow Island

Meet twelve-year-old Timothy Scott as he discovers a hidden world behind an antique mirror. Plagued by bullies, ostracised by his peers and seeking solace in his only friend who is invisible. Thrust into this new world he must learn to overcome his own self-doubt in an epic coming-of-age fantasy adventure.

Born from the style of adventure in Harry Potter and the Chronicles Of Narnia, be prepared to enter a whole world of adventure for all ages.

Available now

Timothy Scott: The Torn Mountains

Timothy must return through the mirror to help save his younger sister. When a familiar voices beckons from the shadows, Timothy must steel himself to return except this time he will not be alone. Mielikuvitus has changed, the foreboding shadow of the Darkness has started to lift but Timothy knows there is something else at play.

Travelling once again through the mirror we join Timothy and a most unexpected ally as they venture to the mythical Torn Mountains in the hope of saving his sister from the hands of a sinister creature.

Available now

In the Blackout Series

Blackout

Michael Swann is a man haunted by his past. After the untimely death of his son, he has withdrawn from his family and seeks a life of danger and solitude. After an uneventful free-climb Michael crosses paths with a mysterious woman that sees him dragged from modern-day Greece to the battlefields of the First World War. Somehow, Michael has travelled back in time.

Waking in a cold and sterile military facility, Michael finds himself recruited into the Tempus Project, a secret project researching movement through time. All is not as it seems as Michael soon discovers more to the secrets behind Tempus and its intentions. Through his journey Michael will not only question his world, his beliefs but also his sexuality.

Available now

Collapse: A Blackout Time Travel Novel

Michael Swann is back. Having turned his back on Tempus and the clandestine military project he now lives on the run with his partner Adrian. When a surprising face from his past drags him back, Michael must unravel a series of seemingly unconnected events if he is to piece together the world that is crumbling around him.

Spanning even more epic locations throughout history, Michael will need guidance and help from those who understand the ability of time Leaps if he is to secure leverage to restore his life and save his newfound family.

Available now

Aaron Raven Series

Gridlock

What connects a retired Metropolitan Police detective, a chemical attack on a train and the unsolved murder of an Eastern European mob boss twelve years ago?

Aaron Raven must piece together the interlaced events if he is to help prove the innocence of his hospitalised sister who is the prime suspect in the chemical attack. Be prepared for a heart-racing thriller spanning Europe as Aaron skirts the line between right and wrong as he fights to save his reputation and family.

Available now

Printed in Great Britain
by Amazon